The Girl He Used to Know

Tracey Garvis Graves

TRAPEZE

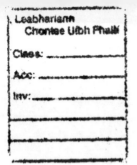

First published in Great Britain in 2019 by Trapeze Books,
an imprint of The Orion Publishing Group Ltd
Carmelite House, 50 Victoria Embankment,
London EC4Y 0DZ

An Hachette UK company

3 5 7 9 10 8 6 4 2

All the characters in this book are fictitious, and any resemblance to actual persons, living or dead, is purely coincidental.

A CIP catalogue record for this book is available from the British Library.

ISBN (Paperback) 9781 4091 8369 3

Printed and bound in Great Britain by Clays Ltd, Elcograf S.p.A.

MIX
Paper from responsible sources
FSC® C104740

www.orionbooks.co.uk

The Girl He Used to Know

[redacted]

For anyone who's ever felt like they didn't belong

And for Lauren Patricia Graves, who is the light of my life

1

....

Annika

CHICAGO
AUGUST 2001

I run into him at Dominick's, of all places. I'm poking around in the freezer case, searching for the strawberries I put in my morning smoothie, when a man's voice somewhere off to my right says, "Annika?" He sounds unsure.

From the corner of my eye, I catch a glimpse of his face. It's been ten years since we've seen each other and though I often struggle to recognize people out of context, there's no need for me to question whether or not it's him. I know it's him. My body vibrates like the low rumble of a faraway train and I'm grateful for the freezer's cold air as my core temperature shoots up. I want to bolt, to forget about the strawberries and find the nearest exit. But Tina's words echo in my head, and I repeat them like a mantra: *Don't run, take responsibility, be yourself.*

I draw an uneven breath that doesn't quite fill my lungs, and turn toward him. "Hi, Jonathan."

"It *is* you," he says.

I smile. "Yes."

My hair, which used to be waist length and usually in need of a good brushing, is now shiny and straight and stops a few inches below my shoulders. The tailored shirt and slim-fitting pants I'm wearing are a far cry from my college wardrobe of skirts and dresses two sizes too big. It's probably thrown him a bit.

At thirty-two, he still looks the same to me: dark hair, blue eyes, broad swimmer's shoulders. He's not smiling, but his brows aren't knitted together in a scowl, either. Though I've vastly improved my ability to read facial expressions and other nonverbal cues, I can't tell if he's harboring any angry or hurt feelings. He has every right to feel both.

We take a step forward and we hug, because even I know that after all this time—and all we've been through—we're supposed to hug. There is an immediate feeling of safety and comfort when Jonathan's arms are around me. That hasn't changed at all. The smell of chlorine that used to cling to his skin has been replaced by something woodsy and, thankfully, not too heavy or cloying.

I have no idea why he's in Chicago. A prestigious financial services firm in New York had whisked Jonathan out of Illinois almost before the ink finished drying on his diploma, when what had once been a planned move for two turned into a solo endeavor.

When we separate, I stumble over my words. "I thought you lived . . . Are you here on business . . . ?"

"I transferred to the Chicago office about five years ago," he says. It astounds me that all this time, as I've walked around the city I now call home, I never knew bumping into him was a possibility. How many times have we been within a certain-mile radius of each other and not known it? How many times were we behind or in front of each other on a busy sidewalk, or dining in the same restaurant?

"My mom needed someone to oversee her care," he continues.

I'd met his mother once, and I liked her almost as much as I liked my own. It had been easy to see where Jonathan's kindness had come from. "Please tell her I said hello."

"She died a couple of years ago. Dementia. The doctor said she'd probably been suffering from it for years."

"She called me Katherine and couldn't find her keys," I say, because my recall is excellent and it all makes sense now.

He acknowledges my statement with a brief nod. "Do you work downtown?" he asks.

I close the freezer door, embarrassed that I've been holding it open the whole time. "Yes, at the Harold Washington Library."

My answer brings the first smile to his face. "Good for you."

The conversation sputters to an awkward halt. Jonathan has always done the heavy lifting where our communication is concerned, but this time he doesn't let me off the hook and the silence is deafening. "It was great to see you," I finally blurt. My voice sounds higher than it usually does. Heat rushes to my face, and I wish I'd left the freezer door open after all.

"You, too."

As he turns to go, a pang of longing hits me so hard my knees nearly buckle, and I gather my courage and say, "Jonathan?"

His eyebrows are raised slightly when he turns back around. "Yes?"

"Would you like to get together sometime?" I tense as the memories come flooding back. I tell myself it's not fair to do this to him, that I've done enough already.

He hesitates but then he says, "Sure, Annika." He removes a pen from the inside pocket of his suit coat and reaches for the grocery list in my hand, scrawling his phone number on the back.

"I'll call you. Soon," I promise.

He nods, his expression blank again. He probably thinks I won't go through with it. He'd be justified in that, too.

But I will call. I'll apologize. Ask him if we can start over. "Clean slate," I'll say.

Such is my desire to replace the memories of the girl he used to know with the woman I've become.

2

Annika

CHICAGO
AUGUST 2001

At my initial therapy session with Tina it took my eyes almost five minutes to adjust to the dimly lit room. When I could finally see my surroundings clearly, I realized it was intentional, and that everything in the room had been placed there based on its ability to soothe. The floor lamp in the corner—the only source of light—had a cream-colored shade that threw muted shadows against the wall. The brown leather furniture felt buttery-soft under my fingertips, and the thick rug covering the floor made me want to kick off my shoes and wiggle my toes among its soft, fluffy fibers.

"I ran into Jonathan," I tell Tina before she's even shut the door when I show up for my weekly appointment. She sits down in the armchair and I sink into the overstuffed couch across from her, its cushions enveloping me in a way that has always eased my anxiety about being there.

"When?"

"Last Tuesday. I stopped at Dominick's on my way home from work, and he was there."

We've spent many hours discussing Jonathan and she must certainly be curious, but knowing what Tina's thinking by the look on her face is a nut I'll never crack. "How did it go?"

"I remembered what you said I should do if I ever saw him again." I brightened, sitting up a bit taller despite the couch's continued attempt to swallow me. "We had a conversation. It was short, but it was nice."

"There was a time when you wouldn't have done that," Tina says.

"There was a time when I would have escaped out the back door and then taken to my bed for two days." I *had* felt drained when I'd finally made it home with my groceries. And then, when I was putting them away, the grief I'd felt about the death of Jonathan's mother finally caught up to me and I had myself a good long cry because now he doesn't have any parents at all. I'd also neglected to tell him how sorry I was even though I was thinking it in my head. Despite my fatigue, it had taken me a long time to fall asleep that night.

"I thought he was in New York?"

"He was. He transferred here to take care of his mom before she died. That's all I really know." Jonathan's appearance had been so unexpected, so random, that I hadn't been capable of articulating many questions. It had occurred to me belatedly that I had no idea if he was married. Glancing down at a man's ring finger is the kind of subterfuge that occurs to me later—and in the case of Jonathan, two full days after the fact.

"What do you suppose was going through Jonathan's mind when he saw you in that grocery store?"

Tina knows how difficult it is for me to understand what others are thinking, so her question does not surprise me. In the ten years since I've seen Jonathan, I've replayed the final weeks of our relationship, and the last message he left on my answering machine, over and over in my mind. Tina had helped me see these events through Jonathan's eyes, and what I'd realized made me feel ashamed. "He didn't seem hurt or angry," I say, which doesn't really answer her question. Tina knows everything there is to know about the situation, and she could probably tell *me* what Jonathan was thinking. She just wants to hear my take on it. One of the things I like most about our sessions is that I'm the one who determines what I'm comfortable discussing, so Tina won't push. Not too much, anyway.

"How *did* he seem?"

"Neutral, I guess? He smiled when I told him about the library. He started to walk away, but I asked him if he wanted to get together, and he gave me his number."

"You've made real progress, Annika. You should be proud."

"He probably thinks I won't call."

"Will you?"

Though it fills me with anxiety to envision the road I'm about to travel, I answer firmly. "Yes."

I study Tina's face, and though I can't be certain, I think she might be pleased.

3

Annika

THE UNIVERSITY OF ILLINOIS
AT URBANA-CHAMPAIGN
1991

In college, if you wanted to find me, you'd need only to look in three places: the Wildlife Medical Clinic, the library, or the student union, where my chess club meetings took place.

With the amount of time I spent volunteering in the clinic, one might think I aspired to a career in veterinary medicine. Animals were one of the few things that brought me extreme happiness, especially those in need of my attention. The other volunteers might have assumed the animals provided a respite from the loneliness and isolation that surrounded me during my college years, but few would understand that I simply preferred the company of animals over most humans. The soulful look in their eyes as they learned to trust me sustained me more than any social situation ever would.

If there was one thing I loved almost as much as animals, it was books. Reading transported me to exotic locales, fascinating periods in history, and worlds that were vastly different from my own. My mother, frantic with worry one afternoon when I was eight, found me outside in our tree house on a snowy December day engrossed in my favorite Laura Ingalls Wilder book, the one where Pa got caught in the blizzard and ate the Christmas candy he was bringing home for Laura and Mary. She'd been searching for me for half an hour and had called my name for so long she'd lost her voice. Though I explained it to her repeatedly, she couldn't seem to grasp that I was simply playing the part of Laura waiting in the cabin. Sitting in the cold tree house made perfect sense to me. When I'd discovered I could pursue a career that would allow me to spend my days in a library, surrounded by books, the joy I'd felt had been profound.

Until my dad taught me to play chess at age seven, there wasn't a single thing I was good at. I did not excel at sports, and I was all over the board academically, earning either the very highest or the very lowest marks, depending on the class and how much it interested me. Debilitating shyness prevented me from participating in school plays or other extracurricular activities. But much like books, chess filled a void in my life that nothing else had been able to satisfy. Though it took me a long time to figure it out, I know that my brain does not work like other people's. I think in black-and-white. Concrete, not abstract. The game of chess, with its strategies and rules, matched my worldview. Animals and books sustained me, but chess gave me the opportunity to be a part of something.

When I played the game, I almost fit in.

The Illini Chess Club met in the food court area of the student union on Sunday evenings from 6:00 to 8:00 P.M. The number of attendees varied widely. At the beginning of the semester, when members weren't yet bogged down by their course loads or busy studying for exams, there might be thirty students. By the time finals drew near, our numbers would plummet and we would be lucky to have ten. The Sunday chess club meetings were casual, consisting mostly of free play and socializing. The chess team meetings—for members who wanted to participate in competitive play—were held on Wednesday evenings and focused on competitive training games, the solving of chess puzzles, and analyzing famous chess matches. Though I possessed the necessary skills and would have preferred the more formal structure of the chess team meetings, I had no desire to compete.

Jonathan joined us on a Sunday evening early in my senior year. While the rest of the club mingled and talked, I fidgeted in my customary spot, board set up, ready for play. I'd kicked off my shoes as soon as I sat down, pressing the soles of my bare feet down on the cool smooth floor because it felt so *good* to me in a way I could never explain to anyone no matter how hard I tried. I watched as Jonathan approached Eric, our club president, who smiled and shook his hand. A few minutes later, Eric called the meeting to attention, raising his voice to be heard above the din.

"Welcome, everyone. New members, please introduce yourselves. Pizza at Uno afterward if anyone's interested." Eric turned back to Jonathan and then pointed toward me. The gesture filled me with dread, and I froze.

I almost always played with Eric, for two reasons: One, we'd joined the chess club on the same day our freshman year and as the two newest members, it made sense for us to partner up for our first game, and two, no one else ever wanted to play with me. If Eric and I finished our game quickly, he moved on to play with someone else and I went home. I liked playing with Eric. He was kind, but that never stopped him from playing his hardest. If I beat him, I knew I'd earned it, because he spared me no handicap. But now that Eric had been elected president and spent some of the meeting answering questions or handling other administrative functions, he wasn't always available to play with me.

My stomach churned as Jonathan walked toward me, and I calmed myself by flicking my fingers under the table as if I were trying to remove something unpleasant from the tips. When I was a child, I would rock and hum, but as I got older, I learned to keep my self-soothing methods hidden. I nodded my acknowledgment of his presence when he sat down across from me.

"Eric thought we could partner tonight. I'm Jonathan Hoffman."

His jaw was square and his eyes were bright blue. His short dark hair looked shiny, and I wondered if it would feel soft and silky under my fingertips. He smelled faintly of chlorine, and while I hated most smells, for some reason that one didn't bother me.

"Annika Rose," I said, my voice barely above a whisper.

"Monica?"

I shook my head. "No M." The confusion surrounding my name had been a constant my whole life. In seventh grade, a particularly vile girl named Maria had shoved my head into a locker. "A weird name for a weird girl," she'd hissed, sending me fleeing in tears to the nurse's office.

"Annika," Jonathan said, as if he were trying it on. "Cool. Let's play."

Eric and I alternated who played white and therefore took turns enjoying the slight advantage that came with it, and if we'd played together that night it would have been his turn. But since I'd been paired unexpectedly with Jonathan, the pieces in front of him were white and he went first.

His opening sequence displayed his affinity for the moves of World Champion Anatoly Karpov. Once I identified his strategy, I chose my defense accordingly and immersed myself in the game, the sounds and smells of the food court fading away along with my nervousness. I no longer heard snippets of the students' conversations as they ate their burgers and fries, or the sizzle of the wok from a fresh batch of chicken fried rice. I didn't smell the pepperoni pizza hot out of the oven. I played ruthlessly from the start, because every game I played was a game I played to win, but I also took my time and concentrated on my next move. Neither Jonathan nor I spoke.

The game of chess is largely silent, but to me there is great beauty in the lack of sound.

"Checkmate," I said.

There was a long pause and then he said, "Good game." He looked around, but only a few of our members remained. Everyone else had left for dinner while we were still playing.

"You too," I replied, because the victory had been as hard won as any I'd earned from Eric.

"You going out for pizza and beer?"

I stood up, grabbed my backpack, and said, "No. I'm going home."

The lingering smell of sandalwood incense and Lysol greeted me when I opened the door of the campus apartment Janice and I had lived in for the past two years. The incense was to cover up the faint scent of pot that always clung to her boyfriend's clothes. Janice would never have allowed Joe to get stoned in our apartment, and she couldn't detect the smell on him herself. But I had a very sensitive nose and I knew what it was the moment she introduced us. Janice understood that the memories it triggered were something I simply couldn't handle.

The Lysol was to counteract the aftereffects of whatever Jan cooked for Joe. She loved to experiment with recipes and spent hours in the kitchen. Her palate ran toward the gourmet side of things, while mine aligned more closely with the dietary habits of a six-year-old. More than once, I'd seen Joe staring at the grilled cheese or chicken nuggets on my plate while Janice stirred something complicated on the stove. I appreciated her willingness to keep the smells in our apartment to a minimum, but didn't have the heart to tell her that the Lysol and incense only *added* two of them to the mix. And because I wasn't the easiest person to live with, I never would.

"How was chess club?" Janice asked when I came in, threw my backpack on the floor, and flopped onto the couch. It would take hours for me to fully unwind, but being home allowed me to relax slightly and my breathing to grow deeper.

"Horrible. There was a new member, and I had to play with him."

"Was he good-looking?"

"I'm super exhausted."

She sat down next to me. "What's his name?"

"Jonathan." I kicked off my shoes. "I'm so mad at Eric. He knows we always play together."

"Who won?"

"What? Oh. I did."

Janice laughed. "How'd that go over?"

"The same way it always does."

"You want me to make you a grilled cheese? I made one for Joe earlier. I had everything in the fridge to make chicken Florentine, but that's what he wanted. And you said you had nothing in common with him."

"He didn't take me seriously." Jonathan had made the mistake that others who'd come before him had frequently made: he'd discounted my abilities while being overconfident in his own. I would soon learn that it would be the first and last time he ever made that mistake with me.

"Next Sunday, you'll play with Eric."

"I'm too tired to eat."

"I have no idea what the two of you are saying to each other," Joe had said the first time he witnessed one of our conversations. To be fair, it wasn't only because I suspected he was high at the time. Janice had had three years to learn how to communicate with me, and to her credit, she'd mastered my native language like an expert linguist.

Unable to sustain further conversation, I wandered down the hallway into my bedroom, face-planted onto the bed fully clothed, and slept straight through until the next morning.

4

Jonathan

CHICAGO
AUGUST 2001

My phone rings and the caller ID flashes an unknown number as I walk down the street on my way to meet Nate for an after-work drink. I've been stuck in meetings all day and the only thing I'm interested in at the moment is an icy cold beer. August in Chicago can be brutal, and my dress shirt clings damply to my back under my suit jacket. When I hear the chime indicating that whoever called has left a voice mail, I figure I might as well find out what it is so I can put out the fire now and enjoy my beer in peace.

Annika's voice stops me in my tracks. The odds that she would actually call were only marginally better than my ex-wife and I seeing eye-to-eye on anything now, so they weren't that great. I move out of the flow of pedestrian traffic, holding a finger against the opposite ear so I can hear her better, and start the message over from the beginning.

"Hi. I was wondering if you might want to meet for breakfast on Saturday or Sunday morning at Bridgeport Coffee. Whatever time is convenient for you. Okay, bye." I can hear the tremble in her voice.

There's another message.

"Hi. This is Annika. I should have mentioned that in the other message." The tremble is still there, along with an embarrassed sigh.

There's one more message.

"I'm sorry for all the messages. I just realized I didn't give you my phone number." Now she sounds frustrated as she rattles it off, which is unnecessary because I can retrieve it from my incoming call log. "So just call me if you want to meet for coffee. Okay, bye."

I imagine her slumping into a chair after leaving the messages, spent, because I know how difficult these things are for her.

The fact that she did it anyway tells me something.

The dark bar smells faintly of old cigarette smoke and men's cologne. It's the kind of establishment newly single men go to to unwind before heading home to the underfurnished apartments that have never seen a woman's touch. I hate places like this, but Nate is still in the daily-drinking phase of his divorce, and I remember all too well what that's like. He's sitting at the bar peeling the label from a bottle of beer when I walk in the door.

"Hey," I say as I sit down beside him, loosen my tie, and gesture to the bartender to bring me the same.

Nate points toward the window with the mouth of his beer bottle. "Saw you out there. You better shut that phone off if you want to enjoy your beer in peace." Nate and I don't work for the same firm, but their mission statements are identical: *All work and no play makes this company a shitload of money.*

"It wasn't work. It was a voice mail from an old girlfriend I ran into the other day. She said she'd call. I wasn't sure."

"How long's it been?"

"I was twenty-two the last time I saw her." And if I'd known there was a possibility I wouldn't see her again for ten years, I might have handled things differently.

"How'd she look?"

The bartender hands me my beer, and I take a long drink. "The years have been very kind to her," I say when I set the bottle back down on the bar.

"So was it serious or just a fling?"

"It was serious for me." I tell myself it was serious for her, too, but there are times I wonder if I'm lying to myself.

"Think she wants to rekindle?"

"I have no idea what she wants." That part is true. I don't even know if Annika's single. I don't think she's married, because she wasn't wearing a ring, but that doesn't mean she's not in a relationship with someone.

"Still hung up on her?"

Every now and then, especially right after Liz and I split up, when I was lying in bed alone unable to sleep, I would think of Annika. "It was a long time ago."

"I know a guy who never got over the girl who dumped him in eighth grade."

"That's probably not his only issue." Though it *has* been a long time, it sometimes feels like it was yesterday. I can hardly remember the names of the girls who came before her, and after her there was only Liz. But I can recall with unbelievable clarity almost everything that happened during the time I spent with Annika.

Probably because no one has ever loved me as fiercely and unconditionally as she did.

I look over at Nate. "Did you ever fall in love with a girl who was different? Not just from any girl you'd ever dated before, but from most people in general?"

Nate signals the bartender for another beer. "Marched to the beat of a different drum, did she?"

"She marched to the beat of an entirely different *band*. One you've never heard of and under no circumstances ever expected to like." When Annika would frustrate me, which was pretty often, I would tell myself there were lots of other girls out there who were not so challenging. But twenty-four hours later, I'd be knocking on her door. I missed her face and her smile, and I missed every one of the things that made her different.

"She must have been hot because that kind of thing never flies when the girl's just average."

When John F. Kennedy, Jr.,'s plane crashed into the Atlantic a few months before Liz threw in the towel and went back to New York without me, his image—along with his wife's and sister-in-law's—had been plastered all over the TV screen for days. Because I had no interest in celebrity news, I'd never realized until then how much Annika looked like Carolyn Bessette Kennedy. They shared the same bone structure and blue eyes, and hair so blond it was almost white. They both possessed the kind of striking beauty you'd notice in a crowd. When I ran into Annika at Dominick's, the resemblance had been even more pronounced. Her hair is shorter than it was in college and now it lies smooth and straight, but she still wears the same color of lipstick, and when my brain registered that fact, a certain memory thawed the ice in my heart a little bit.

"Annika is beautiful."

"So the crazy didn't matter."

"That's not remotely what I said." The words come out more harshly than I intended and there's a beat of awkward silence as we both take a drink.

I'd be lying if I didn't admit, at least to myself, that the way Annika looked *did* play a part in my initial attraction and my willingness to look past a few things. When Eric pointed at her that day in the student union, I couldn't believe my luck, although I did wonder why such a hot girl was sitting all alone. It would have been easy to dismiss her the way the others had, find someone else to play with next time. But I sought her out again and again because I felt beaten down by the trouble I'd gotten into at Northwestern and bitter from the boulder-sized chip I'd been carrying on my shoulder ever since. I wasn't feeling very self-confident and losing to a girl didn't help. I cringe at the memory, and it is only now, ten years later, when I realize how much energy I wasted fighting the inconsequential battles that really aren't meant to be fought. Annika didn't know it at the time, but she was exactly what I needed in order to believe in myself again. And in time, I realized she was so much more than just a pretty face.

"You gonna see her again?" Nate asks.

Whenever I think of Annika, my mind returns to the way we left things and the same unanswered question. It's like a pebble in my shoe, uncomfortable but not unbearable.

But it's always there.

I take another drink of my beer and shrug. "I haven't decided yet."

When I get home from the bar, I pour a whiskey and stare aimlessly out my floor-to-ceiling windows as the sun goes down. When the whiskey's gone, I play Annika's messages again because I'm officially drunk and I've missed hearing her voice. Not returning her call seems juvenile and petty, and maybe I'm just feeling sorry for myself because the last two women I've loved decided they didn't love me anymore. By the time Liz filed for divorce, I didn't love her anymore either, but Annika's a different story.

I reach for my phone, and when her answering machine picks up I say, "Hey. It's Jonathan. I can meet you for coffee on Sunday morning at ten, if that still works for you. See you then."

Maybe Annika called because she's finally ready to remove the pebble from my shoe once and for all. Aside from that, I want to know—despite how I feel about the way our relationship ended—that she's okay. Though I sensed by the way she carried herself that she's doing fine, at least on the outside, I need to know if she's still shouldering the weight of it on the inside.

Besides, it's not like I'd say no to her.

I never could.

5

Jonathan

CHICAGO
AUGUST 2001

When I arrive at the coffee shop, Annika's standing on the sidewalk shifting her weight from side to side, bouncing on the balls of her feet. She stops immediately when she sees me.

"Good morning," I say.

"Good morning." She's wearing a sundress, but unlike the clothes she used to wear, this one fits her body. My eyes are drawn to her narrow shoulders and the hollows at her throat and collarbone. "Are you ready to go in?"

"Sure." She takes a step toward the doorway, hesitating when she sees the size of the crowd packed tightly inside the small coffee shop. She picked the venue, but I'm the one who chose the time and maybe she would have preferred to meet earlier or later to avoid the rush. If memory serves, this particular location has a spacious outdoor patio, so maybe it doesn't matter. Instinctively, I stretch my hand toward her lower back to guide her, but at the last minute I pull it away. I used to be one of the few people whose touch Annika could tolerate. In time she grew to love the feeling of my arms around her, my body becoming her own personal security blanket.

But that was years ago.

Slowly, we make our way to the counter and place our orders. In college, she would have asked for juice, but today we both order iced coffee.

"Have you eaten breakfast yet?" I ask, pointing toward the pastry case.

"No. I mean I didn't know if you'd already eaten so I ate a little but not really enough to count as a full breakfast, but I'm not hungry now."

As the words tumble from her mouth, she looks down at her shoes, over my shoulder, toward the barista. Anywhere but at me. I don't mind. Annika's mannerisms are like slipping into a comfortable pair of shoes, and though I feel bad admitting it, even to myself, her nervousness has always made me feel at ease.

I try to pay, but she won't let me. "Is it okay if we sit outside?" she asks.

"Sure." We sit down at a table shaded by a large umbrella. "You look great, Annika. I should have told you the other day."

She flushes slightly. "Thanks. So do you."

It's instantly cooler due to the umbrella, and the color on Annika's cheeks fades away. When I lift my glass to put the straw in my mouth, she tracks the movement of my left hand and it takes me a second to realize she's checking for a wedding ring.

"How's your family?" I ask.

She looks relieved that I've started with something so neutral. "They're fine. My dad retired and he and my mom have been traveling. Will's still in New York. I saw him a few months ago when I flew out to see Janice. She lives in Hoboken with her husband and their six-month-old daughter."

"So you've stayed in touch with her?" Janice was always more than just Annika's roommate, so it shouldn't surprise me that their friendship is still going strong.

"She's my closest friend even if I don't get to see her that often." She takes a sip of her coffee. "Do you live around here?"

"West Roosevelt."

"I'm on South Wabash," she says.

A ten-minute walk is all that separates us. "I wonder how many times we've come close to running into each other."

"I wondered that too," she says.

"I wouldn't have pegged you for an urban dweller."

"It's only a twenty-minute walk to work, and if the weather's bad, I can take the L. I have a driver's license, but I don't own a car. It's not like I really need one to get around."

"How do you like working at the library?"

"I love it. It's all I ever wanted to do." She pauses and then says, "You must like your job, too. You're still working there ten years later."

"It's a solid company, and they've made good on all their promises." I'm even a bit further along on the career path they laid out for me during the interview process, and most days I like my job just fine. Some days I hate it, but then I remind myself that, just like Annika said, it's all I ever wanted.

"Do you still swim?"

"Every morning at the gym. What about you? What do you like to do in your free time?"

"I volunteer at the animal shelter when I can, and I have a part-time position at the Chicago Children's Theatre. I help teach an acting class on Saturday mornings. I wrote a play."

"You wrote a play? That's amazing."

"It was just a fun thing to do. The kids did a great job with it. I'm working on another one right now, for them to perform at Christmastime."

"How old are they?"

"I work with several different age groups. The youngest are four and five and the oldest are in the nine-to-eleven range. They're a great bunch of kids."

"Do you have any of your own?"

Her eyes widen. "Me? No."

"Are you married? Or in a relationship?"

She shakes her head. "I've never been married. I was seeing someone, but we broke up. Are you married?"

"I was. We divorced about a year and a half ago."

"Were you married to that girl? The one you told me about on my answering machine?"

So, I guess she did get the message after all. "Yes."

"Do you have kids?" She looks apprehensive as she waits for my answer.

"No."

Liz had very clear goals in mind when it came to her career, and she wasn't going to stop climbing the corporate ladder until she shattered the glass ceiling. Her passion for business was like a homing beacon when I first arrived in New York, beckoning me toward her. I was all for Liz climbing the corporate ladder, but each rung had a timeline attached and when she informed me she wouldn't be ready to start a family until she was forty-one, and what did I think about freezing her eggs—I thought she was kidding.

She wasn't.

It's funny how the very trait that attracts you to someone is the same trait you can't stand when you're untangling yourselves from each other. And not funny ha-ha. Funny like how in the world could you not have seen it?

I'd agreed to meet with Annika today because I'd hoped for some answers, but by the time we finish our coffee we've progressed no further than idle small talk. She is in no way prepared to revisit what happened between us, at least not yet, and it would be unnecessarily harsh to push her.

"Ready?" I ask when nothing but melting ice remains in our cups. She stands in response and as we walk, she mentions how much she loves her apartment's proximity to the park and museums, and points out her favorite places to grab takeout or go shopping. Her neighborhood provides everything she could ever want, and Annika the urban dweller makes perfect sense now. She lives in a bubble where nothing takes her out of her comfort zone, and everything is within her reach.

I should have realized it immediately: Annika is doing fine. There's no one here to save.

As we approach her apartment building, her bouncing stride and nervous chatter ramps up as her anxiety reaches a fever pitch. Has she been waiting for me to say something and now that we're almost home, she's afraid a confrontation is imminent?

I grab her hand because I don't know how else to still her, and the memory that slams into me stops me in my tracks. We're not on S. Wabash anymore but rather the doorway of her college apartment building. Her palm is small and soft in mine, and it feels exactly the way it did when I held it for the first time.

"We don't have to talk about it." She stops moving and the look of sheer relief on her face tells me I was right. There won't be any explanations today, but I'm not sure I have the fortitude to keep peeling back Annika's layers in order to obtain them. "I just wanted to know if you were okay."

She takes a deep breath. "I'm okay."

"Good." I glance toward the entrance of her building. "Well, I should get going. It was great seeing you again. Thanks for the coffee. Take care, Annika."

Though she has trouble deciphering other people's facial expressions, her face is an open book and no one would ever have trouble understanding hers. I've always wondered if she exaggerates them to help people understand what she's thinking, the way she wishes they would for her. I find it endearing. When she comprehends that one coffee date is the extent of our reunion, she looks crushed. Though it isn't intentional and it's certainly not retaliatory, I have the fleeting thought that this is the first time I've ever done anything to hurt *her.*

And it feels awful.

But maybe my failed marriage isn't far enough behind me. That's the thing no one tells you about divorce. No matter how much you and your spouse agree that the relationship is broken, it hurts like hell when you go your separate ways, and the pain follows you around until one day, it doesn't. It's only recently that I've noticed its absence, and I have no desire to gamble on replacing it with more heartbreak.

I don't want to leave.

I want to pull Annika close, twist my fingers in her hair and kiss her the way I used to.

Instead I walk away from her feeling more than a little lonely and very, very tired.

6

Annika

THE UNIVERSITY OF ILLINOIS
AT URBANA-CHAMPAIGN
1991

One week after I beat Jonathan at chess, Eric sat down across from me a few minutes before Sunday night's club meeting began, thus restoring order to the chaos he'd inflicted upon my world.

"Tell me this is the year you're going to agree to compete," Eric said.

"You know it's not."

"You could if you wanted to."

"I *don't* want to. I don't like being away from home."

"You'd only have to travel a couple times. Three if we make it to the Pan-Am. There's going to be a practice meet in St. Louis in October. You could go to that one. Feel it out. Drive home afterward."

"I don't drive."

"You could ride with someone."

"I'll think about it."

Eric nodded. "Good. I bet you'd like it."

I would totally hate it, and I purged the thought from my mind immediately.

I was studying the board, already formulating my strategy and pondering which opening move would be most effective, when a voice said, "Would you mind if I played with Annika again?"

Jonathan was standing there looking down at us. Why would he want to play with me again? On the rare occasions when Eric missed a meeting, the other club members rarely sought me out to play, and I usually ended up slipping away and going back home.

"Sure, man. No problem," Eric said.

Jonathan sat down across from me. "Is that okay with you?"

I wiped my palms on my jeans and tried not to panic. "I always play with Eric."

"Is he your boyfriend?"

"What? No. I just . . . I always play with him." But Eric had already taken a seat two tables away across from a junior named Drew.

"I'm sorry. Do you want me to ask him to switch back?"

That was exactly what I wanted, but what I wanted even more was for the two of us to start playing so we could stop all this talking. So I did the only thing I could to make that happen.

I picked up my white pawn and made the first move.

This time, he won. I'd drawn on every bit of skill and experience I possessed, but it still wasn't enough, and he deserved the victory. "Thanks," he said. "That was a great game." He whistled as he packed up his things.

Our game had gone on for so long that once again, everyone had already left for dinner. When I picked up my backpack and turned to go, Jonathan grabbed his and fell in beside me. I fervently hoped it was because we were both headed in the same general direction of the exit and that it would be a largely silent endeavor, but I was wrong.

"Do you want to catch up with everyone? Get some pizza?"

"No."

"You're really good at chess."

"I know."

"How long have you been playing?" he asked.

"Since I was seven."

"How long have you been a member of the chess club?"

"Since freshman year."

He was probably six-two to my five-four, and his legs were much longer than mine. I had to walk briskly to match his pace in order to answer the questions he kept firing, which hardly seemed fair since I didn't really want to answer or keep up with him in the first place.

"Did you always know you were going to join the club?"

"No."

I'd discovered the chess club by accident three weeks after I moved into my dorm room, on the same day I'd called my parents, told them I was dropping out, and asked them to come get me the next morning. I'd spent the preceding twenty days swirling in a paralyzing vortex of loud sounds and bad smells, overwhelming stimuli, and confusing social norms, and I'd had just about all I could take. My parents had taken me out of school halfway through my seventh-grade year, and my mother had homeschooled me for the rest, so the transition had been especially jarring and confusing for me. Janice Albright, a chatty brunette from Altoona, Iowa, who the university had randomly assigned to be my roommate, seemed to float effortlessly through the rapid-fire onslaught of college life while I kept getting stuck in the maze, taking wrong turns and backtracking. I trailed behind her like a wisp of smoke she could never quite shake, a lone figure in a sea of bobbing twosomes and foursomes laughing and joking their way to class. I followed Janice to lectures, to the library, and the dining hall.

On that particular Sunday, Janice and two of her friends returned to our dorm room shortly after I made the tear-filled call to my parents. One of them sat down with Janice on her bed, and the other settled herself at the end of mine. I was sitting cross-legged near the top and the girl's presence drove me under the covers with my book and the penlight I'd been using since I was a child when I was supposed to be sleeping and not reading. It was September and our unair-conditioned dorm room felt like a sauna most of the time; under the covers it was nearly unendurable, the air stifling and hot.

"Just because you look like that doesn't mean you can be weird," the girl said. I froze, hoping she wasn't speaking to me but knowing instantly that she was. I'd heard some variation of this sentiment more than once when I would do something people thought was strange or out of the ordinary. *But she's so pretty,* they'd marvel, as if the way I looked and the way I acted were mutually exclusive.

I *am* pretty. I know this for two reasons: People have been telling me my whole life, and I own a mirror. Sometimes I wondered how much worse people would treat me if I were ugly. I never thought about it for long because I was almost certain I knew the answer.

"Be nice," Janice said.

"What?" the girl said. "It's weird."

Though Janice had rarely spoken to me in the three weeks we'd shared a living space, she had never been unkind. And once during our second week in the dorm, when I was running dangerously low on clean clothes, she showed me where the laundry facilities were and taught me how to use the machines. Silently, we stood side by side and folded our clean clothes, stacking them in the same basket that she carried back to our room.

Suddenly I was in middle school again, and the kind of terror I hadn't felt in years enveloped me. I just wanted them to leave me alone, and I trembled as my eyes filled with tears. Beads of sweat prickled my hairline, and the air under the covers became unbearable. But there was no way I could show my face now.

"Why don't you guys take off without me," Janice said. "I've got some studying to do."

"Jesus. You really struck out in the roommate department," one of the girls said.

"Forget about her," said the other. "She's not your problem."

"I don't mind looking out for her. Besides, it would be like kicking a puppy." She said it quietly, but I heard it.

The soft click of the door signaled their departure, and I came out from under the covers and took deep breaths of the cooler-only-by-comparison air. "Why would anyone *ever* kick a puppy?"

"They wouldn't."

"Then why would you *say* that?"

"It's just an expression."

I wiped my cheeks with the back of my hand. The more I tried to stem the flow of my tears, the faster they fell. Neither of us spoke for a while and my sniffling was the only sound as I tried to get myself under control. The ringing phone saved me from further humiliation when Janice rose to answer it.

"Hi. Yes, it's Janice," I heard her say and then she stretched the cord to its limit so she could take the phone out into the hallway and talk to whoever it was in private, away from me. After a few minutes, she returned, hung up the phone, and sat down on the end of my bed.

"Sometimes I miss my old room. I have six brothers, but I'm the baby, and they're all out of the house now. But I remember what it was like when they all lived at home. They drove me crazy. It's hard not to have a space where you can be alone."

I hadn't uttered a word, and yet Janice somehow seemed to know exactly what I was thinking and how I was feeling. *How in the world did she do that?*

"It's so hot out. I was thinking of walking to the union for a lemonade. Why don't you come with me?"

I didn't want to. My parents had promised they'd be there in the morning to take me away from this nightmare, and I wanted to dive back under the covers and count down the minutes. But there was a part of my brain that understood what she'd done for me, so I said, "Okay."

As we walked to the union, Janice pointed out the Wildlife Medical Clinic. "I've heard they need volunteers there. You should go talk to them. They probably want people who would be kind to animals." I nodded but didn't have the courage to tell her I'd be gone in the morning.

While we were standing in line waiting to order our lemonade, I noticed the chessboards. There were at least fifteen of them sitting on the nearby tables, pieces set up, waiting for play. Students sat in front of them, talking and laughing.

I must have been staring because Janice said, "Do you play?"

"Yes."

"Let's go check it out."

"I don't want to."

"Come on."

She handed me my lemonade, and I followed her over to an older student standing next to one of the chessboards. "What is this? My friend plays chess and she'd like to know."

"This is where the chess club meets," he said, looking at me. "I'm Rob. We're here every Sunday from six until eight. What's your name?"

Janice nudged me, and I said, "Annika."

He turned to the boy on his right. "This is Eric. He's new, too. If you stay, we'll have an even number and everyone can play."

"She'd like that," Janice said.

I had been looking off in the distance and Janice moved into my line of vision so she could look me in the eye, which made me very uncomfortable. "I'll be back at eight to pick you up. I'll come right here, to this table, and we'll walk home together."

"Okay." I sat down across from Eric, and the only thing that kept me from bolting in terror was him moving his first piece. Instinct took over as I formulated my strategy, and as we played, I forgot how much I hated college, and how stupid I felt trying to do the things that came naturally to everyone else. I took out all my frustrations on that game, and I played hard. Eric proved to be a worthwhile opponent and by the time I ceded victory to him—but just barely—I felt almost human again. For the first time since I arrived on campus, I did not feel quite so out of place.

"Great game," Eric said.

"It was," I said, my voice barely above a whisper.

Rob handed me a sheet with some information about the club. "So just come back here next Sunday."

I took the sheet and nodded, and at eight o'clock on the dot, Janice arrived to walk me back to the dorm. One of my worst days had turned out to be one of my best. For the first time in a long time, strangers had showed me kindness, and I dared to hope that one day, Janice and I might become actual friends. And thanks to the serendipitous discovery of the chess club, I had an outlet, and a reason to stay.

Later that night, when Janice went down the hall to study, I called my parents back and told them not to come.

My thoughts drifted back to the present when Jonathan and I reached my apartment building. It had been a while since I'd reflected on the events that led me to chess club. If not for Janice and the members of the club, and the kindness they showed me that day, I would not be a senior in college. Though I still had far to go, I'd learned so much about people and life, and that there were very good and very bad things about both.

"Is this where you live?" Jonathan asked as I made my way up the sidewalk toward the front door.

My back was to him, and I didn't turn around when I responded. "Yes."

"Okay. Have a good night. I'll see you next week," he said.

7

Annika

CHICAGO
AUGUST 2001

"What's bothering you today, Annika. Can we talk about it?" Tina asks when I arrive for my appointment and we've settled into our seats. For the first time since I started therapy, I want to lie and fabricate an excuse for why my hair looks like I combed it with my fingers (because I did), the dark circles under my eyes (not sleeping well), and my unmatched clothes (pink skirt, red T-shirt). But that would honestly take more energy than the embarrassing, humiliating truth, so I spill it, and I spare no detail.

"Jonathan doesn't want anything to do with me. And that's exactly what I deserve."

"I think you're being incredibly hard on yourself."

"It's the truth."

"Why do you think he doesn't want to see you again?"

"Because," I say, fully aware that I sound like a petulant teenager yet unable to stifle my frustration because things with Jonathan had not progressed in the way I'd expected. "I thought we could just pick up where we left off."

"You mean the way he felt when he was waiting for you in New York?"

"Yes. I'm ready now."

"What about Jonathan? Do you think he's still ready?"

I barely understood my own thoughts and had no clue about Jonathan's. "I thought he was until he left me standing on the sidewalk."

"Do you think he's punishing you in some way because of the past?"

"Isn't he?"

"Could there be another reason? Ten years is a long time. I'm sure there have been lots of developments in his life, the way there have been in yours."

One by one, I pull the Jonathan facts out of my brain where I've committed them to memory. "He's divorced. No kids. I think he works a lot. He lives in an apartment not far from me."

"Divorce is a major, and often very stressful, life change. Jonathan may have always seemed invincible to you, but he's human and he feels pain just like anyone else. Could it be that it's his current situation that's influencing his decision whether or not to see you again, and not the past?"

Tina and I have spent hours working on the difficulties I have putting myself in other people's shoes, and after I watched Jonathan walk away, I spent all day trying to figure it out on my own. My frustration grew because for the life of me, I could not put my finger on it no matter how hard I tried. I just assumed he was mad at me for what I'd done. Then I couldn't relax and therefore couldn't sleep, and I've been at a deficit ever since. Yet in less than fifteen minutes, Tina has effortlessly unraveled it for me, and I finally understand. All these extra steps are exhausting. I remember feeling stunned when Tina explained that most people can draw these conclusions instantaneously, without any extra analysis at all. How amazing but also heartbreaking, because I'll never be one of them.

"I just . . . I wanted so badly to have the chance to show him that I'm different now. That I'm not the same girl I was back then."

"But that's something you want. He gets to have a say, too." Tina scribbles something on the legal pad that rests on her lap. "Do you think Jonathan would have wanted you to change?"

"Doesn't everyone? How could you not want someone to change after they hurt you?"

"Changing how you deal with something is not the same thing as changing who you are as a person. Jonathan isn't here so I can't answer for him, but I've spoken to a lot of people in my years of providing therapy. The one thing I hear them say the most is that the other person changed. And not one of them has ever said it like it's a good thing."

"What do you think I should do?"

Tina shakes her head. "That's your homework for next time. I want you to tell me."

8

Annika

THE UNIVERSITY OF ILLINOIS
AT URBANA-CHAMPAIGN
1991

Jonathan was walking out of Lincoln Hall when Janice and I passed by on our way to class. He smiled and said hi. I did nothing.

"Who was that?" Janice asked.

"Jonathan. Chess club."

"The guy you beat?"

"Yes." I didn't want to talk about Jonathan. The thought of talking to Janice about any guy stirred up too many unpleasant memories. I could think about Jonathan in my head, but I wasn't ready to talk about him out loud.

Janice elbowed me. "Is there a reason you didn't mention how good-looking he was?"

"Are you hungry? Do you want to get some lunch? I'm hungry."

"Oh, Annika. It's funny that you think I'm going to let you off so easily."

"I really wish you would."

"Not a chance."

"I can't do it again. I won't."

"Not every guy is bad. A lot of them are very good."

"Well, we both know I'm not capable of spotting the difference on my own."

"Don't worry. This time he'll have to get past me first."

"That won't be necessary. I'm sure he doesn't think of me like that."

"Where do you want to eat lunch?"

"Actually, I'm signed up for a shift at the clinic. There's an opossum with a broken arm I want to check on. Poor thing. He's so cute. You should see his little splint."

"Then why did you suggest lunch?"

"I just wanted to change the subject."

"I'm disappointed in myself. I can't believe I fell for it."

The University of Illinois Wildlife Medical Clinic accepted native wild animals in need of care due to illness and injury, or because they'd been orphaned. The goal was to rehabilitate them and release them back into the wild. Veterinary students made up the bulk of the volunteers, but there were a few—like me—whose undying love for animals, and not our future vocations, had led us to the clinic behind the veterinary medicine building on the south side of campus. I had a tendency to gravitate toward the smaller animals, but I also felt a special affinity for the birds. They were majestic creatures, and there was nothing more satisfying than releasing one and watching it soar off high in the sky.

The small animal I cradled in my gloved hands—the aforementioned opossum, who I'd decided should be called Charlie—had a long road ahead of him, but with the right care and attention, he had a good shot at returning to his natural habitat.

Sue, a senior who'd been volunteering at the clinic almost as long as I had, and whom I felt very comfortable with, walked into the room. "Hey, Annika. Ah, look at that little guy."

"Isn't he adorable? I just want to take him home with me. Do you know opossums don't actually hang by their tails? People always think they do, but they don't. They have Mickey Mouse–shaped ears and fifty teeth, but they're not dangerous." The other day when I was at the library studying I got sidetracked by a book on opossums, and I learned so many fascinating things. It took almost ten minutes to get through them all, but I shared every last one of those facts with Sue because I was certain she'd want to know.

"Clearly, he's in good hands." Sue glanced at her watch and squeezed my arm. "I've got to get going. I'll see you later, okay?"

"Okay."

I spent the rest of my shift cleaning cages, helping to administer medicine, and giving attention to any animal that needed it. Before I left for the day, I returned to Charlie's cage to say good-bye. I thought about how much I would miss him when it came time to let him go, and I wondered for just a moment if I would ever feel as attached to a person as I was to the animals.

And I wondered how much it would hurt if I was ever the one they had to let go.

9

Annika

CHICAGO
AUGUST 2001

"I'm going to eat lunch," my coworker Audrey says. She and I share the small office that houses our desks and computers and a couple of file cabinets. There have been several times when she's walked into the room and caught me staring off into space. She jokes about how I need to stop slacking off, but it doesn't sound like she's teasing when she says it. And I'm not slacking off. Staring into space is how I clear my mind so I can work through whatever problem I'm trying to solve.

"Okay," I say, because Audrey hates it when I don't acknowledge her statements. It's just that I'm not sure what she wants me to say. I didn't announce that I was going to eat lunch when I took my peanut butter sandwich out of my bag the way I do every single day. It's lunchtime. Eating is what we do.

As soon as Audrey leaves, I pull a piece of paper from my desk drawer. On it I've written everything I'm going to say when I call Jonathan, and all I have to do is read it out loud. I've thought long and hard about what Tina said, and I want Jonathan to know that I understand where he's coming from but that I'd like for us to spend some more time together. Jonathan was so many things to me, but he was also my friend, and I don't have very many of those.

I'm relieved when I get his voice mail, because that will make this so much easier, but just before the beep, Audrey walks back into our office. I don't want her to see me reading from a script, so I shove the paper under my desk blotter and wing it.

"Hey, Jonathan. It's Annika. Again. I just, um . . . thought you might be interested in doing something on Saturday." My throat feels dry and I take a fast sip of water, dribbling it down my chin in the process. "The weather's supposed to be nice so maybe we could pick up some lunch and take it to the park. If you're busy or you don't want to, that's okay too. I want you to know I *understand* where you're coming from. I just thought I would ask. Okay, bye."

I disconnect the call and gasp for air.

"Was that a personal call?" Audrey asks.

"It was nothing," I say. I need a minute to regulate my breathing and vent the adrenaline racing through my bloodstream from one stupid phone call.

"It didn't seem like nothing. Who is Jonathan?" I don't report to Audrey, but she's been here three years longer than I have and acts like she's entitled to know all of my business, professional or otherwise.

"He's just someone I used to know."

She leans against the edge of my desk. "Like an old boyfriend?"

"This is my lunch hour." Why didn't I say that before? And can't she see the sandwich on my desk?

"What are you talking about?" she asks in a bitchy voice, the one she uses when she thinks I've said something particularly strange.

"I just meant . . . when you first came in and asked if it was a personal call. This is my lunch hour." I shut my eyes and rub my temples.

"Are you getting sick or something?" She talks to me like I'm a toddler. Her voice is always very loud, so it feels like she's yelling at me.

"I'm just getting a headache."

"Will you be able to finish out the day? I can't cover for you this afternoon like I had to last week when you were gone. I had to stay late that night."

"I'm sorry," I sputter.

"It was a lot of extra work."

"I won't need you to cover for me. I'll take something for my headache." Audrey stares at me, making no move to leave. I pull out my desk drawer and shake a couple of pain relief capsules into my hand. I choke a little when I try to swallow them because I didn't take a big enough drink from my water bottle.

Audrey sighs and reaches into her desk drawer for some crackers. "I'm sure my soup is cold now," she says as she leaves the room again, and though I had nothing to do with it, it somehow feels like my fault.

When Audrey returns, I slip into the break room to make a cup of tea and I see my coworker Stacy. She always has a smile for me and her voice is very calming. When Stacy burns her finger on the meal she takes out of the microwave, I tell her I'm sorry and give her a little side hug.

"Oh," she says. "Hi, Annika. Just give me a second to put this down." She sets the meal on the counter. "What was that for?" Her voice doesn't sound as calm as it usually does. It's higher pitched now.

"I feel bad that you burned your finger."

"You're always so sweet, but I'll be fine. Thanks, Annika." She grabs her lunch and leaves the room in a hurry. She must be late for a meeting or something.

It isn't until the end of the day when I'm shutting down my computer to go home that I remember the only reason Audrey had to cover for me last week was because of an off-site meeting I attended at the request of our boss.

My headache never really went away and I'm completely worn out when I get home from work. I'm fostering a mother cat and her five kittens, and they're currently in a cardboard box under my bed. I spend an hour lying on the floor next to it listening to their calming little meows as my headache finally fades away. For dinner, I pour a bowl of cereal, and when I finish eating, I put on my pajamas and crawl into bed with a book, even though it's only eight thirty.

The phone rings an hour later. I don't have caller ID because not very many people call me, and I usually let my answering machine screen the ones that do so I have time to decide if I want to talk to them. It drives my mother absolutely nuts. It drives Janice nuts, too, so she always yells, "Pick up the phone, Annika. I know you're there and I know you want to talk to me."

I want to hold out so the answering machine can do its thing, but then I remember that it might be Jonathan, and I snatch the handset with only seconds to spare.

"Hello?"

It *is* him, and I'm flooded with happiness. Plus, I've always found the sound of Jonathan's voice to be very soothing. He never speaks too loud and there's something comforting about the way he strings his words together. To me, they sound like a melody. Audrey sounds like a foghorn whenever she blows into the room, and the way she strings her words together does *not* sound melodious. It sounds like screaming death metal.

"I didn't wake you, did I?" he asks.

It's only nine thirty, but if there's one person who's familiar with my sleep patterns, it's him.

"No. You didn't wake me. I'm reading in bed."

"I can get together on Saturday," he says.

"That's great!" I say it way too loud.

"Yeah, well. It's just lunch, right?"

"That's what I said in my message. I said it was lunch."

"Yeah, I know. What I meant was . . . never mind. Lunch is fine. Lunch will be great. Do you want me to pick you up at home?"

"I'll be at the Children's Theatre Saturday morning. Can you pick me up there? Around noon."

"Sure."

"Okay. I'll see you then."

"Good night," he says.

"Good night."

We hang up, but I don't go back to my book right away. I spend the next half hour thinking about Jonathan, replaying the highlights of our relationship like a "best of" reel, and when I wake up the next morning, he's the first person I think about.

10

Annika

THE UNIVERSITY OF ILLINOIS
AT URBANA-CHAMPAIGN
1991

The sound of footsteps echoed loudly on the sidewalk, and I turned around in time to see Jonathan sprinting toward me. When I left, he'd been talking to Eric and a few of the other players, and I assumed he would be going to dinner with everyone. We had played each other again, and I'd managed to win this time. Jonathan must not have minded too much, because he said, "I like playing with you, Annika."

A warm feeling had spread through me, because no one but Eric had ever said that to me before, and I didn't remember it having an effect on me the way it did when Jonathan said it. It was becoming easier for me to talk to him without clamming up or stammering my reply. I'd just needed a little time to ease into it, the way I always did with new people.

"Hey," he said when he caught up to me. "You forgot your book." He thrust out his hand and I spotted my dog-eared copy of *Sense and Sensibility* nestled in his large palm.

"Thanks."

"It's getting dark. You should always try to walk home with someone."

"Everyone always goes out to dinner."

"Why don't you?"

"I don't want to." I put the book in my backpack and we crossed the street. Usually I abhorred small talk, but my curiosity got the better of me. "Why don't *you* go out to dinner?"

"I have to work. I bartend at the Illini Inn on Saturday and Sunday nights. Do you ever go there?"

"No."

"You should come in some time. Like when I'm working."

"I don't go to bars."

"Oh." He hoisted his backpack higher on his shoulder, and we walked in silence for a minute.

"Have you ever thought about joining the competition team? Eric asked me to consider it, and I think I'm going to."

"No."

"Why not?"

"I don't want to."

"There must be a reason."

"It would just be too much for me."

"Because of your course load?"

"I can handle the academic load, but I volunteer twice a week in the Wildlife Medical Clinic and then there's chess on Sunday night. That's enough for me." I required more downtime than most people. I needed to be able to read and sleep and be alone. "If you're so into chess, why did you wait until your senior year to join the club?" I asked.

"This is my first year here. I transferred from Northwestern."

"Oh."

He stopped walking suddenly. "Thank you for being literally the only person I've told that to who didn't immediately ask why."

I stopped, too. "You're welcome."

He stared at me with a blank expression for a few seconds and then we started walking again.

"Why do you always smell like chlorine?"

"*That's* the question you want me to answer?"

"Yes."

"I swim almost every day. It's what I do for exercise. I had my growth spurt later than everyone else, so I didn't go out for football or basketball. If you don't start early, you can never really catch up. I'm good at swimming though. I'm sorry if the smell bothers you. Seems like it never quite goes away, even after I shower."

"I don't mind it."

We'd arrived at my apartment building by then, so I left Jonathan standing on the sidewalk and walked toward the door. Before I reached it he called out, "You should think about joining the competition team."

"I'll think about it," I said.

But I wouldn't.

11

Jonathan

CHICAGO

AUGUST 2001

I'm waiting outside the theater at noon when Annika walks out the door surrounded by children. She's holding the hand of a little boy, and she crouches down to give him a hug before he runs into the waiting arms of his mother. The children scatter toward their respective parents, waving and calling out good-bye to Annika before they go. She waves in return, a smile lighting up her face. The smile grows bigger when she sees me, and I tell myself that accepting her invitation was the right thing to do. Like I told her on the phone, it's just lunch. What I won't tell her is that I'd been having an awful day when she'd left the last voice mail, and hearing her voice had taken the edge off of it. Annika's the perfect antidote to any bad day.

She walks up to me. "Looks like you've got quite a fan club," I say.

"I find children more enjoyable than most adults."

Her statement does not surprise me. Children are born without hate, but unfortunately, some of them learn by an early age to wield it like a weapon, and no one knows that more than Annika. She has always had a childlike air about her, which probably makes her highly relatable to the kids. It's also the reason adults are often unkind to her, because they mistakenly believe it points to a lack of intelligence or ability, neither of which is true.

"I picked up lunch," I say, holding up the bag from Dominick's. The grocery store has a great take-out counter, and since that's where I ran into her, I figured it was as good a choice as any.

"But I invited you. I'm the one who's supposed to pay."

"You paid last time. It's my turn."

The humidity has dropped considerably in the last week and the air feels halfway bearable as we head toward Grant Park. Annika remains silent on the walk over.

"Is anything wrong? You're kind of quiet," I ask.

"I talked too much last time. I was nervous."

"Don't be. It's just me."

It seems all of Chicago has decided to come to the park today. We pick our way through the crowd and find an empty patch of grass to sit down and have our lunch. From the bag, I pull out sandwiches and chips. I hand Annika a bottle of lemonade and crack open a Coke for myself.

"You brought your board," she says, pointing to the carrying case that had been slung over my arm and that now rests on the grass beside us.

"I thought maybe you'd be up for a match." Mostly I thought it would put her at ease. Chess has always been one of the ways we communicate best.

"I'd like that. I'm rusty, though. You'll probably win."

"I'll probably win because I'm better than you." It takes her a second to comprehend that I'm teasing and she smiles.

She's beautiful when she smiles.

Around us, people play Frisbee on the grass, many of them barefoot. A bee buzzes around Annika's lemonade, and I swat it away. When we're done eating I open the board and we set up.

Almost everything about Annika seems delicate. Her hands are so much smaller than mine, and when I first met her I spent enough time studying them as she contemplated her next chess move that I couldn't help but wonder what they might feel like if I held one. But when she plays chess there is an absolute ruthlessness about her. She could barely look at me the first time I walked her home, but she has always stared at the pieces on a chessboard with laser focus, and today is no different. It's a good game. She *is* rusty, but she plays hard, and I concentrate, because I've never forgotten the first time we played, when she wiped the floor with me.

Today I manage to come out ahead, and I move my knight into position. "Checkmate."

There's nowhere for her to move her king and she can't block me or capture my piece. I can tell by her creased forehead and the way she's staring at the board that she's already beating herself up for the loss. "I let you win," she says.

I laugh. "No, you didn't. You played well, but I played better."

"I hate that you beat me."

"I know."

As we're picking up the pieces and putting them away, Annika says, "After we went to coffee, you didn't act like you wanted to see me again." My teasing smile fades, but I'm not sure if Annika will pick up on the hesitant expression that replaces it.

"I did want to. I just wasn't sure if it was a good idea."

"But we're in the same city now. I'm ready and I'm making things happen this time. I'm not leaving it all up to you."

"There are things we haven't talked about yet. Because I don't think you *want* to talk about them."

"I thought we could skip over everything that happened and start fresh."

"That's not how it works."

"It would be so much easier if it did." She stares down at the blanket and neither of us says anything for a minute.

"I go to therapy once a week. I started as soon as I moved to the city. Her name's Tina. She's really helped me understand why I . . . why I see things the way I do. I told her you probably didn't want anything to do with me because of what happened between us, but she said maybe it was because of the divorce."

"It's a little of both, I suppose." It's a hard pill to swallow when you have to admit, even to yourself, that you were wrong about the person you were certain was perfect for you. It was even harder to admit that part of Liz's allure was that she was the polar opposite of Annika. At the time, I'd convinced myself that it meant everything until the day it backfired on me, and I realized it hadn't meant as much as I thought it did. "You get cautious after a divorce. Second-guess yourself a little," I say. But Annika was right to accept some of the responsibility for my hesitation, because it was definitely a factor. "What about you? Any breakups in your past?"

"I dated one of my coworkers at the library. He's a nice guy and we got along so well. We tried to make a go of it romantically for about six months, but he was too much like me." She looks into my eyes and then looks away just as suddenly. "It was a disaster. People like us need people who are . . . not like us to balance things out. We're just really good friends now. I dated the next man for over a year. He said he loved me, but he could never quite accept me for who I am and treated me as if I wasn't worthy of his attention and affection because of it. Sometimes I worried that if we'd stayed together, I might have started to believe it."

"Maybe he *did* love you, but you wouldn't let him."

She shakes her head no. "It's because of you that I know what it feels like to be loved and accepted." Her eyes fill with tears and she blinks them away.

"Maybe I'm the one who needs to take it slow this time."

"I can do slow, Jonathan. I'll wait for you, the way you always waited for me."

Annika is wearing slip-on shoes without socks. I reach over and gently take them off. She looks at me and smiles as the memory hits, and she wiggles her toes in the grass like it's the best feeling in the world.

I smile, too.

12

Annika

THE UNIVERSITY OF ILLINOIS
AT URBANA-CHAMPAIGN
1991

Jonathan campaigned relentlessly in his effort to convince me to join the competition team. It didn't help that Eric was now in on it, and I was receiving pressure from both of them.

"What if I came to your apartment and picked you up for the meeting on Wednesday?" he asked. "Then would you go?" I'd only just begun to feel comfortable talking to Jonathan. I wasn't ready to add another activity, especially a higher-stress activity like competitive chess.

"Maybe." I wished I could protest that I didn't need a babysitter, but the truth was that I avoided trying new things at any cost, and that's exactly the role Jonathan would have to play.

We packed up our things and left the student union together because Jonathan now walked me home every Sunday night after chess club ended. The others would head out for dinner and we would fall in step side by side until we reached my apartment.

It was the highlight of my week.

The sky had threatened rain on my way to the union, and now upon leaving the building, I discovered it had arrived as a heavy downpour. I pulled my umbrella out of my backpack and debated calling Janice to ask her to come get me in her car. I didn't know how to drive and despite my mother's urging, refused to obtain a license. The thought of piloting thousands of pounds of metal terrified me, and the closest thing I had to transportation was my old blue ten-speed Schwinn.

"I drove tonight. I can give you a ride home."

Nervousness about being alone with Jonathan in his vehicle almost prevented me from taking him up on the ride, but before I could think too much about it, he pushed open the door, opened his umbrella, and held it over both of our heads as he headed in the direction of the parking lot. The wind was blowing and we walked quickly as he led me toward a white pickup truck. He unlocked my door and ran around to the driver's side and unlocked his.

It was early October and the days had grown cooler. The dampness in the air from the rain made it seem even chillier. I'd forgotten to bring a jacket and I rubbed my hands along my arms in an attempt to generate some friction.

"Are you cold?"

"I forgot my jacket at home."

Jonathan fiddled with a dial on the dash, and air blew from the vents. "It might take a few minutes to get warm."

Traffic slowed at the intersection. It was fully dark and at first I couldn't understand why most of the cars had stopped at the green light, and why a few of them were honking their horns loudly, making me want to cover my ears from the awful sound. But then I spotted the goose and a long row of goslings trailing behind her as they tried to cross the road. Most of the cars were waiting, but of few of them sped through the intersection with no regard for the animals.

I jumped from the truck without a second thought, leaving the door wide open in my haste to assist the geese. Jonathan must have leapt from the car right after me, because I could hear him yelling, "Annika! Jesus! Be careful."

The mother goose hissed as I worked on shepherding her and her offspring to safety. The rain pelted me, and Jonathan, too, because he'd begun directing traffic, holding out his hands like a policeman to stop the motorists from coming any closer. I walked alongside the geese and shielded them with my body as they slowly made their way single file through the intersection and down into the safety of the ditch on the side of the road. I flapped my hands in excitement because we had saved them, but then I put them over my ears to block out the cacophony of angry car horns. Jonathan and I got back in the truck and he pulled into the line of traffic when the light turned green. I turned around, craning to see the geese in the dark and feeling relieved when I located the bobbing head of the mother. They were heading away from the road, and I hoped they would continue on their way toward wherever they would settle for the night.

"That was wild," Jonathan said. "I had no idea you were going to jump out of the truck like that. You scared the crap out of me."

"Did you see those cars? Some of them seemed like they were going to run right over those poor animals. I don't know why those geese were so off course."

"Some people need to chill out."

"Do you want to meet my roommate?"

"You mean now?"

"Yes."

"I have to get to work, and I need to go home first to change into dry clothes."

"Oh, that's right. I forgot."

"I mean, I can spare a few minutes if you really want me to meet her."

Jonathan parked his truck and followed me up the stairs to my apartment. Joe and Janice were sitting on the couch watching TV. "That smell is incense," I said.

"Okay," Jonathan said.

I could read Janice's expressions fairly well because I'd been studying them since the day I'd met her, and she was looking at us with her "I'm delighted" smile. "Annika! Who's this?" she asked.

"This is Jonathan. He drove me home because of the rain."

"Hi," Jonathan said.

"That's my roommate, Janice, and her boyfriend, Joe. He smells like pot which is why we burn the incense."

Joe grunted a hello, but Janice and Jonathan shook hands. "Nice to meet you," she said.

"You, too."

"Why are you guys soaking wet?"

"We had to help the geese. A mother goose and her goslings were trying to cross the road by the union and people weren't even stopping!"

"So you jumped out of the car to help them," she said.

"Of course. No one else was going to help them." I turned to Jonathan. "Okay. You can go now."

No one said anything for a few moments. Jonathan walked to the door, but before he opened it, he turned around and said, "Don't forget to take a jacket with you tomorrow. It's supposed to be even colder than today."

"I won't." But there was a good chance I would. Organization was not my strong suit. Shortly after Janice took me under her wing during those disastrous early days of our freshman year, she tried to help me get organized and soon discovered I was a lost cause. My side of our dorm room looked a lot like my bedroom at home: Clean clothes in one pile, dirty in another. Papers everywhere. To some, it looked like chaos, but to me it was organized chaos, and Janice learned not to disrupt it after she tried to help me while I was at class by folding all my clothes. I'd become so visibly upset that she never attempted it again.

Matching clothes and proper grooming were things I rarely thought about, but Janice was able to convince me that being color-coordinated was a good thing, and she gently reminded me to comb my hair whenever I started to resemble a mad scientist. There were still times I'd retreat under my covers with my penlight and a book, and Janice would ask if I was upset or depressed. Eventually I was able to assure her that sometimes, I just needed to be left alone. There *were* things I was confused about, mostly the proper responses in social situations, and as I grew more comfortable with Janice, I asked her about them.

Living with her had been like a crash course in how to be normal.

After Jonathan left, I shut the door and sat down on the couch next to Janice. "What do you think?"

"Well, for starters, he's very polite."

"He's a giant nerd," Joe said.

"No he's not," I said.

"Annika wasn't asking you, Joe."

"I bet he just loves to play chess," Joe said.

"I love playing chess."

Joe snorted and shot Janice some sort of look. She shot one back at him. It was a fairly recent addition to her expression catalogue, but I knew it meant "Shut up right now, Joe."

"Why are you still dating him?" I asked Janice.

Janice shushed me and pulled me into the kitchen. "I don't know. He's very, very pretty."

"And so dumb."

"It's okay. It's not like I'm going to marry him."

Was Jonathan a nerd? Just because he had short hair and didn't play every sport didn't mean that he was a nerd. He was really smart, and intelligence had always made guys seem more interesting to me than they might be to others. Plus, he *was* really good-looking and sometimes while we were playing chess I stared at him, mesmerized by how perfect his face looked. He had the whitest teeth I'd ever seen, which made me think his kisses would taste like Pep O Mint Life Savers. Joe's kisses probably tasted like pot and Funyuns.

And failure.

"Do you like Jonathan?" Janice asked. "Like, *like* him like him?"

"No."

"It's okay if you do," Janice said.

"I don't."

"Just don't jump in with both feet this time. Until we know for sure."

I turned to her, exasperated. "But *how* will we know?"

"Sometimes we won't. But if a guy reminds you to carry a jacket because he doesn't want you to get cold, it's a pretty good indicator he won't try to hurt you. That doesn't guarantee that he won't, and you still have to be careful, but it's a good start."

"I don't want to be wrong again," I said, because I had been, once, midway through our sophomore year. A guy named Jake, who I'd met in one of my lectures, had taken a liking to me, and to say I reciprocated with vigor would have been an embarrassing understatement. What started as silly doodling on each other's notebooks while the professor droned on soon morphed into walking to our next class together, me wearing the biggest smile that had ever shown itself on my face, and Jake with his arm casually thrown over my shoulder or resting on my ass. Having a boyfriend was as great as I'd always thought it would be, and it was easy! For over a week, I rarely left Jake's side. I sought him out in the student union and the dining hall, and took my rightful place at his table the way any girlfriend would. I did his laundry and helped him with his homework because that's what you do when you're in love with someone and they're in love with you. And he was very busy, so I was grateful he could spend time with me at all. Whenever we ran into his friends, which seemed to be all the time because he was apparently very popular on campus, he would point at me and say, "Have you met Annika? She sure is *something*." Then they would all laugh and my smile would grow even wider because it felt so good to fit in.

And then, a short while later when things turned bad, my roommate was there once again to pick up my pieces and put me back together.

Janice laid a hand on my shoulder. "I don't think you're wrong this time. I think Jonathan genuinely likes you. He seems like a good guy. Let yourself have this. Don't let one bad experience take the happiness in meeting a great guy away forever. If you're not quite ready to admit it to me, at least admit it to yourself."

"Do you really think he likes me?"

"It sure seems like he does. Does he flirt with you?"

Jonathan hadn't done any of the things Jake had done, like drawing on my notebook or putting his arm around me. "I'm not sure. He does smile at me a lot."

"That's a good sign."

"I'll have to pay closer attention."

I thought about Jonathan later that night when I was lying in bed, and I tried not to mentally catalogue all the things that could go wrong. Instead, I thought of how he almost always chose to play with me at chess club. I liked that he always walked me home. I liked that he cared whether or not I was cold.

I liked all of those things.

I liked them a lot.

13

Annika

THE UNIVERSITY OF ILLINOIS
AT URBANA-CHAMPAIGN
1991

The sun had barely risen when Jonathan and I left campus for the drive to St. Louis. My empty stomach churned. I was so nervous, I hadn't been able to fathom the thought of breakfast and I worried I might dry-heave in the passenger seat of Jonathan's truck.

"I'm sorry there's no music," Jonathan said. "The radio has never worked."

"I like the quiet," I said. Being trapped in a car where loud music was playing was one of the things that could send me into a tailspin. I couldn't handle the overstimulation and would need hours of silence to counteract the noise. Jonathan's truck looked old and it rattled softly as we drove down the highway, but to me it was perfect.

Jonathan had not only convinced me to join the competition team, he'd talked me into participating in the practice match. Eric had been thrilled. So had Janice. I was the only one who still had reservations. At the last chess team meeting—and only the second one I'd attended—I'd overheard some of the others questioning Eric about whether I was cut out for tournament play. That was another thing I'd discovered over the years. If you're quiet and don't make a lot of sound, for some reason people think it means there's something wrong with your hearing. But there was nothing wrong with mine.

Eric defended me. "I've been playing with Annika for three years, and I'd bet money that she could beat every one of you. She'll be an asset to us." The last thing I wanted to do after an endorsement like that was let Eric down.

There were twelve of us competing that day, and if I'd had to drive over with the others, packed six to a car like sardines, surrounded by noises and smells, I would not have agreed to do it.

"We can drive over by ourselves if you want, Annika," Jonathan had said. "And we don't have to spend the night. We can leave as soon as our matches are over." Once again, he'd removed every obstacle in my way as if he'd known exactly what to do to make me comfortable.

"He does know," Janice said when I told her about his offer. "And he's doing it because he likes you, and because he truly is a nice guy."

"I'm very nervous," I admitted to Jonathan, tucking my hands up under the hem of my shirt so I could hide the flicking of my fin gers.

"You'll do great," he said. "They'll take one look at you and forget how to play the game."

"I don't think so," I said. "These players are really good. I can't imagine they'd suddenly forget how to play."

"I meant because you're so pretty. They'll be too busy looking at you and it will blow their concentration."

"That probably won't happen."

He let out a short laugh. "Just me then, huh?"

My brain figured out what he meant a few minutes later and I yelled "Oh" loud enough to make Jonathan jump in his seat a little. "Were you flirting with me?"

"I was trying to. I thought I was halfway decent at it, but now I'm not so sure."

"Jonathan?"

He took his eyes off the road for a second and looked over at me.

"I totally thought you were flirting. I was just making sure."

Then he gave me another one of those smiles I'd told Janice about.

The competition was being held in a large conference room at a local hotel. Though we were traveling as a team, we would be competing individually. The weather that day was unseasonably warm for late October, as it often is in the unpredictable Midwest, and I'd worn a long baggy skirt and even looser T-shirt knowing I wouldn't be able to handle clothing that wasn't lightweight and comfortable. I still felt overheated and had already started to sweat a little.

"You doing okay?" Jonathan asked. I hadn't uttered a word since we'd walked into the hotel, and I'd remained close by his side even though I really needed to go to the bathroom. My bladder didn't handle nervousness well at all.

"When will we start playing?" I hated not knowing exactly how things worked, and I should have asked Eric what to expect from tournament play before I'd committed. If I could get past the part where I had to exchange small talk with my opponent, and start playing, I could lose myself in the game and block out the rest. All the butterflies in my stomach would disappear and I'd stop feeling like I had to throw up.

"The first round will start at ten o'clock. Eric has the sheet with our brackets and who we'll be playing. Don't worry. I'll explain everything."

His words calmed me and I nodded. "Okay."

For the next half hour, we warmed up and Eric shared everything he knew about the other teams. I would potentially be playing three times, depending on whether I won and advanced to the next round. My first opponent was a girl from Missouri, and I studied her stats and pondered my opening.

A little before ten, we filed into the conference room and took our spots in front of the boards that had our names next to them on small cardboard signs.

"Hello," my opponent said. She was a dark-haired girl named Daisy and when she extended her hand, I shook it quickly and turned my attention back to the board. My nervousness over competing for the first time affected my opening, and I faltered, making two careless moves in a row. Her capitalization on them was all it took for me to realize she would be a formidable opponent, and it was exactly the motivation I needed to banish the butterflies and send me into fighting mode. We battled until the finish, but in a move she didn't see coming, I captured her king. "Checkmate."

"Good game," she said.

The next match seemed easier by comparison; I'd expected it to be harder. Maybe it was the luck of the draw, but I dispatched my opponent—a tall boy from the University of Iowa—with relative ease, although it took me nearly two hours to do it.

"Wow. Okay," was all he said before he moved on.

By the time I sat down across from my third and final opponent, I had been playing for almost four hours, and the combination of an early wake-up time and the mental energy required to sustain this level of play had begun to catch up with me. My opponent kept his focus on the board when we sat down across from each other. We didn't look at each other, and neither of us said a word. Our match went on for a long time and we drew a crowd as the others finished. It was truly the hardest match I'd ever played in all my years of dispatching opponents, and it was only because my opponent botched his final move that I was able to triumph. I felt depleted, almost limp, as I captured his king. "Checkmate." Jonathan came up and placed his hands on my shoulders, squeezing gently as I exhaled in relief.

Our fellow teammates gathered around us, celebrating their wins and lamenting their losses. We lingered for a while until Eric suggested we leave the hotel and go to dinner at a nearby diner. The team enthusiastically agreed.

"What do you think, Annika?" Jonathan asked. "Are you hungry?"

"Yes," I said. It was almost six o'clock by then, and my opponents had probably been able to hear my stomach growling while we played. "I need to use the restroom and then I'll be ready to go."

When I was washing my hands, I looked in the mirror. My cheeks were pink and my eyes had a brightness I'd never seen in them before. Maybe this was what it felt like to be happy, I thought. In the hallway, after I left the bathroom but before I walked to where Jonathan was waiting for me, I quickly slipped off my shoes and tucked them into my bag. Janice had convinced me to swap my usual tennis shoes for a pair of her flats, and I hated the way my feet felt inside them. No one would be able to see my bare feet under my long skirt.

He was standing by the door, and he held it open and followed me outside. The late-fall grass had gone mostly dormant and there was a texture to it, a slight crispness that felt incredible under my feet as we cut across the hotel's lawn on the way to Jonathan's truck so we could catch up to the others, who'd already begun pulling out of the parking lot. I wanted to sit down on the grass and curl my toes in it. I would never be able to explain how much satisfaction that would give me, or how effective it would be in helping me disperse the stress from the crowded room and a full day of competition.

Jonathan started the truck and pulled out of the parking lot. "How is it that you've been a member of the chess club for over three years, and no one but Eric and I know how good you are?" he asked. Only seven of us had won all of our brackets, and Jonathan and I were two of them.

"When Eric can't play with me, I usually go home."

"Why?"

How could I make him understand that I was mostly invisible to others? Most of my fellow club members had written me off a long time ago as the weird, shy girl, and they would have been right. For most of them, the club provided a social outlet and the chess part was a way to add a pleasurable activity they also enjoyed. It was so much more for me. Concentrating on the game eliminated a lot of the anxious clutter that constantly took up real estate inside my brain. "I don't know. I just do."

At the restaurant, Jonathan parked the truck and we went inside to join the others. As we waited in line, I slipped my hands into the pockets of my skirt and swished the fabric back and forth. There was something about the movement that soothed me, and I liked the sound it made.

"Miss, you can't come in here like that," a voice said. I didn't realize it was directed at me until Jonathan said, "Annika, where are your shoes?" It felt like one of those moments when you're talking too loud because you're in a noisy place but then the noise stops suddenly and everyone looks to see who's shouting. Except I wasn't shouting. I was standing in line at a diner in my bare feet, and everyone was looking down at my hot pink painted toenails. I hadn't done it intentionally; I'd just forgotten to slip my shoes back on before we got out of the truck.

My face flamed, and I turned toward the door, panicking when I tried to pull it open instead of pushing. It rattled as I shook it and when I finally comprehended how it worked, I burst through it and fled to the parking lot. Jonathan caught up to me as I jerked on the door handle of his truck. "Hold on, it's locked," he said. He put in the key and opened the door for me. "Don't worry about it. Just put on your shoes and we'll go back in."

I climbed into the truck and wiped the tears that spilled from my eyes with the back of my hand. Jonathan stood patiently next to the door, waiting.

"I can't go back in there."

"Why not?"

"You go ahead. I'll wait here."

"Annika, it's no big deal."

"Please don't make me go in," I cried.

He placed his hands, palm side down, on my legs, and his touch comforted me in a way I'd never felt before. He made me feel protected, as if he'd never let anything bad happen to me. "Stay here. Lock the door, and I'll be back in a minute."

He closed the door, and I pushed down on the lock as he walked back into the diner. Through the glass, I watched him talk to the team and then make his way to the counter. He returned to the truck five minutes later carrying a white paper bag.

I reached over and unlocked his door. "I told them you were tired and that the competition really took it out of you so we decided we'd head back. They were totally cool. Wanted me to tell you again how great you did today. I got sandwiches and pie. Do you like pie?"

I no longer had any doubt about the kind of guy Jonathan was.

"I love pie."

"The sandwich is ham. The pie's apple." He handed me a foil-wrapped sandwich and a Styrofoam container of pie, along with a fork and napkin.

It was something that Janice would do, and I wondered if I would always need someone to take care of me. "Thank you." I was never intentionally impolite, but I often forgot to say thank you, and I would have been so embarrassed if I hadn't remembered until after he dropped me off at home.

Jonathan unwrapped his sandwich and took a bite. "You don't strike me as someone who'd have hot pink toenails."

"Janice did it. She said if I insist on going barefoot so much, the least I could do was make my feet prettier for people to look at." I took a bite of my pie because I always ate dessert first if given the chance, and I was so hungry I had to force myself to pause between bites. "I don't like shoes."

He let out a short laugh but it sounded kind. "Yeah, I gathered that."

"They feel restrictive and I can't wiggle my toes."

"What do you do in the winter?"

"Suffer in boots."

"You don't play games, do you?"

I took another bite of my pie. "Chess is the only game I know how to play."

After we finished eating, we drove down the dark highway in silence, and by the time we reached Urbana, I'd returned to as calm a state as I'd ever be in outside the walls of my apartment. Jonathan pulled up in front of my building and turned off the truck. I opened the door and climbed out without saying good-bye, focusing only on reaching the safety and comfort of my bedroom, where I planned to spend the rest of the evening in solitude trying to forget the whole mortifying experience. To my surprise, Jonathan got out, too, and he caught up with me as I reached the doorway of my building. He grabbed my hand and I stopped short. He squeezed it gently but didn't let it go. His touch grounded me and made me feel as if nothing bad could ever happen as long as Jonathan had ahold of my hand.

"Do you want to go out with me Friday night?"

"Go out with you where?" I asked.

"On a date. We can go wherever you want."

I couldn't believe he still wanted to be seen with me, let alone take me someplace willingly. Jake had never asked me to go anywhere with him, and the food Jonathan had just shared with me had been the closest I'd ever come to having a meal with a member of the opposite sex.

It was the closest thing I'd had to a date of any kind.

"Why would you want to do that?" *Why would anyone?* My humiliation felt palpable by then, and I instantly regretted asking the question. Why heap more embarrassment on top of what I'd already brought upon myself?

"Because I think you're really pretty, and I like you." When I didn't say anything, he dropped my hand and shoved his into his pockets. "I feel like I can be myself with you."

All my life, I'd been waiting for someone I could be myself with. It had never occurred to me that I could be that person for someone else. His words choked me up and made me feel like crying.

"I would like to go out with you."

He smiled, and my eyes met his fleetingly before I looked away. "Great. Well, I'll see you tomorrow at chess club."

I looked down at the ground and nodded. Then I walked inside, and though I was exhausted and wanted nothing more than to escape into the comfort of a deep sleep, I couldn't stop thinking about when he might hold my hand again.

14

Jonathan

CHICAGO
AUGUST 2001

I last all of five days before I break down and call Annika. I'm leaving the day after tomorrow to spend two weeks in the New York office, and I want to see her again before I go.

"It's Jonathan," I say when she answers the phone. "I can't believe you picked up. I thought for sure I'd get your machine."

"I thought it was Janice calling me back. She hates it when I screen her calls."

"I wanted to see if you could have dinner tomorrow night. I know it's short notice."

"I can have dinner. I would love to have dinner."

"Okay. What's your number at work? I'll call you tomorrow afternoon." She gives it to me, and it's hard to miss the unmistakable joy in her voice.

So, I guess I'm willing to peel back a few layers after all.

I'm swamped at work, so when I call Annika the next day to confirm, I tell her I'll have to come straight from the office. She says she's working late, too, so she asks me to pick her up at the library and says she'll be ready by seven. That's an early night for me, but I can get away with it because I'll be on a plane long before the sun comes up tomorrow.

She's having a conversation with a man when I arrive, presumably a coworker because they're both wearing lanyards around their necks. Annika is gesturing excitedly with her hands, and she doesn't seem at all like the shy girl I met in college and had to draw out of her shell. This man is someone she's comfortable with. I can tell by how close he's standing to her and the way she almost looks right at him when she's talking. I wonder if this was the man she said was "too much like" her. She hasn't spotted me yet, and it feels slightly voyeuristic to observe her like this, but I'm still learning about present-day Annika, and one thing I've noticed is that she seems more confident than she was back then. I guess that's what ten years will do to a person.

She sees me and stops talking abruptly, walking toward me without saying good-bye to the man. He doesn't seem to mind and ambles off in another direction.

"Hi," I say.

"Hi."

"Are you ready to go?"

"Yes. I just need to grab my things." She walks off and doesn't turn around to make sure I'm following, but of course I am.

In her office, I lean against her desk as she shuts off her computer and gathers her things. A stocky, unattractive woman with frizzy black hair stomps into the room. "Did you leave your cart in the reference section, Annika? Someone abandoned theirs and it's blocking the row." She stops talking when she realizes there's someone else in the room.

"No," Annika says. "Mine is back where it belongs."

The woman studies me and smooths her hair. "Hi. I'm Audrey. Annika's superior." She thrusts out her hand and her chest.

"She's not my superior," Annika says. "I don't report to her."

Audrey gives an embarrassed smile with a touch of irritation carefully hidden underneath.

But I notice it.

"Jonathan." I shake her hand quickly.

Audrey shoots Annika a pointed look. "So that's who you were leaving the message for the other day, Annika." She turns back to me, coy. "And you are . . ."

That's not really any of your business. "Annika's college boyfriend."

Audrey's eyes get big.

I look at Annika, warmly. "I was her first love."

"He was my first everything," Annika says matter-of-factly.

"And now you've reconnected?" Audrey asks. She can barely contain her curiosity.

I smile cryptically. "Something like that."

"I don't like Audrey," Annika says as we make our way toward the exit.

"I can't say I blame you."

"She isn't very nice to me, and the more I try to stand up for myself, the worse it gets."

It makes me sad that Annika still has to deal with this kind of crap after all these years, but I see it every day at my own workplace. The jockeying for power. Behavior more suitable to high school than the business world.

"Do you know how sometimes you think of the perfect rebuttal but by the time you come up with it, it's hours later?" she asks.

"Sure."

"That's how it always is with me and Audrey."

"I bet you can hold you own," I say, but she shrugs and looks down at the ground.

We grab a cab outside the library. I'd asked Annika if she liked the food at Trattoria No. 10 and told her I'd booked a table. "But I can change it if you'd rather go someplace else."

"I love the food there," she'd said. "Especially the stuffed shells."

"How was your day?" I ask once I've given the cab driver our destination.

"It was good. Busy. I spent most of the day weeding."

"Weeding?"

"Our collections are like our gardens and we go through them looking for damaged or outdated books. I take my cart and pull off a big section to make sure the selection is something my patrons would like. I would never just leave my cart in the row," she mutters.

It's nice to see her so passionate about her job, and even more than that, so comfortable with me. Her demeanor has changed significantly, and for the better, since our coffee date. She's not the only one who seems more relaxed, because Annika has always had that effect on me. Currently, there are very few people in my life I can be one hundred percent myself around, but she's always been one of them. I don't have to put on a show or try to impress her the way I did with Liz. It's very liberating.

"How was *your* day?" she blurts a bit loudly and unexpectedly, as if she just realized she should ask and is trying to make up for it with urgency and enthusiasm. It startles me a little.

"Also busy." I should still be at work, toiling away in my office until midnight so I can complain about it the next morning the way my peers will, for the sole purpose of making sure everyone knows how late we were there. The dog and pony show we all have starring roles in drives me insane, but choosing not to participate really isn't an option.

The cab pulls up to the curb, and I pay and follow Annika into the restaurant.

The hostess greets us with an unusually big smile and an enthusiastic "Hello!" She comes around from behind the podium and walks toward Annika, arms outstretched. I tense for a second, because Annika doesn't like it when strangers touch her, but she's smiling and flapping her hands at the hostess. "Claire! Hi!" They hug.

"It's so good to see you. It's been a while."

Annika nods her head. "I know. It has."

"We have a reservation for two under the name Hoffman," I say.

Claire checks my name off the list and leads us to a cozy table for two. "I'll send Rita over with your drink," she says to Annika.

Annika sits down, beams like a child at Claire. "I've been looking forward to it all day."

"Still cherry?"

"Yep."

I'm not entirely sure what Annika's connection is to this woman, but I'm starting to formulate a few theories.

"For you, sir?" Claire asks.

"Gin and tonic, please."

"Right away." She squeezes Annika's shoulder and heads back toward her podium.

"So," I say. "Is that a friend of yours or did you forget to mention you're a VIP-level customer here?" I use a joking tone.

Before she can answer me, a man dressed in chef's clothing barrels toward our table. Annika lights up. "Nicholas!"

"Annika!" he says. "We weren't sure you'd be back."

"Well, I haven't been since that night. But Jonathan asked me if I liked the food here and you know how much I enjoy the stuffed shells so . . ." She looks at him like, ta-da!

What is happening here?

"I don't think he's been back either."

"I'm not surprised. He prefers Mexican food."

"Well, I'm happy to see your beautiful face at one of my tables." He glances at me and then back to Annika. She completely misses the cue, and after an awkward silence, I extend my hand and he shakes it. "Jonathan."

"Nicholas."

Rita, a middle-aged, kind-looking motherly type, arrives with our drinks. "Honey, you sure are a sight for sore eyes," she says, and sets down our drinks. "I'm so happy to see you here again."

"Hi, Rita," Annika says, and takes a long pull on her straw. "This is where I discovered Italian sodas," she says as Rita moves on to the next table. "They're so good. I usually get the cherry, but lemon is my second favorite. Do you want a sip?"

"No thanks." I take a rather large drink from my own glass. "Can you fill me in?"

At first she looks like she doesn't understand what I'm asking, but then realization dawns on her face. "Oh! My ex-boyfriend and I made quite a scene the last time we ate here. Well, he did. He could be quite loud when he was annoyed. Janice called him high-strung. Well, she called him a lot of things, but that was the nicest."

"Why didn't you say something? We could have gone to a different restaurant."

"You asked if I liked the food here, and I do. It's probably my favorite menu in the entire city. I like that they don't change it a lot, but if the owner ever takes one of my favorites away, Nicholas said he'd make it special. All I'd have to do is ask him."

"You're not bothered by what happened the last time you were here?"

"That wasn't the restaurant's fault."

"So, you had a fight?" I gesture with my hands as if I'm actually trying to pull the story out of her.

"It started in the cab on the way over. Ryan—that was his name—wanted us to go on vacation with his best friend and the friend's wife who I once overheard say I was weird, so I said I didn't understand why she would want to go on vacation with us in the first place. And I had already told him I didn't think I could go on a cruise because I get seasick easily." I nod, because I know Annika has a delicate stomach.

". . . Plus you know how much I would *hate* the feel of sand under my toes."

I did. Grass was good, but sand and dirt were deal breakers. A cool tile floor on a hot day was her favorite, but soft carpet ran a close second.

"But the thing is, he never listened to me. He would always say things like 'It's not that big of a deal' or 'You'll be fine.' But I knew I would *not* be fine. We were still arguing about it when Claire seated us. Then he said that he would ask his friend to reconsider the cruise but that the beach part was nonnegotiable because his friend's wife really loved the water, and I snorted and said she really loved vodka because the last time we went out for dinner with them, she drank so much she passed out right there at the table. I kept poking her, but it was lights out.

"Then Ryan said, 'Can't you for once just *try*?' and I had no clue what he was talking about because all we were doing is sitting at that table over there"—she points to a small table directly across from us—"eating dinner. Try what?

"I guess I didn't tell him what he wanted to hear because then he said, 'Do you know what it's like to be with someone who looks like you but then opens her mouth and ruins everything?' and I told him I did not and that I had no idea what that even meant, and then his face turned red. 'It's a complete fucking waste,' he said. 'I can't take it anymore.' Then he stood up and started yelling really loud about how crazy I was, and the restaurant staff made him leave."

"Annika, that's *horrible*. I can't believe he talked to you that way." No wonder everyone here is so kind to her.

"Usually, he didn't. And when we first started dating he was actually very sweet. Tina said our problems were due to the fact that we don't speak the same language. Janice told me that he probably snapped and that he was an asshole and she had never liked him."

"Then what happened?"

"Claire came over to make sure I was okay and suggested a big piece of cheesecake. Their desserts are really good here."

"And after that?"

"I ate the cheesecake and went home. Janice was right. Ryan *was* a jerk. He was waiting for me in my apartment when I got home because he had a key. He seemed calmer, but he kept bringing up all the times I'd said or done the wrong thing. It made me feel like crying. But then I remembered that no one can make me feel inferior without my consent."

"Did Janice tell you that?"

"Eleanor Roosevelt did. But Janice is the one who gave me a whole book of her quotes, and I memorized all of them. I also really like the one that says 'A woman is like a tea bag; you never know how strong it is until it's in hot water.' Then I told Ryan I didn't like the way he treated me and the only time he was actually nice was when he wanted to have sex." She says it really loud, and the heads of the couple next to us whip around. I turn my back to them slightly.

"Then I told him it was over and that he had to give me my key back."

"Jesus."

"I know. I should have never given it to him in the first place. Anyway, I haven't seen him since."

At the end of the evening, I had anticipated pointing out how much better this date had gone than the first time we tried it in college, but I'm not sure that's true any longer.

"You could have asked me to take you someplace else. I certainly would have."

"Why?"

"You and your most recent boyfriend experienced a very public and—from what I gathered—extremely loud breakup here."

"You're right. It was kind of a disaster." She looks around at our fellow diners. "I don't think any of these people were there that night, though. It was almost a year ago."

"I'm glad you told him it was over." I must have stared at her a beat too long, because she averts her eyes, but she smiles and her cheeks flush slightly. She puts down her menu. "I don't even know why I'm looking at this. There's no way I could order anything but the stuffed shells."

We split a piece of the cheesecake for dessert and Annika says goodbye to everyone on our way out the door.

"1333 South Wabash," I tell the driver when we slide into the backseat of a cab. "Is it okay if I come in for a while?" I ask Annika.

"Yes. I have something I want to show you." She sounds incredibly excited.

"Consider my curiosity piqued." Knowing Annika, it could be any number of things.

She lives on the sixth floor and when we enter her apartment, there's an immediate sense of familiarity. The rooms are in a state of organized chaos that reveals its order only to her. Everything is clean, because Annika doesn't like her living space to be dirty, but I could not begin to make sense of it. There's a row of breakfast cereal boxes on the counter in the kitchen. They're all Cheerios, but every one of them is a different variety. Bright blue bowls are stacked next to the cereal boxes, each one with a spoon already in it. Travel cups for transporting smoothies are lined up in a row next to a blender. There's a teapot on the stove, and on the counter to the left are mugs with the string of a tea bag hanging over the side. It's like her own little breakfast assembly line.

In the living room, the couch and chair have several throw pillows and blankets piled on them, and there's a leaning tower of crossword-puzzle books stacked haphazardly next to an ottoman. I would bet money that every single crossword puzzle has been completed, in ink.

In addition to the overstuffed furniture, covered in soft fabrics, there are several shelves overflowing with hardcover and softcover books. The titles spill out onto the floor. A large rug covers the ceramic tile floor in front of the couch, and there are several plants on tabletops, and one hanging from a hook on the ceiling. A TV sits on a low table across from the couch.

"Come with me," she says, and grabs my hand, pulling me toward the bedroom, and, once inside it, toward the bed. Now I really am wondering what she wanted to show me, and if I've somehow completely misread the situation. But then she kneels in front of the bed and lifts the bed skirt. It's hard to see at first because it's dark, but there's a cardboard box, and in it are a cat and five small kittens. I don't have any pets, and if I had to choose, I'd probably consider myself a dog person. But I can't deny how cute the kittens are. The love Annika feels for these tiny animals transforms her face, and I'm reminded of how protective and nurturing she can be.

"How old are they?"

"Three weeks. The cat's a stray that had been brought into the shelter. They needed someone to foster it until the kittens were born and old enough to be adopted. I'm going to keep the mom. Usually I foster an animal that's sick or injured and awaiting surgery or whatever. That way I get the chance to help more than one. Lately it's been harder and harder to give them up so I decided I'd keep the next one. I wouldn't feel right adopting a dog because I'm gone all day, but I think a cat will make a perfect companion for me."

"Do you like living alone?"

"I got used to it when I went back to campus after you and Janice graduated. I hated it at first, but eventually I grew to love it."

"Was it hard for you without Janice there?" I swallow. "Without me?"

Her face falls a little. "There were times when it was very hard. But it was necessary for me. It prepared me. I would never have been able to contemplate moving to the city on my own if I hadn't tried it on for size first."

"Was the guy I saw you talking to at the library when I picked you up the other person you were in a relationship with?"

"Yes. That was Monte. I'd been flirting with him for months and I got tired of waiting for him to ask me out, so I invited him to go to the aquarium one Saturday. He would never say anything unkind to me the way Ryan did, but I just got so frustrated with him while we were dating. He mostly wanted to communicate via email, and when we did speak in person, I had to spell everything out for him all the time and it made me tired."

I've been smiling so hard since she started talking about Monte that my face actually hurts. How could any man ever be unkind to this woman? The affection I once felt for Annika might have gone dormant for a while, but it roars out of hibernation and makes me feel better about life than I have in a long time. There's something so hopeful about being around her again.

I glance at my watch. It's almost nine and I can already tell she's tired by the look in her eyes and the way she's leaning her head back against the edge of the bed. "I should go. Let you wind down and get some sleep."

She walks me to the door. "Thanks for dinner. Sorry about the Ryan thing. I guess I just don't ever think about that relationship anymore."

For a second, her statement feels like a tiny ice pick to the heart. Is that how it works for her? Is that how she felt after me?

She catches me off guard when she throws her arms around my neck and hugs me. I groan softly when I register the smell of her skin. Liz had been a big believer in pheromones and though her scent hadn't done much for me, I have a feeling she wasn't all that drawn to mine either. I don't know if I buy into that kind of thing, but whatever the cause, catching a whiff of Annika has always had a strong effect on me. I can't explain what she smells like because it's indescribable. On the rare occasion when she wasn't spending the night in my bed at my college apartment, I would switch pillows and lay my head on hers. The odd thing is that Annika couldn't stand perfume and only used unscented soap, so whatever I detected had to be coming straight from inside *her.*

This obviously isn't our first date, and following some sort of protocol seems arbitrary and juvenile. I mean, we've seen each other naked. I know the sounds she makes when she's turned on. There aren't many places on her body that my fingers and mouth haven't explored.

I hug her back and though it's hard to let her go at the end, I do.

15

Annika

THE UNIVERSITY OF ILLINOIS
AT URBANA-CHAMPAIGN
1991

"What are you going to wear?" Janice asked. She was standing in front of my closet sliding hangers to the left as she surveyed the offerings of my college wardrobe. What I wore had always been more important to Janice than it was to me. Before I started living with her, I chose a top and bottom based on how they would feel against my skin. The fact that they didn't match and often clashed horribly had literally no bearing on my choice, and I couldn't recall a single instance where my parents or brother had commented on my choice of clothing. Janice gently pointed out that I'd been walking around campus looking like a fashion "don't" for weeks and helped me put together complete outfits so I could dress myself if she wasn't around. It was yet another example of all the things I felt stupid about.

"A skirt," I said. I wasn't paying a lot of attention to what she was doing, because I had my nose buried in a book.

"That's all you ever wear."

"Then why did you ask if you already knew what I'd say?"

"Because I thought you might want to wear something different for your first date. I thought I saw a pair of jeans in here once. Where did they go?"

"I left them in the laundry room and someone took them."

"You never told me someone stole your jeans."

"I left them there on purpose because I hate jeans. You already know that."

"What about a dress? I have a really cute floral dress and you can wear my little white T-shirt underneath it. It's long. I bet you'd like it."

"The T-shirt will be too tight."

"You're smaller than I am. There's no way it will be too tight."

"I don't want to wear a dress."

"Do you know where he's taking you? Maybe that would help me decide."

"Was I supposed to ask?"

"He didn't mention it?"

I'd given Jonathan my phone number a few days before the practice tournament and he'd called last night to confirm our date. "He said we would go get something to eat."

"If you insist on wearing a skirt, can I at least pick out the top? And do your hair and makeup?"

I'd taken a shower and washed my hair, and that had been the extent of my pre-date beauty routine. I hadn't bothered to get dressed and instead I'd put on the bathrobe I'd owned since I was fifteen and had been lounging in it most of the day. I figured I'd select one of my usual outfits a few minutes before Jonathan was due to arrive, and we would go. Already this was becoming more complicated than I'd expected. Janice treated me like her own live-version Barbie doll sometimes, coaxing my hair into elaborate styles and painting my face with things that felt heavy and goopy and smelled weird. If I acquiesced on the hair and makeup, she'd probably get off my case about the outfit. "I don't care."

"Stay here. I'll be right back."

She returned with a makeup case the size of a tackle box and sat down on the bed next to me. "I don't want any of that foundation stuff," I said, in case she'd forgotten how much I hated it.

I put down my book and did what she asked, closing my eyes when she stroked shadow across my lids and opening them as she applied two coats of mascara to my lashes. They felt heavy and I tried not to blink. "Are you almost done?"

"Just a little blush and you'll be all set. Do you want lip gloss?" Janice loved lip gloss.

"No! Last time you put it on me the wind whipped my hair around when I got outside and some of the strands stuck to my lip." It had been the grossest feeling ever and I'd freaked out and wiped the lip gloss off on the sleeve of my shirt.

"Oh. I forgot about that."

Janice picked up my brush and had me turn around so that my back was to her. I hated brushing my hair, but Janice couldn't handle seeing it tangled, so I'd long since agreed to comb it every morning before I left the apartment if she'd stop trying to get me to do anything else with it. Usually that meant a few haphazard strokes with my brush, and I'd call it done. Janice had asked me more than once why I wore my waist-length hair so long if I didn't like styling it, but I was never able to articulate why I didn't want to cut it. It just *felt* right to me the way it was.

"I know you don't care for perfume, but it might be nice to wear a little on a date," she said as she brushed my hair and then began French-braiding it into a single plait down the center of my back. "It will only give me a headache," I said. Smells were mostly bad, except when they weren't. "Don't make my hair too tight, okay?"

"I won't. I'm going to leave it a little loose so it looks polished, but soft and romantic."

Janice handed me a mirror when she was done. "There. You're all set. What do you think?"

"I can hardly tell I'm wearing makeup, but I look really pretty."

Janice laughed as I crossed to my closet, dropped my robe, and pulled on my favorite elastic-waist skirt and the thin cotton sweater she'd picked out for me to wear with it. Socks and knee-high boots with a flat sole would complete the outfit, and no one but me would know the socks didn't match underneath. Janice smiled when I turned around, because she'd given up the fight about my clothes a long time ago. I knew the outfits I wore were shapeless, but wearing them felt like having a security blanket with me at all times, one that I happened to wear on my body.

"You look great," she said. "You're going to have a wonderful time."

Jonathan knocked on the door at six o'clock exactly, and when I opened it, he took one look at me and said, "Wow."

It made me feel so good, and since it was clearly an acceptable thing to tell someone on a first date, I said it back to him.

He smiled, and I told myself that maybe this wouldn't be so hard after all.

He drove us to an area of campus lined with bars and food carts and parallel-parked at a meter on the street. I had never driven a car before, and attempting to fit a vehicle into a tiny space between two other cars would have paralyzed me, but he made the maneuver seem effortless.

We bought meatball sandwiches at one of the food carts and because the evening was crisp but not too cold, we sat at an outdoor table to eat them. It was sort of like sitting across from Jonathan at chess club, except there was food in front of us instead of a game board. No one would know it was my first date, because we looked like all the other couples eating together, and I relaxed a little.

"What would you like to do next?" he asked.

The question threw me. I struggled when presented with too many choices, but being given none at all was almost worse, and I had no idea how to answer him.

"Whatever people normally do on dates is fine with me."

"We could go have a beer?"

"Okay."

Jonathan threw away our trash, and we walked down the street. He stopped in front of Kam's. It was *the* place to be seen on campus; at least, that's what Janice was always saying. She spent a lot of time there, but I'd only made it as far as the sidewalk out front.

Jonathan and I were having such a good time that I didn't want to tell him the reason I never went to bars was because they were way too loud and smoky for me. Janice had tried a couple of times, but I never lasted more than five minutes before I gave up and went home. I told myself that I could handle it just this once and that it wouldn't be a big deal, but the minute he held the door open for me and I stepped inside, I knew it was a mistake. Billy Idol's "Cradle of Love" assaulted my ears, and the cloud of cigarette smoke we walked into felt like a one-two punch to my senses. It was standing room only, and we were shoulder-to-shoulder with half of the student body as Jonathan took me by the hand and pulled me through the crowd. I clung to him, feeling as if I might throw up.

He carved out a small pocket of empty space for me. "I'll be right back. Wait here," he said, and he went to stand in line at the bar.

It was so loud that the only way to communicate was by shouting or letting someone talk directly into your ear. How did everyone do this? How could they *stand* it? Was this really what people thought was fun? Though Jonathan had situated me out of the line of traffic, it didn't stop a girl from weaving her way toward me and clipping me with her shoulder as she stumbled by. More followed, and pretty soon several people began to invade my tiny slice of personal space. They stepped on my feet, and someone's beer sloshed onto my hand. I wiped it off immediately, hating the smell and how cold and wet it felt on my skin. Jonathan was still waiting his turn three people deep at the bar.

I was hanging on by my fingernails when I saw Jake, the guy I'd had the massive crush on my sophomore year, and who I'd mistakenly thought was my boyfriend. He was sitting at a table with a group of guys, and when he saw me he elbowed the one sitting next to him. R.E.M.'s "Losing My Religion" was now playing on the sound system, but suddenly all I could hear was Nirvana's "Smells Like Teen Spirit" and instead of a bar, I was in Jake's room at the fraternity house.

He'd slipped me a note in class and asked me to come over that night, and I could hardly contain my excitement because I'd been waiting for him to find some time for us to be alone. For the rest of the day, I didn't pay attention in class. I daydreamed about our first kiss, and how he'd probably invite me to one of the fraternity's parties or formal dances. When I returned to my dorm room after my last class, I scribbled my own note for Janice and left it under the Kermit the Frog magnet stuck to the front of our dorm fridge so she'd be sure to see it and wouldn't worry when she came home and discovered I wasn't there. *With Jake. In his room,* it said, and I'd drawn a little heart next to it.

I knocked on the door of the frat house and told the guy who answered it that I was there to see Jake. "Jesus, there's, like, seven Jakes. Which one?"

"Weller," I said proudly, and waited for him to say, "Oh, you must be Annika," because Jake probably talked about me all the time.

"Upstairs. Third door on the left."

Jake answered my knock, and I smiled when he dropped a quick kiss on my mouth. He'd never done that before, and it made me feel warm all over. "Hey, babe."

He closed the door and led me over to the bed. There were three other guys in his room, but Jake would ask them to leave now that I'd arrived. A pungent, smoky smell hung in the air, but no one was holding a cigarette.

"You were right," the one who was sitting at Jake's desk said. The other two were sitting on the bed across from Jake's. "She's hot. What about her body?"

"Don't know yet," Jake said. "Can't see it under those baggy clothes."

Everyone laughed. I did, too, although I didn't know why. If Jake didn't like my clothes, Janice would jump at the chance to help me pick out an outfit he'd like better. I made a mental note to ask her about that.

"I thought we could hang out for a while," Jake said. "Relax a little." He held a Bic lighter in his hand, and I will never forget the scraping sound it made when he sparked the little wheel and the flame shot straight up. One of the guys handed him a glass tube with a little bowl on the top, and Jake put the flame down inside it and sucked the smoke into his mouth. He passed it around and one by one, the boys took their turn. The small room filled with smoke, and I stifled a cough.

Jake's bed was pushed up against the wall, and he'd slung his arm around me when they began smoking, which felt nice. "Now you try," Jake said, holding the pipe up to my mouth.

I shook my head. "No. I don't want any."

He shrugged and put the pipe to his lips, but after he sucked in the smoke, he acted like he was going to kiss me but blew the smoke into my mouth instead. It tasted horrible, and I coughed and sputtered while they laughed. But then Jake kissed me again, and it was the kind of kiss I'd been waiting for all my life, soft and gentle and sweet. Somehow during the kiss we'd ended up almost horizontal on the bed as the pipe made another round. I should have been happy, but something didn't feel right, and I couldn't put my finger on exactly what it was. I wanted Jake to kiss me again, but only after he told his friends to leave. It wasn't fair that they were keeping us from being alone together. Then Jake took another puff on the pipe and when he blew the smoke in my mouth again I found it harder to struggle even though I still didn't want it.

Someone knocked on the door and one of Jake's friends opened it. I felt floaty and odd, and for the life of me, I couldn't comprehend why Janice would be standing there. "Yeah?" Jake said.

There was a long pause where no one said anything, and then Janice said, "I need Annika to come with me right away."

"She doesn't want to go with you."

He was right. I didn't want to go with her. Or maybe I did? I was having such a hard time keeping my thoughts organized. The kiss was so nice, but the pot and Jake's friends were not.

"There's an emergency at the wildlife clinic. They need Annika to come in right away. She's on call."

I didn't think I was on call. I would never have agreed to go to Jake's if I had been, but maybe I'd forgotten. A hawk with an injured wing had been brought in the previous week, and I'd taken to it with an enthusiastic zeal, doing whatever I could to nurse the hawk back to health. I was one of the few people it trusted, and when I wasn't tending to Charlie, the injured opossum, I tried to help with the hawk's feeding and the care of its wound. I sat up, which was a struggle because my body suddenly felt very heavy. "Is it the hawk?"

"Yes. Yes, it is the hawk and you need to come with me right away because everyone is waiting for you."

Jake put his hand on my elbow. "Come on, are you sure you need to go?"

"I have to. It's the hawk."

Janice crossed the room and grabbed on to my hand, which was good because there was no way I was getting off that bed and upright under my own power. My legs felt wobbly and Janice practically carried me out of the room and down the stairs.

Outside, she pulled on my arm. "Come on. I had to park at the end of the street. It's not much farther."

It seemed like we walked for miles before she opened the passenger-side door and poured me inside. She walked around to the driver's side and got in, but instead of starting the car, she rested her forehead on the steering wheel.

"We have to go," I said. "They need me at the clinic." But how could I help the hawk when I could barely walk?

"They don't need you. I just had to get you out of there. Don't you understand what was going on?"

I think it was safe to say I didn't understand *anything* that was going on.

"What did *you* think was going on?" I asked her.

"I don't know for sure. I only know what it looked like," she said.

"What did it look like?" I cried.

She turned to me, and I knew what the expression on her face meant, because I'd seen it a couple of times before. Once, when she was waiting to hear how she'd done on an important test our freshman year, and the next when her grandmother had gone in for open-heart surgery and they'd given her a twenty-percent chance of living through it. "It looked like he might have told his friends they could watch."

"Watch us kiss?"

"Annika, I think he was planning to do more than kiss you."

The fear and shame that washed over me when I finally understood what she was getting at, and how horribly wrong I'd been about the situation, shattered me. I shook and cried and Janice leaned over the gearshift and put her arms around me until I stopped crying. When we got back to the dorm she put me to bed to sleep off the effects.

The next day, when I arrived at class, I took a seat on the other side of the lecture hall. Knowing how scared I was that Jake might seek me out, Janice attended the lecture with me.

That's the day I discovered what it felt like to have not only a friend, but a best friend.

Now, at Kam's, in a situation that had already pushed me clear out of my comfort zone, I had the added misery of coming face-to-face with someone I'd hoped never to see again. I must have been staring at Jake while I relived the painful memory, because he raised his glass and crooked his index finger at me, beckoning. He wasn't smiling this time.

The terror I'd felt that day bubbled up from the place deep down inside where I'd hidden it away, never to be thought of again, and I bolted, fighting my way through the crowd as if I were swimming upstream against a strong current. It was like being in the diner without shoes, but worse because this time, there was nothing preventing me from being there but my own bad memories. On the outside, I looked like everyone else. But on the inside, I remembered that I didn't belong.

I burst through the door onto the sidewalk, and I kept going.

"Annika! Wait!" Jonathan caught up to me and grabbed my wrist moments before I would have darted in front of an oncoming car. "Jesus," he said. "You have to stop doing that. Please just stop for a second." He waited until the street cleared and then interlocked our fingers and led me gently to his truck. "Are you okay? What happened in there?"

"It's too loud. And I can't handle the smoke and there was a guy—"

"What guy?"

"Nothing. He was just this guy I used to know. He was sitting at a table with some people." Tears sprang to my eyes, and I was glad it was dark and that Jonathan couldn't see them.

"Would you rather go to my place? It's quiet there."

I couldn't help but compare it to what had happened the one time I'd accepted a similar invitation. But I felt safe with Jonathan and knew he wouldn't hurt me, so I said, "Yes."

He lived in a studio apartment on the middle floor of an old three-story house in an area that was technically considered off-campus. It must have been quite a trek on foot and he'd probably had at least a twenty-minute walk ahead of him whenever he'd brought me home after chess club. He parked on the street, and we walked up the path to the front of the house and climbed the stairs, which were on the outside like a rickety wooden fire escape. He jiggled his key in the lock of a small door that had peeling paint, the color of which I wasn't sure. Tan, or maybe it was just dirty. "It always sticks," he said.

He flipped on the lights, and I got my first look at the place he called home. It was small, that much I had expected considering the apartment was located in a house, but it was clean and orderly, much more so than it would be if I lived there.

I stood still as he closed the door and tossed his keys on a small table. There was a couch and a coffee table. A small TV sat on a piece of plywood spanning two milk crates that were full of books. Something about Jonathan's place put me instantly at ease. It felt cozy, and it was every bit as quiet as he'd promised. I could see myself living in a place like this.

"I like your apartment," I said.

He smiled. "Thanks. This was about all I could find on short notice. Do you want a beer? I'm going to have one."

I sat down on the couch. "Okay." I'd tasted beer before. I didn't really care for it, but Janice said it was an acquired taste. She kept our fridge stocked with wine coolers, which we both preferred if given the choice, but I didn't often drink them. Drinking alcohol made it harder for me to understand people; I had a hard enough time following along when I hadn't drunk anything at all.

Jonathan opened the beer and handed it to me. Then he sat down beside me and popped the tab on his own. We each took a drink, his considerably bigger than mine. The beer tasted pretty much like I remembered from the last time, and I must have still had a long way to go before I reached the acquired-taste stage.

"What happened at the bar with that guy? I turned my back to order and when I turned around, you were gone. Did he say something to you? Something he shouldn't have?"

"I don't want to talk about it."

"Okay. You don't have to tell me."

I took another sip of the beer and grimaced. "It's just that people take advantage of me sometimes because I have trouble understanding their intentions."

"Did he hurt you?"

I don't know why I decided to tell him, but I did, the whole story tumbling out in fits and starts. I rocked and flicked my fingers. "I thought he liked me, but he really didn't. I don't like to think about what might have happened if Janice hadn't shown up."

I will not cry.

Jonathan placed his hand on my arm and it surprised me how much the small gesture calmed me. I stopped rocking and put my hands back in my lap. "Is that why you wanted me to meet her?"

Still unable to look at him, I nodded.

"I would never do anything like that to you."

"I don't like bars, Jonathan. I don't like crowds or loud sounds or cigarette smoke. I'm really bad at dating because this is the first one I've ever been on."

"You've never been on a date before?"

"No."

"I don't really like bars either. I spend enough time working in one so I don't really want to go to them if I don't have to. But I liked being seen at Kam's with you."

If I lived to be one hundred, I would never be able to understand what he meant by that. All my life, I'd been an embarrassment to myself. How could he want other people to see him with me, especially after the way I acted?

"Why?"

"Because I could tell when I picked you up that you were excited to see me. And that made me feel really good because I'm pretty sure if you weren't interested, you'd straight-up tell me. There's something about having a pretty girl on your arm and knowing she's into you that makes you feel like showing her off."

"I didn't know that," I said.

"Which part? That you're pretty or that I wanted to show you off?"

"I know I'm pretty. My face is aesthetically pleasing. I didn't know about the other thing."

"I've never known anyone like you."

"I honestly don't know what you mean by that. Is it a good thing or a bad thing?"

"It's good, Annika."

I wrapped my arms around myself. "It's very cold in here."

"I'm sorry. The apartments don't have their own thermostats so I can't control the heat. And I'm really starting to question whether this house was ever insulated. I think it's pretty old. Winter might be rough, but at least I won't have to live here next year."

His apartment did seem drafty, as if the house had been poorly constructed or was simply showing its age. I snuggled deeper into the cushions on the couch in an attempt to warm myself.

Jonathan left the room and returned with a sweatshirt that said NORTHWESTERN on the front. "Why don't you put this on."

I took the sweatshirt and pulled it over my head, but I knew within seconds I wouldn't be able to wear it. Jonathan went into the kitchen for another beer, and when he came back into the room he saw that I'd folded it and placed it next to me on the couch. "Don't you want to wear it?"

"I'm okay. It's not that cold."

"I'm pretty sure it's clean." He picked it up and sniffed it. "It smells clean to me."

"I like the way it smells, but it has a tag in it. Tags bother me."

"Do you cut the tags out of all your clothes?"

"It's the first thing I do when I get them home."

Jonathan went back into the kitchen, and when he returned he had a pair of scissors in his hand. He cut out the tag and said, "Here. Try it now."

It was one of the nicest things anyone had ever done for me. I might not always understand what people are saying, but I know when they've been kind.

"Thank you," I said, pulling it over my head.

"You're welcome."

Half an hour later, I'd managed to choke down a third of the beer before giving up on it. Jonathan offered to swap out my can for a fresh one, but I admitted I really didn't care for the taste. After he finished his second, he didn't have any more either. Now that we'd left the bar, our date was going better than I'd expected, and talking about our favorite TV shows and bands had left me in a fairly comfortable state. I knew enough about both to be able to talk about them with Jonathan. Plus, he was really easy to talk to. Maybe he was the reason I'd finally been able to get this far with a guy.

"What are your plans for after graduation?" he asked. He already knew I'd be completing my undergraduate work with a bachelor's degree in English because we'd traded information about our majors on the drive down to St. Louis. Jonathan was a business major, and he told me he would start working toward his MBA as soon as he was hired by a company that would pay for it.

"I want to work at a library someday," I said. "I want to spend every waking day of my adult life surrounded by books." I also planned to earn a master's degree—in my case, library science—in order to pursue the career I'd coveted since my freshman year, and I planned to get started on it as soon as I'd finished my undergraduate studies.

"Really? That's cool. I've never met anyone who loved books so much they wanted to be surrounded by them. I want to move to New York and work in the financial district. I want to make a lot of money and not have to worry about paying for things." He looked around the room. "I don't ever want to live in a crappy old drafty apartment."

"Does your family not have a lot of money?" I asked.

"It's just my mom and me. My dad died when I was six, and I'm pretty sure we've been struggling ever since. There wasn't any life insurance or anything like that. Someday I'll earn enough money to take care of myself and my mom."

"Are you putting yourself through school?" I was lucky, because my parents had saved enough for my brother and me to go to college. We'd be on our own for our graduate studies, but we'd been given a wonderful head start on our educations.

"I had a pretty sizable academic scholarship to Northwestern. Grants and loans covered the rest. It was the only way I was going to get the education and the life I wanted."

I remembered that Jonathan had told me he'd transferred to Illinois, and he'd thanked me for not asking about it. But why? Maybe I was supposed to? Maybe it was yet another social cue I'd missed and it had been rude of me not to show interest in the subject. Why were there so many things to think about? To remember? Why couldn't I figure anything out in the moment instead of days or weeks later?

"Did you not like it at Northwestern?"

"I did like it. I felt like I belonged there. I didn't set out to . . . I was trying really hard to keep myself afloat, and I promised myself I'd only do it once or twice. But writing the papers was such easy money and I was acquiring so much student-loan debt. I had to grovel, for days, but the university's ethics committee finally agreed not to make it part of my permanent transcript if I just left."

"You wrote papers for other people? That's cheating."

"Yeah, well. It's not like I asked people to write them for me. I was the one who did the work."

"But cheating is wrong," I said.

Jonathan looked away. "You're right. It is. And this shitty, drafty apartment is probably more than I deserve. I'm just trying to put the whole thing behind me."

Jonathan didn't talk as much after that, and around ten o'clock I started yawning.

"Are you not having a good time?" he asked.

"I'm having a wonderful time, but I'm very tired."

"Do you want me to take you home?"

"Okay."

Jonathan turned off his truck and walked me to the entrance of my building. I had to really concentrate in order to remember everything Janice had told me. "Thank you I had such a great time and I really like being around you and dinner was so good." It came out all at once, and when I finally reached the end of that long, rambling statement, I had to gasp for air.

"I had a great time, too."

"For real?"

He grabbed my hand and held it gently in his large palm. "Yes."

"Are you going to kiss me?"

He laughed. "I was planning on it, yes."

"Okay. I'm ready."

He laughed again, but it wasn't the mean kind of laugh; at least, I didn't think it was. He cupped my jaw in his hands and pressed his lips to mine. He closed his eyes, which was good, because I could leave mine open so I wouldn't miss anything. I felt the same warmth I'd felt when Jake first kissed me, but it was so much better with Jonathan. He opened his eyes and I looked away as fast as I could.

"Have you ever been kissed?" he asked.

"Only by Jake but that doesn't count because he only did it to trick me. Did I not do it right?"

"You did it right," he said.

I wanted to believe him. "Do it again."

So he did.

Janice was waiting up for me. I had barely walked in the door and hadn't even taken off my coat when the questions started. "How was your date? Do you like him? Where did you go? I want to hear all about it."

"Most of the date was good. I liked the meatball sandwiches, but I still hate bars. We went to Kam's and Jake was there. When I saw him, I freaked out. I almost got hit by a car because I ran right into the street. I just wanted to get away from him. Jonathan ran after me and we went back to his place. It was nice. Quiet. I told him about what had happened with Jake and he was nice about it. I felt comfortable with him. Like I could tell him things that I've only been able to tell you. I drank part of my beer but couldn't finish it. When he walked me to the door I told him I had a great time and liked being around him and then he kissed me. It was so great!"

Janice made this noise like a loud sigh. "There's nothing quite like a first kiss. What else did you do?"

"We mostly talked. He wants to move to New York someday and make lots of money. I found out he had to transfer here because he let people cheat off him at Northwestern because he was broke."

Janice put her hand on my arm. "Annika. What did you say to Jonathan after he told you about the cheating?"

"I told him cheating was wrong because it is. It's horrible."

"And how did he seem after that?"

"I don't know. He didn't say anything for a while, I guess. I didn't mind, though. Sometimes it's nice to sit quietly with someone."

"Sometimes it's important to let the people we care about know that a single incident doesn't have to define them. He shouldn't have cheated, I'm not saying that was okay. But it sounds like he made an error in judgment based on his circumstances. It happens. And then we learn from our mistakes and we don't make them again."

"I did it all wrong, didn't I? I said the wrong thing and he'll probably never want to see me again. Do you think I hurt his feelings?" The thought of that made me want to cry, because Jonathan had always been so careful with mine.

"I think he probably just wanted to be understood. You told him about Jake, which was a very personal thing for you to share. He probably felt like he could tell you something personal too, and he mentioned the cheating because that was a difficult situation for him."

"How do you know these things? You weren't even there!"

"I just do. And I'll help you so that the next time you see him, you'll say all the right things."

But would I? Now I'd be constantly worrying about the next dumb thing that might fly out of my mouth. "The thing I don't understand is why Jonathan would like me? And don't say it's because I'm pretty."

"I think you have a lot of wonderful things to offer people if they'll just give you a chance. I learned that our freshman year. Others can, too."

"I like him. I really, really do."

It was the first time in my life I'd ever felt this way about anyone.

16

Annika

THE UNIVERSITY OF ILLINOIS
AT URBANA-CHAMPAIGN
1991

Jonathan had told me on the phone that he'd come by after lunch to walk me to class. He'd called almost every night since our date, and twice we'd gone to lunch together. I'd felt an incredible thrill when he grabbed my hand as we walked to class afterward, because no one had ever done that. Whenever I walked alone on campus, I would stare at the couples walking hand in hand, wondering what it would feel like, and now I knew.

"Annika?" Janice said, knocking on my door. "Jonathan is here."

My bed was in the corner of the room and I'd been lying on my side facing the wall, because that was my favorite position for reading. I was in the middle of a chapter and didn't really want to stop. My back was to Jonathan, so I couldn't see him as he approached the bed, but I knew he was there, because I could smell chlorine.

"Are you ready?" he asked.

"I'm not going to class."

"Are you sick?"

"No. But I'm very tired."

"Did you stay up late studying?"

"I was up late reading. I never finished my assignment."

"Do you need help?" I could hear Jonathan shuffling through the pile of papers strewn across the bed.

"I knew how do to it, but I didn't feel like working on it. It's boring."

More shuffling of papers. "Is this . . . is this in Italian?"

"Yes." I'd spent an hour the night before translating an old essay I'd written last year, the synapses in my brain firing in absolute joy at the task. So much more enjoyable than my unfinished homework.

"What are you going to do with it?"

"I don't know. Save it, probably." I was still reading my book while I answered his questions.

"Can you turn around so I can see your face?"

"Sure."

I put down the book and rolled onto my other side. "Hi," he said.

"Hi!"

I remained lying on my side, so Jonathan stretched out on the bed in the same position, facing me. Looking directly into his eyes—or anyone's, really—made me uncomfortable, so I stared at his nose. "Do you want to kiss me?" For so long, I'd envied the affection other people seemed to acquire effortlessly. Holding hands and kissing someone felt like finally being able to nibble at a buffet that had delicacies I had yet to fully sample, and I was eager to try every one of them. After years of loneliness and isolation, receiving attention and affection from another person boosted my spirits unbelievably. It was an infinitely preferable way to go about life.

"I wanted to kiss you the minute I walked into your room."

"Then why didn't you?" I couldn't comprehend why he would wait when he clearly wanted to do it. There were probably a whole bunch of rules about kissing I didn't understand and would have to muddle my way through, and that took a little bit of the joy out of it, replacing it with anxiety, my constant emotional companion.

"Because it might have seemed rude not to at least talk to you for a while first. And I want you to know that I'm not like Jake."

"I never think you're like Jake. I like you, and I liked kissing you the other night. As soon as it was over, I wanted to do it again as soon as possible."

"I liked kissing you, too."

"I need to tell you something. I wasn't very understanding about the cheating. Sometimes I don't say the right things, but you've been so nice to me, and I know you're a good person. Everyone does something at least once in their lives that they regret later. I'm sorry you had to transfer here."

"Oh. Okay. Well, thanks for that. It hasn't been *all* bad."

"It hasn't?" It had sounded pretty bad.

"No."

"Okay. Do you think we've talked enough?"

Jonathan laughed. "Yes."

He kissed me then, and it was different from before, but in a good way. Our good-night kiss at the door had been shorter, but these kisses were longer, and each one seemed to melt into the next. He did, in fact, taste a little like Pep O Mint Life Savers, and his kisses weren't sloppy or too rough. He took frequent enough breaks that I didn't feel like I was suffocating, and he was careful not to crush me with his body. Jonathan slipped his arm under my head, and his palm rested on my hip, but other than those two contact points, he did not try to touch me.

"Are you still going to class?" I asked.

"No."

"Why not?"

"Uh, because I'd rather keep doing this."

"Me too!"

Jonathan let out a short laugh, but I wasn't trying to be funny. He kissed me again and I could study his face because his eyes were closed. His eyelashes were as long as mine, but it was the angles and planes of his face that intrigued me. Such perfect symmetry and balance. I extended the tip of my index finger toward his smooth unblemished skin and lightly traced his cheek. He opened his eyes a little, and I had to go back to looking at his nose. But it was straight and perfectly proportioned so I didn't mind at all. "I'm tired too," he said. "Let's take a nap."

"Okay," I whispered. How strange it felt to *want* to fall asleep next to someone. Normally it would bother me to have someone in my bed, because I had a very specific way I liked to sleep, which didn't include another person sharing the space. But I wanted Jonathan to stay, and it gave me a special kind of thrill to realize he wanted to fall asleep with me. It seemed even more intimate than the kissing. More grown-up, somehow. Janice often had someone sharing her bed, but this was yet another first for me. I reveled in the sensations washing over me and tried not to dwell on how much I'd miss them if he were to decide I wasn't worth the trouble.

It would be a real shame if that happened, because Jonathan made me feel comfortable and safe in a way that no one else had ever bothered to, not that many had tried.

17

Jonathan

CHICAGO
AUGUST 2001

Annika looks incredible when she opens the door. My department is celebrating the addition of a new client and, more specifically, the client's very large investment portfolio. We will spare no expense to welcome them, and tonight's event includes a cocktail hour followed by a formal sit-down dinner in the party room of a trendy, overpriced restaurant. It's the kind of event where not having a plus-one would seem out of place. As a star player on the team, I'm expected to look the part at all times, and though no one has ever said it outright, a beautiful woman on my arm is certainly part of the persona. I tried to come up with a good reason why I shouldn't bring Annika, but I couldn't.

The burgundy dress she's wearing stops just above her knees, showing the perfect amount of leg, but the sleeves are long and covered by some kind of lace overlay. It is the ideal attire for a corporate dinner party. Annika has the kind of body that isn't overtly noticeable. Her breasts never feel like they're in your face, but they make you wonder what they look like under her clothes. Her legs are only slightly longer than average, but they're toned. She is the most perfectly proportioned woman I've ever had the pleasure of seeing naked, and has the softest skin I've ever run my hands across. Tonight, she looks both sexy and conservative, and I look forward to introducing her to my fellow team members. I'd brought two other women to work functions after Liz and I split up. They were attractive, but they were also smart and successful. Unfortunately, I hadn't felt a spark with either one of them.

I hadn't felt much of anything at all.

In the cab on the way over, I give Annika the rundown on who I'll be introducing her to.

"Bradford is my boss. I know someone who went to college with him back when he was just Brad. He's married to the company but also has an actual wife who I gather spends most of her time raising their children alone. He's very tall." Brad seemed to enjoy having conversations where he was standing but his employees were seated and he could tower over them even more. "He works more hours than everyone, and he never passes up the opportunity to let us know it. He also doesn't understand why this would bother anyone."

We walk into the restaurant, and I lead Annika toward a pair of open French doors where my teammates are gathering, drinks in hand. Brad is standing alone just inside the room.

I watch as he notices Annika. She's wearing her hair up, which draws my attention to her neck. I want to kiss it. Actually, I want to suck it the way I used to in that old, lumpy bed in my college apartment. Maybe Brad does, too, because he's looking at the exposed skin a little longer than he should. It's subtle, but I've seen him do it a hundred times with my coworkers' wives and girlfriends. Brad knows that no man who reports to him will ever call him on it, which is why he'll never stop doing it. It bothers me to see him do it to Annika, and because of it my greeting is clipped and my handshake short and perfunctory. If Brad notices, he doesn't show it.

Let it go, Jon.

"This is Annika," I say.

"What an exotic name," Brad says. "It's a pleasure to meet you."

"Thank you. It's a pleasure to meet you, too. Jonathan said you were very tall." I tense because of the other things I'd said, and sometimes when Annika repeats what I tell her, she doesn't always apply the appropriate edits. I needn't have worried, as I watch Brad puff himself up another half inch as he shakes Annika's hand and holds it a beat longer than necessary. He studies her, checking things off an imaginary list, and smiles when she passes the test. She meets his smile with one of her own, and holds his gaze for a few seconds before smoothly looking away.

I take Annika's arm and lead her to a group of my peers standing next to the makeshift bar that has been set up in the room. Annika handles the introductions like a champ, repeating each man's name as she clasps their hands, smiles, exchanges small talk about her occupation.

"What can I get you to drink, miss?" the bartender asks.

For a minute, I expect her to ask if they serve Italian sodas, but Annika smiles and says, "Club soda with lime, please." It's not that Annika can't or won't drink, but she doesn't really enjoy the way it makes her feel. Now she can sip on the virgin drink and no one will question it.

When the cocktail hour ends, we make our way to our seats at a table for ten. Several of my coworkers and their significant others join us, and Annika handles the introductions with the same ease she demonstrated with Brad.

There's a subtle stiffness to her posture, and I'm probably the only one who notices the slight pause she takes before she answers their questions, or how diligently she observes the other women and patterns her behavior after theirs. I also notice that a few of the glances thrown her way by the women are meant to scrutinize. The smiles are just a little too wide and calculating, and the first time I'd ever seen one in a corporate setting, it had been on the face of my ex-wife. My coworkers notice her, too, for reasons that are different from their wives. Annika appears confident, as if she attends these kinds of functions regularly and is no longer impressed by them. It gives her a sophisticated edge even though I know that Annika *isn't* impressed by this kind of thing and never will be, and therefore isn't pretending at all.

"I love your dress," Jim's wife says, leaning toward Annika to briefly touch the lace.

"Thank you. The lace is very comfortable on my arms because of the fabric underneath. Otherwise I'd never be able to wear it." Annika says it very matter-of-factly and takes another sip of her club soda and lime.

"Oh, I know what you mean. I had a lace dress once that didn't, and it was so uncomfortable. I ended up giving it away." Jim's wife, Claudia, who is rather quiet and is routinely cold-shouldered by the other, more boisterous wives, has finally found some common ground, and she studies Annika with quiet reverence. Annika's cool aloofness, which is entirely unintentional, has afforded her the upper hand slightly, and I don't think she even realizes it. But even if she did, Annika would never capitalize on it to make herself seem more important. It simply would never occur to her.

"You should try silk," Annika says. "I have a blouse that feels absolutely wonderful against my skin."

"I will," Claudia says. "Thanks for the tip."

The waiters serve two different wine pairings with the meal, and I'm surprised when I see Annika sipping the white. She only drinks half, but she's eaten a full meal and it doesn't seem to have affected her. Everyone at the table has consumed enough that I doubt they're paying attention anyway.

Brad catches me on my way back from the restroom. "I like her," he says, as if I should care about his opinion on any aspect of my personal life. I don't, and I haven't forgotten what he said to me when I told him Liz and I were splitting.

"Just remember, there's no need to bring your personal life to work with you," he told me, despite the fact that in an attempt to avoid going home to my depressing and empty bachelor apartment, I'd been working more hours than I ever had.

Thanks for being sympathetic to my personal, life-changing event, Brad.

You asshole.

"I like her too," I say to Brad, hating myself for playing the game. "She's got so many great qualities."

"You were wonderful tonight," I tell Annika as we leave the hotel and walk hand in hand into the warm, late-August night. She smiles and squeezes my hand.

"I'm glad I didn't mess anything up for you."

"Of course you didn't. Don't think that way."

One of the best things about reconnecting with Annika is how natural it feels to be with her. Standing on the sidewalk, I wonder if she remembers how it felt to be in love with me.

I haven't forgotten how it felt to be in love with her.

As soon as we're settled in the back of the cab, she snuggles up next to me. Her body relaxes until I can feel her melting into me. She goes limp and falls asleep with her head on my chest. I don't mind at all, and I hold her until we get home. With my arms around her, she feels like mine again.

It's only when we're inside her apartment that I realize the evening—and the performance required of her to endure it—has taken everything she had and there's simply nothing left.

She's done.

She walks into the bedroom, and I follow. She pulls a T-shirt out of a dresser drawer and turns her back to me, not because she's upset that I followed, but so that I can unzip her dress. I oblige, and as soon as I've lowered it, the dress hits the floor. Her bra and underwear follow, which tells me that modesty is still a completely foreign concept to her. I'm not going to ogle her like the horny college student I once was, but I appreciate the view of her naked backside just the same. She turns around and when I see the front view, maybe I ogle just a little.

I mean, I'm human.

She pulls on the oversized T-shirt. It says WWJD on the front, but there's no picture or explanatory text underneath.

"'What would Jesus do'?" I don't recall that Annika was particularly religious in the past, but that doesn't mean she isn't now.

"'What would *Janice* do.' She sent it to me a few years ago, on my birthday. It's a joke because she always had to tell me what I should do." She sits down on the edge of the bed and shakes a couple of pills into her hand from the Tylenol bottle on the nightstand, washing them down with a sip from the water bottle next to it.

I smile. "Yeah, I got that." I also realize with sudden clarity that the reason Annika has done so well tonight is likely due to the coaching she still receives from Janice. How exhausting it must have been for her to attend a dinner like this. No wonder she has a headache.

"Can you stay awake for a few more minutes, Sleeping Beauty? I need you to walk me out so you can lock up."

At the door, I say, "I had a great time tonight. I'll call you tomorrow."

"I had a great time too," she says.

I drop a kiss on her cheek and step into the hallway, waiting until she closes the door behind me and I hear the tumble of the lock.

It occurs to me on the way home, when I'm smiling and thinking about Annika and our evening and about the T-shirt Janice sent, that Jonathan also begins with "J."

18

Annika

THE UNIVERSITY OF ILLINOIS AT URBANA-CHAMPAIGN 1991

"Someone called in sick so I have to work tonight," Jonathan said as we walked home from our afternoon classes.

"Okay." My good mood deflated, because I'd started looking forward to Fridays with Jonathan. He bartended on Saturdays and Sundays, but the last couple of weeks we'd hung out at his place on Friday night, playing chess and kissing. I liked that he didn't seem to mind taking things slow. Sometimes we'd read books, my head in his lap as he played with my hair or stroked my head. Jonathan had started to alleviate some of the loneliness I faced on a daily basis, and the time I spent with him highlighted how much better it was to experience things with someone who cared about you in a way that was different from your roommate or family. For years, I'd ordered my hamburgers plain and never entertained the possibility of eating them any other way until Janice gave me one with ketchup, and I realized how much better it tasted. "You're like the ketchup in my life," I'd told Jonathan one night on the phone, and he laughed.

"I don't know what that means, exactly, but if it makes you happy,

I'm honored to be your condiment." That was another thing I really liked about him. He never made me feel stupid about the weird things that came out of my mouth.

"Do you want to wait for me at my place? We could grab something to eat before my shift and then I'll drop you off."

"But you won't be there."

"No, but you'll be there when I get home and that will give me something to look forward to. It might be kind of late."

"That's okay." I often took late-afternoon naps, which meant I spent many hours wide awake in the middle of the night. Usually I read a book until I got tired again.

"All right. I'll pick you up in a few hours and we'll go to dinner. You should pack a bag so you can stay overnight." He kissed me goodbye and I hurried inside because I had so many things to ask Janice.

Jonathan's apartment made a lot of alarming sounds. The floors creaked whenever one of the other tenants walked around above, and it sounded like they might crash through the ceiling at any moment. The wind was blowing hard, and the drafty windows rattled in their old frames. I spent the evening wrapped in a blanket on the couch while I looked at my watch every five minutes.

He got home a little after midnight. I'd fallen asleep, and I nearly jumped out of my skin when he laid a hand on my shoulder and said, "Annika." I blinked several times because I'd fallen asleep with all the lights on and the brightness hurt my eyes. "I didn't mean to scare you."

"Hi," I said.

He smiled the way he always did when I said that. "Hi. I'm going to take a shower. I'll be quick."

I hated the way Jonathan smelled after he'd been working at the bar, especially the cigarette smoke that clung to his skin. He hated it, too, and he said he always took a shower the minute he got home. He kissed me, and I could taste that he'd had a beer or two during his shift, but I didn't mind.

He locked up and turned off the lights in the kitchen. "Why don't you wait for me in my room."

The bathroom was across the hall. I listened to the water running, thinking about the fact that Jonathan was naked. I felt the same way about his body that I did about his face: I knew there would be angles and planes I'd find pleasing there, too. He was also strong, and I liked watching his biceps flex when he lifted something heavy.

I was sitting cross-legged on his bed when he walked back into the room. He was wearing a T-shirt and a pair of sweatpants, and he rubbed at his wet hair with a towel. He sat down on the bed and leaned over and kissed me. The taste of beer had been replaced by toothpaste, and he smelled so good.

"Are you tired?" I asked.

"I'm not tired at all. Are you tired?"

"I've been sleeping for the last three hours."

"What do you want to do?" he asked, nuzzling my neck in a way that felt different, but different good. Not different bad.

"We could play chess."

"You want to play chess?"

"Maybe for just a little while." The last few times Jonathan and I had kissed, his hands had roamed to places they hadn't before, and our bodies were pressed so tightly together that nothing would have fit between them. I felt things I'd never felt with anyone. I knew what was coming and I wanted it to happen. I just didn't want to do it wrong. Chess would calm my nerves the way it always did.

"It's okay. We can play chess." He'd been leaning toward me, one arm slung over my lap, but he sat up quickly. I watched as he left the room and returned with his chessboard, and we set it up between us on the bed. The only light in the room came from the lamp on the nightstand and I felt soothed by the atmosphere. The sound of the wind rattling the windows seemed to have disappeared now that Jonathan was home, and the other occupants of the house must have been asleep, because there were no sounds coming from above. Some of my nervousness dissipated, replaced by happiness and a feeling of closeness toward Jonathan.

He'd given me white, so I made the first move. It wasn't until years later that I figured it out, but chess had become our foreplay, and we'd started that enticing dance the first time we played together in the student union. Watching him concentrate thrilled me, because he wanted to win every bit as badly as I did. There was a ruthlessness about both of us when we played, and it translated into something that put us on an equal playing field. I never had to worry about saying the wrong thing when we played. Chess, I knew.

I made a careless error, one I'd still be beating myself up over days later, and Jonathan picked up my rook and set it down next to his side of the board.

Jonathan had started leaning over and kissing me every time he captured one of my pieces, and this time, he pulled the collar of my sweater aside and kissed his way from my mouth, down the side of my neck, and finally to my collarbone.

"Is that okay?" he asked.

"Yes."

"Every time you lose a turn, I'm going to do it again."

"I won't lose," I said, because I believed it. But then I realized I wanted Jonathan to keep doing it. Not enough to lose on purpose, because the concept of intentional deception wasn't something that would have occurred to me. It was only the next day when I recounted the whole thing for Janice and she asked me if I was tempted to lose on purpose that I realized I could have pretended.

He made a careless mistake that was uncharacteristic of him, and when I placed his bishop next to my board, he said, "Now you kiss *me*."

I leaned toward him, placing my lips softly on his. It felt so good that, emboldened by the sensations, I kissed him harder. His hair felt damp and cold under my fingers as I ran them through his hair, but his mouth felt warm.

The next time he captured one of my pieces, he kissed his way down my neck again. Then he sucked on it. It felt electric and I gasped. I wanted more but didn't know how to tell him. Somehow he knew because he sucked harder and pulled my oversized sweater over my head. I was wearing a baggy long-sleeved T-shirt underneath it, and he took that off, too. Janice had helped me pick out the bra. It was made of cotton, with no underwire or uncomfortable pattern, but it was light pink with demi cups, and Janice said Jonathan would probably like it a lot. I couldn't read Jonathan's expression, because he appeared to be in some kind of trance.

"Will you . . . Can you stand up next to the bed?"

I did as he asked. I was wearing my favorite item of Janice-approved clothing that wasn't a skirt, a pair of thin baggy cotton pants with a drawstring I could cinch to exactly the right tightness, which for me wasn't very tight at all. I'd tied the drawstring in a bow, and he grabbed the end and pulled gently. Immediately, the pants slid down my hips a few inches, and when he untied them the rest of the way, they fell down and pooled at my feet. My pink underwear matched the bra. Jonathan stared. "I had no idea this was what your body looked like. I really want to take off the rest of your clothes."

"Are we going to finish our game?"

"We will if you want to finish it. Absolutely. Do you?"

I did want to finish, because I found it difficult to abandon any match that hadn't been played to the end, but the sensations coursing through my body were slightly stronger than my desire to return to the board. "We can finish the game tomorrow."

He put his hands on my hips and looked into my eyes, and for the first time I looked into his for a few moments before shifting my gaze to his nose. "So it's okay if I take them off?"

"Sure. Go ahead."

Modesty was a completely foreign concept to me. When I was younger my mom would often find me outdoors without a stitch on. Being naked meant there were no scratchy fabrics touching my skin, no zipper pressing down on me, and nothing could compare to the feeling of only air on my skin. Once, during our freshman year of college, I'd gotten out of bed in the middle of the night to get a drink of water. Janice's boyfriend had been spending the night, and we'd both awakened at the same time and found ourselves standing in front of the sink in our room to fill a cup. I had turned on the small light next to my bed so I wouldn't trip and it cast a yellow glow on us. I was naked, but he was wearing underwear. He did not say a single word as I filled my cup, drank it down, and walked back to my bed and slipped beneath the covers.

Janice, however, had *plenty* to say about it the next morning and told me I had to buy a robe. "You can't walk around our dorm room like that."

"But I live here. He doesn't."

"You still have to cover up," she said.

I held still as Jonathan reached around and unfastened my bra, slipping the straps off my shoulders and letting it fall to the floor. He slid my underwear down over my hips until it dropped to the floor. The same fingers that moved chess pieces so decisively were tentative as they reached out and skimmed along the indentation of my waist. Janice had told me that once I was in this position I should tell Jonathan

I was a virgin. "You can't just spring something like that on him." She hadn't specified the exact timing of this revelation, but since I was standing in front of Jonathan without any clothes on, I figured it was probably an okay time. "I've never had sex before."

That snapped him out of his trance.

"No one has ever wanted to," I said. "You don't have to either."

"Annika, I want to. More than anything."

His tone confused me. Was he mad? Frustrated? I detected frustration, but I didn't know what it meant. Why couldn't Janice be here with me? "Did I wait too long to tell you?"

"No. I'm just . . . Do you really not know how I feel about you?"

I shook my head. "Not really."

"I think you're beautiful, and smart. There's something about you that makes me feel good when I'm with you."

"Do you think it will hurt?"

He took my hand and kissed the back of it. "I don't know. If it does just tell me to stop and I will, okay?"

"Okay."

"Has anyone ever touched you before?"

"No."

"Have you . . . do you know what any of this feels like?"

"Yes." I'd been amazed to discover—quite accidently one day—what happened when I touched myself. I'd felt the beginning flutter of those same sensations when Jonathan and I kissed and pressed up against each other.

Jonathan nodded, exhaling. "Okay, good."

He pulled me down beside him on the bed, trembling slightly. "Have you done this before?" I asked.

"Yes."

"Are you nervous?" I asked.

"No," he said, placing his fingers over my mouth. And whether to calm me or to begin, he replaced his fingers with his lips. I loved kissing Jonathan, and I loved his touch, which was probably the biggest reason we'd made it this far.

He sat up and stripped off his shirt. He glanced over at me like he was waiting for me to say something. I looked at his chest, broad and smooth. His shoulders looked strong and well-defined. *Am I supposed to tell him that?* "You have a nice chest and strong-looking shoulders," I said. He smiled, so I knew I had said the right thing.

He brought us down onto the bed, and I landed on the chess pieces with a yelp. Jonathan lifted me up and swept the board and all the pieces onto the floor, so there was no way we were ever going to be able to finish that game.

When he pulled me toward him the sensation of being skin-to-skin felt so utterly foreign that I tensed. "Are you okay?" he asked.

"Yes." Already I was becoming accustomed to the feel of my breasts rubbing up against his chest. Then Jonathan pulled back a little and skimmed my nipple with his thumb. I felt a tingle between my legs, as if there was some sort of direct current that ran back and forth between the two body parts. Just about the time I got used to that, and was really starting to enjoy it, Jonathan bent his head and drew my nipple firmly into his mouth, which added a twinge of something I struggled to define. Was it pain? Pleasure?

"Am I going too fast?" he asked. His breathing sounded odd and ragged, like he couldn't catch his breath.

"Yes!" I must have said it very loudly because Jonathan jerked suddenly, as if I had startled him.

"Why didn't you tell me to slow down?" he asked.

"I don't know how to tell you," I said, my body now completely rigid.

"Yes you do," Jonathan said. "If I'm going too fast, just say the word 'slow' and I'll know what you mean. Okay?"

"Okay." Jonathan repeated everything he'd done so far—the kissing of my lips, the touching and sucking of my nipples—and I felt my body relaxing. He kissed me again, and put his hand on the inside of my thigh, stroking it. I broke the kiss but only because I suddenly needed more air than I was currently getting. Jonathan's fingers moved slowly toward my center, and when he reached it, I concentrated as hard as I could on blocking everything else out. I felt the first stirring of arousal, and I knew from touching myself that it would grow stronger if Jonathan's fingers kept circling me in the same pattern. But then he began moving his body lower on the bed, which confused me. When I felt his tongue on me, I raised my head and looked between my legs. "What are you doing!"

He looked up, brows knitted together. "I'm going down on you," he said.

"Why would you do that?"

He grinned. "Because I think you're really gonna like it."

I pushed his face away. "No, I won't."

"There's nothing to be embarrassed about," he said.

Why would I be embarrassed? "I'm not. It's just too much for me." There was no way I could handle that much stimulation.

"Are you sure?"

"I'm sure."

"So you don't want me to do that?"

"No."

"What do you want me to do?"

"Just do what you were doing before."

"You mean with my fingers?"

"Yes. That felt good."

He started over for the third time, and he did everything exactly the way I needed him to. As he touched me, lightly and then more firmly, I felt my arousal building again. I didn't think it would, but Jonathan touching me felt ten times better than when I touched myself.

My orgasm was imminent, but I didn't know what to do. Was I supposed to announce its impending arrival or just let it happen? Janice had forgotten to mention this part. But in the ten seconds or so before I came I stopped worrying if the way I felt or acted was right or wrong, because the sensations Jonathan's touch elicited were not only manageable, they were incredible. I stopped thinking entirely, and I put my hand over Jonathan's, holding it tighter against me. When my orgasm arrived I cried out, not caring if it was loud. The sheer pleasure of it washed over me in waves, leaving me boneless and feeling like I was sinking into the mattress.

Jonathan leaned over and kissed me. "I need to be inside you right now, Annika." He got out of the bed and I heard the sound of a drawer opening.

"What are you doing?' I asked.

"I'm getting a condom." I watched with clinical interest as Jonathan took off his jeans and underwear and rolled the condom on. When he got back in bed he settled his body between my legs. Holding himself up on his arms, he started to push into me in infinitesimal increments. He was careful, and gentle, but there was an urgency I could hear in his breathing. "Are you okay?" he asked. "Am I hurting you?"

It wasn't unpleasant, but I felt stretched in a way I never had before. "It stings a little. It's okay. Keep going."

A minute or so later he began to thrust into me faster, going deeper, and then his body began to shudder and shake. He groaned loudly and then collapsed on top of me, his cheek resting on my chest. I could feel the pounding of his heart, his warm skin. He was still inside me, and I wondered how long he planned on staying there. "That was incredible," he said.

"Did I do it right?" I asked.

Jonathan made a sound. Sort of like another groan, but softer this time. "You did it exactly right."

"Do you think you'll want to do it again?"

"Definitely," he said, pressing a kiss to my neck. "Do you want to do it again?"

"Could we rest for a little while first?" In order to handle more touching, I would need a break.

"Absolutely. Whatever you want." He withdrew from my body, which was an incredibly odd sensation, and got out of bed. As he walked toward the bathroom he said, "I'm going to need a few minutes anyway."

When Jonathan returned he slid back under the covers and pulled me into his arms, tucking me into the space under his chin, with his arms wrapped around me. He sighed, stroked my cheek, and rubbed his foot along my leg.

It felt like being trapped in a hot steel cage. I would have rather thrown off the covers and stretched out on the bed, moving my arms and legs as if I were making a snow angel, than be held.

But I'd seen this in movies and read about it in books.

This was cuddling.

Cuddling occurred after sex.

So I stayed put, letting him rub my shoulder and kiss my ear. He seemed drowsy, yawning like he might want to take a nap.

After fifteen minutes of this I started to get out of bed. "Where are you going?" he asked.

"It feels sticky between my legs."

"But I used a con— Oh. Stay here. I'll get a towel."

When he returned I pulled down the covers and spread my legs. Jonathan leaned down to examine me. "There's a little blood," he said. "That's probably what you felt." He must have run the towel under the faucet, because it was warm and damp. I lay back as he ran it lightly over my inner thighs and then between my legs.

"Annika, I think I'm ready again."

19

Annika

CHICAGO
AUGUST 2001

I'm eager to meet with Tina today. I feel like there are so many things I can share that I'm proud of, and I want her to be proud of them, too. Plus Audrey was out sick today, so I had a great day at work.

"Jonathan took me to a work function," I say after Tina leads me into her office and we've sat down. "I didn't say anything stupid, at least I don't think I did. I met his boss and most of his coworkers. It was exhausting and I had a splitting headache afterward, but I did it."

Tina knows that one of my coping mechanisms is to mimic the behaviors of others. She said it's a useful tool and that I should do whatever helps me the most.

"How do you feel when you're out with Jonathan?"

"I feel good. He's always been someone I'm comfortable being with. It feels like it did when we were in college."

"Have the two of you determined the kind of relationship you're comfortable having now?"

"Jonathan said he wanted to take it slow. So that's what we're doing. But we're spending a lot of time together. That makes me happy."

"Have you talked about the past yet?"

Truthfully, I hadn't thought about our past lately because our present was so preferable by comparison. "No."

"Do you think you're purposely avoiding things you find unpleasant because you prefer it when life is running smoothly?"

"Yes. I mean, maybe not avoiding unpleasant things but enjoying our time together and the fact that we've reconnected. I've missed him."

Tina does this thing where she steeples her index fingers under her chin. It took me almost a year to figure out it means she's thinking. Also that she's waiting for me to come to some kind of conclusion on my own. "At some point, you may find your past influencing the progression of this relationship. I think you should consider having the conversation even if it's not something you want to talk about."

"Everything is going so well."

"Which is why now might be a good time."

I don't admit to Tina that part of me hopes Jonathan has stopped thinking about it. Stopped wondering what happened on my end now that I've shown him I'm ready to pick up where we left off. But there's another part of me that understands it's the right thing to do. I owe him an explanation.

"I really like being with him."

"Then you have even more of a reason to talk about it. Something tells me it will go better than you think."

After my appointment with Tina, I eat dinner and read fifty pages of a book. Therapy always tires me out and I'm thinking about taking a bath to kill time until nine, which is the earliest I can go to bed if I don't want to wake up at 4:00 A.M. The buzzer startles me, because I don't have many visitors, but when I hear Jonathan's voice I forget all about being tired. I buzz him in and when I throw open the door, I clap my hands because this is just the best surprise ever. Normally I don't enjoy it when people drop by unannounced, but with Jonathan, I don't mind at all.

"I'm sorry I didn't call first. Have you eaten? I brought dinner," he said, holding up a take-out bag. "I've got just enough time to eat it with you before I have to head back to the office."

"I did eat. But that's okay. I'll keep you company." I beckon him inside before he can change his mind. "You're going back to work?"

He loosens his tie. "I have to. We're not done. Brad's planning to sleep on the couch in his office. I guess he's the winner."

"What will he win?" I'm genuinely curious, as I have no idea what kind of contest they're running down at Jonathan's workplace.

"Oh, no, nothing actually. I just meant he wants to make sure we all know how much harder he's working."

Jonathan could spend hours explaining it to me, but I doubt I'll ever understand the world of investment banking. And even if I did, it sounds awful.

"Won't you be tired tomorrow?"

"Yes, but lately I'm always tired."

We sit down at my kitchen table and he unpacks the food. Jonathan has brought a burger and fries. He pops one of the fries in my mouth.

"My friend Nate—he's the one I told you about that got divorced recently. He's got a new girlfriend and asked if you and I wanted to meet them for dinner."

"You want me to go to dinner with you and your friends?"

"Sure."

The only double dates I'd ever been on were with Janice and whoever she was seeing at the time, and with Ryan's best friend and his alcoholic wife. I had enjoyed double dating with Janice, more so after she finally dumped Joe and started dating a cute guy from one of her classes, but hadn't enjoyed it at all when Ryan and I had done it. But in the end, I'd discovered I really didn't like Ryan either. I liked Jonathan, so maybe I'd like his friend, too. And he wanted me to come! That had to count for something.

"That would be okay with me."

"I'll set something up. Will Saturday work for you?"

"Sure. I don't have any plans."

"I imagine you don't get to see Janice as often as you used to, but do you have other people to do things with?"

"Not really." I hated admitting to Jonathan that I still had difficulty in this area.

"There are probably a few people you get together with, aren't there?"

"I don't have a lot of friends."

"What about your coworkers?"

"Audrey doesn't like me. There's another girl—her name's Stacy. She seems nice, but whenever I try to talk to her, she usually ends up walking away." And I never have any clue why, other than whatever I said must have come out wrong. When I was younger, I preferred the company of boys over girls. They usually said what they meant. My role as someone's girlfriend seemed clearer somehow, and I mostly understood how it worked. But being a friend to someone vexed me. All my life, despite my good intentions, I'd always done it wrong. Women said so many things, often to my face, that I'd later learn they didn't mean. In some cases, they meant the complete opposite. They were rude when I was able to keep up, and nice when I seemed lost.

Keeping to myself, where I knew what to expect, was often much easier.

"Are you lonely?" Jonathan asks.

How could I tell him that my loneliness was crushing? How it felt awful to be lonely but not know how to reach out to people and fill the time I always had too much of? It wasn't that I didn't enjoy being alone, because I did, and could spend hours on solitary endeavors like reading or going for long walks without ever wishing for human companionship. I could visit the animals at the shelter or write another play for the children to perform. But sometimes I craved the presence of someone else, especially if I could be myself. A single father lived in my apartment building and occasionally, when he had his six-year-old daughter for the weekend and something unexpected happened that required his presence elsewhere, I would watch her. I relished it immensely and secretly wished he needed me to watch her more. The last time she was here, we spent two hours making paper dolls, and it was one of the most satisfying afternoons I'd had in a long time.

Shortly after Ryan and I broke up, I returned to the solitude I normally enjoyed, appreciating the simplicity of my life because I no longer had to walk on eggshells around a man. But now that time had passed, the loneliness had started reappearing like a growing tidal wave in the distance. I could feel it building and when it finally reached me, I would spend the rest of the day or night restless and fighting tears. It would eventually pass, but the episodes were becoming more frequent. I tried to fill my days with more social interaction, but that only left me feeling overwhelmed and exhausted. A personal connection with someone was what I craved the most. Someone who understood my needs and was willing to speak my language.

Someone like Jonathan.

I avert my eyes as I answer him. "I don't mind spending time alone, but sometimes I do get very lonely."

Jonathan leans over and puts his arm around my shoulders, pulling me close as I fight back tears. "Not everyone can look past their own hang-ups to see what I see. It's their loss."

When Jonathan said things like that, it propped me up and took away a little of the sting from the people who'd tried to tear me down or make me feel like a second-class citizen because I viewed things differently than they did. Ten years ago, I might not have been clear on what Jonathan was saying, but that had changed. Tina had taught me that it was important to surround myself with people who understood me. People who were secure about their own place in the world. It wasn't always easy to identify who those people were, but I was much better at it now than I had been in the past.

Around nine, Jonathan tells me he'd better get back to work. I yawn because now I'm really tired. I would never make it if I had to work late as often as Jonathan did.

"Want me to tuck you in before I head back to work?"

"Does that mean sex?" I blurt it out without thinking.

He laughs. "Well, that would be a fantastic send-off, but I really do have to get back."

My face flames, and I hang my head. I thought for sure I'd gotten it right. "I'm so embarrassed."

"You shouldn't be. You seemed awfully open to the possibility."

When we reach the doorway, he slides his hand behind my head and places a gentle kiss on my mouth. Then he presses me up against the wall and kisses me again, harder this time. No one else's kisses have ever affected me the way Jonathan's do. There is a gentleness about them that makes me feel safe, but there is something else now, an urgency. He twists his fingers in my hair, and we kiss for a while. I'm breathless when we finish.

"Ryan wasn't a very good kisser. Neither was Monte. Not like you."

Jonathan smiles like what I said made him happy.

"What did it mean?" I ask. I don't want to get my hopes up, because maybe the kiss doesn't mean anything.

"It means I've missed you. It means I've been waiting a long time to do that."

"Are we still going slow?"

He looks into my eyes and I hold his gaze for as long as I'm able before looking down at the floor. "I don't know. Maybe I don't want to go slow anymore."

"I'll be thinking about that kiss for the rest of the night," I say.

"Me too," he says, and then I lock the door behind him.

20

Annika

THE UNIVERSITY OF ILLINOIS
AT URBANA-CHAMPAIGN
1991

Several volunteers were huddled together talking when I arrived for my shift at the wildlife clinic. Sue was standing with them. "Hey, Annika. Can I talk to you?"

"Hi, Sue. I can only talk for a second because I want to check on Charlie." They'd removed the opossum's splint and had started planning for his release back into the wild. I'd become very attached and would miss him horribly.

Sue laid her hand on my arm, which didn't really bother me because I liked her and she only left it there briefly. "I'm so sorry, but Charlie died. He got sick overnight, very rapidly. I know he was special to you."

I couldn't stay there, could not bear the thought of such a tiny living thing suffering the way Charlie must have before he died. I turned on my heel and ran out the door into the cold evening air. Had Charlie taken his last breaths in his cage, or had someone been holding him? I hadn't thought to ask Sue these questions, and they haunted me now. I pictured his injured arm in its tiny little sling, and I burst into tears.

It was the only time in four years that I flaked on one of my shifts.

"Annika?" Janice said. "Jonathan's here. I called him. Is it okay if he comes in?"

I didn't answer her. I couldn't. I was lying on my side facing the wall, but I was under the covers, and I'd pulled them partially over my head.

The bed dipped a little, and I knew he'd sat down next to me. I felt his hand on my shoulder. "Hey. Is there anything I can do?"

I wanted to answer him, but I'd shut down and could already feel the pull of sleep and wanted nothing more than for it to take me away. My mom told me that the day she and my dad yanked me out of school midway through seventh grade I slept for almost seventeen hours straight. Sleep was my self-preservation tactic in response to pain. Jonathan said my name again and so did Janice, but I didn't say anything at all, and sleep took me.

It was pitch-dark in my room when I woke up, and the clock said five thirty. Desperately thirsty after sleeping all the way through until morning, I walked to the kitchen and filled a glass at the sink after making a quick stop in the bathroom. My stomach growled, and I reached into the cupboard for some crackers. Then I remembered that Charlie had died and the crackers got stuck in my throat when I tried to swallow.

I headed back to my room intending to read until it was time to get ready for class and stopped short as I passed through the living room. Jonathan was asleep on the couch, fully dressed in jeans and a sweatshirt, and though I had no idea why he was there, I was happy to see him.

I stretched out alongside his body, and he stirred. "You're still here," I said.

"I could tell you wanted to be alone, but I wanted to make sure you were okay when you woke up." He wrapped me sleepily in his arms, and I pressed my face to his chest.

"I don't like it when tiny living things die. It hurts my heart."

He stroked my hair. That was another thing I'd discovered about Jonathan. There wasn't any kind of touch from him that I didn't like, and it was as calming to me as I hoped mine had been to Charlie. We lay on the couch and he held me as the sun rose and filled the room with light.

"I miss Charlie."

Jonathan kissed the top of my head. "I know."

21

Annika

THE UNIVERSITY OF ILLINOIS
AT URBANA-CHAMPAIGN
1991

I was from a town called Downers Grove and Jonathan lived in Waukegan, about fifty miles to the north. Jonathan drove us home for winter break the day after we took our last finals. We had celebrated the end of the semester the night before by going out for pizza and beer with Janice and Joe. It had gone better than I thought it would. The pizza place Janice suggested was off campus and catered mostly to families with young children, and I found it to be a huge improvement compared to the noisy, student-filled choices closer to campus. Jonathan and Joe got along really well, which Janice said was likely due to Jonathan's ability to blend in with just about anyone and also the number of beers Joe drank.

"Come over here," Jonathan said as he merged onto I-57 to begin the two-hour drive to my house. The pickup truck had a bench seat, and it was just like the movies I'd watched where the guy wanted his girl to scoot over to the middle so he could put his arm around her, which is exactly what Jonathan did after he told me to fasten the center seat belt. I laid my head on his shoulder and every now and then he would give me a little squeeze. I didn't know why he liked me, what he saw in me that others had not. But I was grateful and happy that he did.

When he pulled into the driveway of my parents' house, they were standing there bundled up in their coats waiting for us. When I saw them, I clapped my hands together excitedly and jumped from Jonathan's truck the second he put it in park.

"Annika!" my mom said. She wrapped me in her arms, and I felt the way I always did when she was near: peaceful, secure, safe. Also like I couldn't breathe because she squeezed me so tight.

My dad and I shared a stiff hug. He wasn't big on physical affection, but I never doubted his love for me. From the time I was old enough to understand what the word meant, my mom had been telling me how much my dad loved me. He was a systems engineer and when he wasn't at work, he was either reading or building something for Will or me in the garage. He spent one whole summer building us that tree house in the towering oak in the backyard. Will eventually grew tired of it and ran off to ride bicycles with his neighborhood friends, but my dad and I used to stretch out on the smooth pine floor and read for hours. The two of us were kindred spirits; at least, that's what people had been saying about us all my life.

"Hello," my mom said, extending her hand to Jonathan. "I'm Linda."

I'd completely forgotten Jonathan was there. My dad must not have noticed him either, but when my mom said, "Ron, aren't you going to say hello to Annika's friend?" my dad stuck out his hand. "Hello." He shuffled off into the house after that.

"I hope you can spend some time with us before the two of you have to head back for the tournament," my mother said. The chess team had earned a spot in the Pan-American Intercollegiate Team Chess Championship, which would be held in downtown Chicago and begin a couple of days after Christmas. The Pan-Am was a six-round fixed roster with teams of four players and two alternates. I would be filling one of the alternate roles, which meant there was a good chance I would not see any playtime, barring something disastrous happening to one of the other four.

"I could come back the day after Christmas," Jonathan said. "Then I thought I'd take Annika home to meet my mother on our way to join the rest of the team at the hotel."

"That would be lovely. Maybe you could have lunch with us? Annika's brother will be home then, too."

"Okay. I'll plan on that."

"Would you like to come in?"

"Sure." Jonathan picked up my suitcase and we followed my mother into the house.

Once inside, I plopped down on the living room floor to play with my cat, Mr. Bojangles, whom I'd missed terribly, and became engrossed in our favorite game, which consisted of him batting at a ball that would have had a bell inside it except I'd removed it because I found the jingle incredibly grating. Will said the bell was probably Mr. Bojangles's favorite part of the toy, but I just couldn't handle it. Jonathan and my mom stood nearby talking. It amazed me that they could converse so effortlessly after only just meeting each other.

"Well, I should probably head out," Jonathan said. "My mom's waiting for me."

"Why don't you walk Jonathan out, Annika?"

"Okay." I rolled the ball toward Mr. Bojangles and he sent it shooting across the floor. As soon as Jonathan left, I would return to the cat and likely spend the next hour playing this game.

"I'll call you," Jonathan said when we reached his truck.

I wasn't a big fan of talking on the phone, but it would be the only way for Jonathan and me to stay in touch over the break. "Okay."

He reached into the bed of the truck, lifted the tarp that had protected our suitcases, and retrieved something from his. "I bought this for you. But you have to promise not to open it until Christmas."

It was a small rectangular box wrapped in red paper and tied with a gold ribbon.

I remembered Janice reminding me to buy Jonathan a gift a few weeks ago, and I told her I was going to buy him a sweater, because I'd seen a dark blue one at the mall and I'd thought to myself, *Jonathan looks really good in blue.* I'd forgotten my wallet at home that day so I told myself to come back and buy it, but then I'd completely forgotten to do it. "I didn't get you anything."

"That's okay. It's just something small I thought you might like."

I still felt stupid, but then Jonathan kissed me, and it didn't seem like he minded that I'd forgotten. "Merry Christmas."

"Merry Christmas."

He glanced toward the house and kissed me again. We had slept together almost every day since the first time we had sex, and it was hard for me to describe the feelings I currently had for him. I thought about him all the time. I'd discovered that I *did* like cuddling with Jonathan once I got used to it, and that the feel of his arms around me was something I never got tired of. I felt anxious when he wasn't around and at peace when he was near. I'd talked to Janice about it, and she said it meant I was falling in love with Jonathan. I had to take her word for it, because I had no frame of reference for such a thing.

All I knew as I watched him drive away was that I started missing him before he'd made it halfway down the driveway.

"What is that?" my mother asked when I came back inside the house.

"It's a Christmas present from Jonathan. He said I have to wait until Christmas to open it."

"Oh, Annika. That was so sweet of him. He seems like such a nice young man."

"He has never been mean to me, Mom. Not even once."

My mom didn't say anything right away. But she blinked several times as if there was something in her eye, and then hugged me again. I wriggled away as soon as I could, because this one was so tight I could barely breathe.

I had my parents to myself for almost two weeks before my brother flew in from New York to join us. Will worked on Wall Street and was always trying to regale my parents and me with his accounts of living and working in the big city as if we couldn't possibly fathom it on our own. I found it hard to pay attention, because I barely knew my brother. For most of my life, Will had ignored me. He left home for good as soon as he graduated from college, and I overheard my mother complaining that the only way she could get him back here at all was by playing the holiday card, which had something to do with guilt and nothing to do with the actual cards she sent out to our family and friends.

Now that I was home, I fell into old, familiar patterns of staying up late and sleeping until noon. I puttered around the house and played with Mr. Bojangles. My dad and I spent hours in the den reading our books in companionable silence while my mom baked and wrapped gifts. My dad and I trimmed the tree and we decided to place the lights vertically instead of wrapping them around it, and we grouped the ornaments by category, with all the balls on the top half of the tree, and anything that wasn't a ball on the bottom. When Will walked into the living room two days before Christmas, the first thing he said was, "What the hell happened to the tree?"

My mom answered him. "I think it looks very unique and if you don't like it, you can come home earlier next year and help Dad and

Annika trim it." Then she offered him a frosted sugar cookie and a beer, and he stopped complaining. I nearly gagged thinking about what that combination would taste like.

On Christmas Eve, after our extended family members had gathered up their gifts, said their good-byes, and gone home, I sat down next to the tree to open Jonathan's gift. My mom joined me. "I think I'm more excited than you are, Annika."

I was more curious than excited, because I'd been playing a game with myself where I had to come up with a different guess every night before I went to sleep for what was inside the box. I wrote them all down in an old notebook I found in my room. What if it was full of tiny white seashells from Tahiti? Or forest-green sea glass from the Atlantic Ocean? My favorite guess was that he'd bought me a fossilized flower in burnt-orange amber.

I tore off the wrapping paper, but it was not a fossilized flower in amber, or seashells, or sea glass.

It was a bottle of Dune perfume by Christian Dior, and though Janice squealed when I told her about it later, the brand meant nothing to me, because I would never wear it. Perfume felt like a cloud of poison when it settled on my skin. One day at the mall, when I was twelve, a woman had squirted me with perfume as I walked by with my mother. It had sent me into a tailspin of whimpering tears, and once my mother got me out of the mall and into her car, I ripped off most of my clothing. At home, I threw myself into the shower and didn't come out for almost forty-five minutes.

"What a pretty bottle," my mom said. It was light pink with a shiny cap. I ran my fingers over the smooth glass but did not uncap it or spritz a tiny bit into the air to see what it smelled like. "It's the thought that counts," she said. "Make sure you tell Jonathan thank you."

"I will," I said.

Although the gift was something I would never use, I loved the ribbon he'd used to wrap around the gift, and I spent the rest of the evening absently running my fingers across the curling strands. My mom was right, though. The bottle really *was* pretty, and the perfume ended up in a special spot on my dresser where it would remain, capped and unused, for the entirety of the winter break.

22

Annika

THE UNIVERSITY OF ILLINOIS
AT URBANA-CHAMPAIGN
1991

Jonathan arrived the day after Christmas. My mom spent the morning in the kitchen making a whole new meal even though my dad wanted to know why we couldn't just eat the leftovers from the day before. It sounded like a logical plan to me, but my mom insisted that it would be wrong to do that even though we could barely get the refrigerator door shut because there was so much food in there already.

The five of us sat down to an early lunch of roasted chicken and scalloped potatoes. "Is the team ready for the competition?" my mom asked.

"I think so," Jonathan said. "We're really strong this year. Lots of good players, including Annika."

"What's your major, Jonathan?" Will asked.

"Business."

"I graduated with a business degree from Illinois in 1985. Got my master's two years later. Night school at NYU."

"I hope to follow in the exact same path."

"Really?" Will scowled in my direction. "Why didn't you tell me that, Annika?"

"You never asked," I said. "Plus, I haven't talked to you since last summer."

"Maybe I could put in a good word for you when you start interviewing," Will said.

"I'd appreciate that. Thank you."

"How's the chicken?" my mom asked.

"It's really good," Jonathan said.

"You've outdone yourself, Mom," Will said.

My dad and I kept silent. We'd eaten my mom's chicken a thousand times, and she already knew we liked it.

As I was helping my mom clear the table, Will came up to me and said, "I like this guy. You should really hold on to him."

"I will try to hold on to him," I said. I wasn't sure exactly how to do that, but Will was being nice for once and the last thing I wanted was to lose the only boyfriend I'd ever had. It would have been an easier promise to keep if I'd known how I managed to get one in the first place.

Jonathan came upstairs with me when I went up to grab my things. "Thank you for the perfume," I said, pointing to its place of honor on my dresser. "It was a very thoughtful gift, and I love it." The words came out smoothly, because my mom had made me practice what I would say to Jonathan until I got it right.

He smiled. "You're welcome."

I threw a few more things into my suitcase and zipped it up.

"Is that it?" Jonathan asked.

"Yep."

"You don't need anything else?"

"Nope. That's everything." He picked up my suitcase and headed for the door.

I followed him, but on the way out of my bedroom, I grabbed the gold ribbon lying next to the perfume on my dresser and shoved it into my purse.

Jonathan lived in a small ranch-style home at the end of a cul-de-sac. It was neat and stark inside, unlike my parents' ramshackle split-level with its abundance of knickknacks, cat toys, and books. His mother was waiting for us, and after she hugged Jonathan and kissed his cheek, she turned to me and said, "You must be Katherine. I'm Cheryl."

"Mom, this is Annika. I've said her name like a thousand times."

"Oh. Of course, Annika. I'm sorry. I don't know why I said that."

"It's okay," I said.

She shook my hand. "It's nice to meet you. Jonathan talks about you all the time."

"Mom," Jonathan said.

"Sorry." His mother smiled and winked at me. I had no idea what it meant, but I smiled back. His mom seemed nice, and for some reason, I felt instantly comfortable around her. There was something very unthreatening about her demeanor. Sometimes it was like that when I met new people. Maybe it was their vibe or some kind of aura, but whatever the reason, it always made me happy when I encountered them.

"When are you heading out?" she asked.

"In about twenty minutes. I just need to grab the rest of my things upstairs."

"I'm sorry my mom called you by the wrong name," Jonathan said after we went into his bedroom. "Katherine was my high school girlfriend. Maybe she got confused for a second. You both have blond hair."

"That's okay," I said, because I truly hadn't minded. I wasn't that great with faces and names either.

Jonathan's room looked a lot like mine, although much less cluttered.

He had a lot of high school memorabilia, mostly swimming trophies and team pictures of him standing next to a pool. A stack of yearbooks sat on the floor next to the dresser, and on the wall hung a Waukegan High School banner with a picture of a bulldog. I felt like an archaeologist unearthing relics of a place I'd never visited. I found it fascinating.

"You have so many things from high school."

"Well, yeah. Doesn't everyone?"

"I don't. I was home-schooled."

"Like, always?"

"I went to a regular school until my parents pulled me out midway through seventh grade."

"They pulled you out? Why?"

"My mom said it was to keep me safe."

I sat down on the bed and Jonathan sat down beside me. "What did she mean by that?" he asked.

I had refused to talk about that day with anyone but my parents, and the psychologist the school hastily arranged for me to meet with said it was possible I'd blocked it out. But that wasn't true at all. I remember the day Maria and three other girls came for me like it was yesterday. I told Jonathan how they'd kicked and punched me, bloodied my nose and pulled my hair. How they'd shoved me into a single-stall bathroom in the locker room, turned off the lights, and pushed a chair under the doorknob on the outside so I couldn't leave. I'd cried so hard and yelled for so long that by the time a teacher found me, lip fat and one eye nearly swollen shut, I'd grown so hoarse I couldn't utter a sound.

"Annika," Jonathan said quietly.

"Janice is the only person I've ever told this to. But I'm glad I told you."

Telling him seemed right, in much the same way it had when I'd told him about Jake. It was like letting a dark and dusty secret out, and I liked the way I felt afterward. Unburdened. Lighter. I didn't understand it at the time, but years later I would realize that sharing painful things that had happened to me was one of the ways I strengthened the bond I had with Jonathan.

He hugged me tight. "I don't know what to say."

That surprised me, because Jonathan never seemed at a loss for words. "It's okay." He must have needed a minute or something, because he squeezed me even tighter. When he finally let go of me, he pulled back a little and studied my face, traced my eyebrow and mouth gently with his thumb as if he needed proof that I'd healed sufficiently. "It was a long time ago," I said.

He looked into my eyes and nodded. I turned away, and a shiny gold tube of lipstick on his dresser caught my eye. Pointing at it, I asked, "What's that?"

"It doesn't belong to another girl." He answered quickly, although that possibility had not occurred to me until he said it. "The salesgirl must have thrown it in the bag when I bought your perfume. I didn't realize it until I went to wrap your gift. I didn't know what to do with it so I brought it home."

I picked up the lipstick and removed the cap, becoming instantly captivated by the bright red color and especially the shape, curved and smooth and unblemished, like a brand-new crayon. "Do you like it?" he asked, and I nodded my head.

"You left the perfume at home."

I looked down, embarrassed that I hadn't realized I should bring the perfume with me after telling him how much I loved it. "Most smells are too strong for me to handle."

"I should have given you the lipstick instead. I didn't know. Now I do." He motioned toward the door. "The bathroom's across the hall. Go try it out."

I walked into the bathroom and looked in the mirror. I hoped the lipstick wouldn't feel like the sticky gloss I hated. Was I supposed to color in my lips or trace around them first? This was Janice's area of expertise, not mine, and I'd feel foolish if I had to admit to Jonathan that I didn't know what I was doing. I put the cap back on and set down the lipstick on the counter. Maybe I'd wait until I got back to school and could ask Janice to give me a lesson. Jonathan's face appeared in the mirror next to mine, and I turned around.

"Aren't you going to put it on?"

"I've never worn lipstick before."

"I've never worn it either." I must have looked confused, because he laughed. "It was a joke, Annika."

"Oh!"

"Sit up here," he said, patting the counter. After hoisting myself onto it, Jonathan stood between my legs. "I bet it's just like a coloring book."

Using the pointed side, Jonathan traced my lip line with the precision of a surgeon. Then he used short strokes to fill my lips in completely. I closed them, enjoying the subtle popping sound when I opened them wide again. "Check it out," he said.

I looked over my shoulder, staring in amazement at the girl in the mirror. "Wow," I said. The bright color heightened my features and made me curious about whether a little mascara would balance the effect and improve it even more. Janice was going to be *thrilled* when I asked her.

I turned back around and Jonathan took my chin in his hands, moving my face to the right and then slowly to the left, studying my mouth. "I like it." He looked into my eyes when he said it, and just when it would have been impossible for me to hold his gaze for one more minute, he closed them and pressed his forehead to mine. Maybe other people felt what I was feeling at that moment when they looked deeply into each other's eyes, but when Jonathan and I were joined in a way I could handle, I knew what it felt like to be deeply connected to someone.

Years later, in therapy, when Tina helped me understand that he'd done it on purpose, the sadness I'd felt at losing him had been profound. At that moment, I missed him more than I'd ever missed anything, and the possibility of seeing him again someday seemed highly unlikely. But that day in his bathroom, at his mother's house in Waukegan, I knew that Janice had been right when she said I was falling in love with Jonathan, even if I couldn't completely identify it yet myself.

"I will never let anyone hurt you the way those girls did," he said.

"Okay," I said, because I didn't doubt for one minute that he spoke the truth.

Then Jonathan kissed that lipstick right off me.

Jonathan wanted to leave by four o'clock so we could get checked into the hotel and meet the rest of the team for a pep talk in Eric's room.

"Mom, why is your car in the driveway instead of the garage? It's freezing out, and it's supposed to snow tonight. Give me your keys, and I'll move it for you."

"I seem to have misplaced them."

"Well, just give me the spare key."

"That *was* the spare set. I lost the first set a month ago. I thought they would have turned up by now."

"When did you last have them?"

"I went to the store yesterday, and when I came home, I thought I put them in that little ceramic bowl on the counter. The one my sister brought back from Paris."

Jonathan went into the kitchen, and when he returned, he was holding a set of keys. "You did, Mom. They were in the bowl."

She laughed and shook her head. "Oh, good lord. I think the

holidays have done me in this year. Thank you, honey." She kissed Jonathan on the cheek and took the keys from his hand. "I'm putting these back in the bowl right now. Still can't find the other ones," she said on her way out of the room.

Jonathan's mother stood in the driveway and waved as we backed out. I waved back enthusiastically.

"That was odd," Jonathan said. "My mom never loses anything."

"I lose everything," I said. "Maybe that's why I like your mom so much."

He took his eyes off the road for a second and smiled at me. "You like her?"

"Yeah. She was really nice to me."

"She told me she liked you, too. She called you Katherine again, but what the hell. She likes you."

I laughed, too. "Yeah." *She likes me.*

23

Annika

THE UNIVERSITY OF ILLINOIS
AT URBANA-CHAMPAIGN
1991

The Palmer House Hotel was the venue for the Pan-Am Championship. My mother had insisted on paying for our four-night stay, since Jonathan had been doing all the driving, and she'd given me her credit card and cautioned me not to lose it. I'd told my family about Jonathan's dad dying and his part-time job and how he was putting himself through school. Will had said that he was probably strapped for cash, which made me feel even worse about the money he'd spent on the perfume. I had some money saved up and decided I would take Jonathan out for a nice dinner to repay him for the Christmas gift. My mom thought that was a great idea. Jonathan didn't like the idea of me paying, but when he protested I said "I insist!" with the same tone my mother had used with me.

We deposited our luggage in our room and took the elevator two floors down to meet with the rest of the team in Eric's room. Tournament participants had filled the hotel to capacity, and as we walked down the hall, students milled in and out of the rooms carrying ice buckets, six-packs of pop, and pizza boxes stacked five high. "One

Night in Bangkok" from the *Chess* cast album blared from a boom box in an open doorway. When we arrived in Eric's room, the rest of the team was lounging on the beds drinking cans of Coke.

"Hey, Jonathan. Annika," Eric said. "Ready for tomorrow?"

"Absolutely," Jonathan said.

"Absolutely," I parroted. I often formulated the answers to questions mentally before I said them out loud, but it was hard for me to come up with something on the fly, which is why I preferred, if at all possible, not to say anything at all for fear it wasn't the right thing. No one seemed to be paying much attention to the responses Jonathan and I had given, and I realized later that the question had been mostly rhetorical. Assembled in that hotel room were the best chess players the University of Illinois had to offer. Of course we were ready.

"Do you want some pizza? We have plenty."

"Sure," Jonathan said. "Thanks."

"Thanks," I said.

We sat down on the only remaining space on one of the beds to eat our pizza. It was pepperoni and I didn't like toppings on my pizza, only cheese, but I hid the pepperoni in my napkin and when I was done eating, I balled it up and threw it away.

Eric went over the information for the next day's tournament play. "So let's meet downstairs first thing in the morning," Eric said.

"Sounds good," Jonathan said. He stood up, so I did, too. "See you tomorrow."

"We're going down the hall to meet with some guys from Nebraska. Do you and Annika want to come?"

"Thanks, but we're gonna take off. I'm really tired." It wasn't very late, but maybe the driving had tired Jonathan out.

We walked hand in hand back to our room. It felt so strange to be staying in a hotel room with Jonathan, like we were playing some kind of college version of house. I spent a lot of nights at Jonathan's apartment at school, but this was different. It was *our* bed and *our* dresser. We could take a shower together in *our* bathroom every morning if we wanted to, and I knew from experience that we would.

"I didn't know you were so tired. Do you need to go to sleep?" I asked as Jonathan stuck the key card in the door.

"I'm not tired."

"But you told Eric you were."

Jonathan opened the door and then locked it behind us and slid the chain into place. He responded to my statement with a long, deep kiss that sort of caught me off guard. "I didn't want to announce to everyone that I wanted to be alone with you. It's been almost four weeks. I've missed you. Have you missed me?"

"Oh," I said, finally realizing where he was going with this. "Yes!" There had been so many nights I'd lain in bed thinking about how much I missed being kissed and touched by him. I threw myself into his arms, which made him laugh. He lifted me and I wrapped my legs around his waist and kissed him as he walked toward the bed. We fell onto it, and I didn't mind that he landed on me because the mattress absorbed some of his weight and kept him from crushing me. We kissed for a few minutes and then he took off my clothes.

Jonathan knew exactly how to touch me. He ran the palms of his hands over my skin with a firm touch, because anything lighter tickled me, which was a sensation I couldn't handle. His fingers were bold, searching out my innermost spots. Jonathan always made me come with his fingers, then he entered me and he came, then we cuddled. So it alarmed and confused me when he pulled his hand away, took off all his clothes but his underwear, and said, "Touch me, Annika."

"I don't know how." I'd come to rely on the exact, predictable pattern we had always followed, and I did not want or need variety.

"I'll teach you." He reached for my hand and placed it between his legs, and I could feel how hard he was already. He swallowed. "Please."

It's not like I wasn't used to Jonathan's penis by then. He was every bit as comfortable with nudity as I was, and I knew the size and shape of it well enough to draw it if I'd wanted to. It had been inside of me plenty of times. I'd watched him roll on condoms and I'd watched him dispose of them. He seemed to be always, effortlessly hard and since I never had to touch him to get him that way, it had never occurred to me that he'd want me to. "What do I do now?"

"Rub up and down with the palm of your hand."

I rubbed him gently, the fabric providing a thin barrier to my touch that helped ease my progress on this next step. "Like this?"

"A little bit harder." When I complied he said, "Yeah. Just like that."

"What should I do next?"

"Take off my underwear."

I should have known that, because Jonathan was always taking off mine. I pulled down his black boxer briefs, and as soon as they'd cleared his hips Jonathan reached for my hand and wrapped my fingers around the base of his penis. He put his hand over mine and showed me what to do. Though his penis was rock-hard, the skin covering it felt soft and much silkier than any other part of his body that I'd touched.

He put his hand between my legs again and it felt so good that I stopped touching him, not because I didn't want him to feel good, too, but because it was too much like trying to pat my head while rubbing circles on my belly: I could really only do one of those things at a time. He pressed my hand down on him again and I resumed stroking him, trying as hard as I could to please him and enjoy the way he was trying to please me.

But then he stopped touching me when I was very close. "What's happening?" I said, opening my eyes and looking around to see what had made him stop.

Jonathan was on his knees, rolling on a condom. "Spread your legs."

I did and he entered me. It was better because I only had to concentrate on one thing, but I couldn't get the rising sensations back. Jonathan groaned, so it must have felt good to him, but I didn't know how to find my rhythm again, and everything felt a bit off. I felt like I needed to start again from the beginning, but Jonathan seemed closer to the end.

"I can't hold off much longer," he gasped.

I didn't know what to do. It still felt good with him inside me, but there was no way I was going to have an orgasm.

"Annika, really. I can't."

"It's okay," I said, and I'd barely gotten the words out when he groaned and shook in a way he never had before. He was out of breath and panting into my neck and squeezing me tight, and I could feel him throbbing inside of me.

"Oh my God," he said, and the last word came out soft, like a whisper. It seemed like it felt extra good for him and I was glad about that because I worried I'd messed it up somehow. He kissed my forehead, my cheek, my mouth. "Didn't it feel good to you?"

"It did," I said.

"You didn't come. Did you?"

"No."

"Why?"

"I don't know!"

"I can touch you again. I can start over and make you feel good."

"That's okay."

He was silent then. "Oh."

He got up and went to the bathroom. When he came back, he slid under the covers and put his arms loosely around me. "I'm sorry."

"I'm sorry too," I said. I wasn't sure exactly what I'd done wrong, but I knew I'd done something.

"There's nothing for you to be sorry about. It was my fault."

I had no idea how I was supposed to respond to that, so rather than risk saying the wrong thing, I didn't say anything at all. Jonathan rolled onto his back. Eventually we fell asleep, although it seemed like it took us both an extra long time.

I woke up a few hours later, and I couldn't get back to sleep because I worried that whatever had happened earlier would finally convince Jonathan there was something wrong with me and that I was the worst girlfriend in the world. I replayed what had happened over and over in my mind, right up until the point he'd deviated from our usual routine. A funny thing happened then. The desire I hadn't been able to hold on to earlier suddenly came roaring back. I didn't have enough experience to know that it worked like that sometimes—that it could be unpredictably elusive, and return when you least expected it.

Neither one of us was wearing any clothes. Jonathan was lying on his side—not quite spooning me, because although I'd grown to love cuddling after sex, I'd finally admitted it was difficult for me to fall asleep with his arms around me, but close enough that I could feel the presence of another person when I moved. I turned so that I was facing him and pressed my body against his. There was something thrilling about the feel of his nakedness, the warmth of his skin, and the fact that he was unaware of what I was doing. I pressed against him a little harder, and he stirred but still didn't wake up. I felt him grow hard against me, which I found baffling.

How does that work? What will happen if I touch him?

I fluttered kisses down his neck and, growing bolder, I reached between his legs and wrapped my hand around him, remembering what he'd taught me. He woke up with a groan so loud it startled me.

"Is it okay that I did that?" I yanked my hand away in case the answer was no. He grabbed for it, put it back.

"Yeah, it's more than okay. It's great. It just caught me by surprise." His words came out in fits and starts, as if he were having trouble regulating his breathing. He kissed me, roughly, and I kissed him back with every bit as much force.

Jonathan always wanted the lights on when we had sex. Janice said that was because men were more visual than women. I never minded, but I did struggle with the face-to-face aspect of being intimate with someone. When Jonathan touched me, he often looked deep into my eyes, but I'd have to squeeze mine shut in order to concentrate. The pitch-black darkness of the hotel room did not allow for eye contact, and it unleashed something in me I'd never experienced before. I felt confident, uninhibited, in control. We were a blur of hands and mouths, each of us trying to give more than we took. He kissed his way down my body and when he put his face between my legs, I didn't stop him, because I wanted him to do it. It was intense but it wasn't too much for me after all. As the incredible sensations coursed through me I twisted my fingers in his hair and made so much noise I hoped I never ran into the people in the room next to us.

Jonathan reached for a condom on the nightstand and put it on. "Holy shit, what is happening," he said when I climbed on top of him. He started laughing, and so did I because, for once, I got it. I understood that I was doing exactly what he'd hoped for earlier. Not necessarily the sex, although that was happening, too, but my willingness to break free from familiar patterns and try something different.

It felt so good that I never wanted it to end. I didn't think it was possible to feel closer to Jonathan than I already did, but that night in our hotel room, I learned that the closeness of two people had no limits.

Out of all the firsts I experienced with Jonathan, that was the one I treasured the most.

24

Annika

THE UNIVERSITY OF ILLINOIS
AT URBANA-CHAMPAIGN
1991

When we walked into the ballroom, my palms grew damp. The thrum of the players' conversations filled the area, and my pulse quickened. We were one of the only collegiate teams that was student led and didn't have a coach, so we were on our own and would have to rely on one another for guidance and support. If one of our team members were suddenly unable to compete and I had to step up, I wasn't sure I would be able to.

"Are you nervous?" I asked Jonathan. "I'm very nervous."

He smiled and grabbed my hand, swinging it as if he didn't have a care in the world. "I'm not nervous. I'm ready. We've got an excellent team. I have a good feeling about the tournament." In addition to Eric and Jonathan, a graduate student in physics named Vivek Rao and a phenomenally talented junior from Wisconsin named Casey Baumgartner would round out the team.

I watched Jonathan play that day, in awe of his talent and so proud that this smart and kind guy belonged to me. It was clear from the start that Illinois was a serious contender to go all the way, and as each day of the competition blurred into the next, they kept winning.

I took care of Jonathan the way he often took care of me. I made sure to have something for him to eat or drink between his matches. I kept track of who he would be playing, and when and where. I helped him unwind and it did feel a little like Jonathan and I were playing house when we returned to our hotel room at the end of the day. Though I wasn't the kind of person who imagined things like marriage proposals and what kind of house we would buy, I loved the way it felt to share a living space with Jonathan, even temporarily.

It made me feel secure and happy and calm.

On the last day of the tournament, Vivek Rao defeated Gata Kamsky in seventy-three moves in the fourth-round game, clinching the championship for Illinois. What surprised me the most as we gathered, shouting and cheering, around Vivek was the slight regret I felt at not being called into play after all.

We stormed into the bar afterward, high on our victory, surrounded by a crush of competitors. Jonathan walked in front of me, paving the way with his body, holding tightly to my hand as he pulled me through the crowd to a small table in the back. Once we claimed it, he settled me on a stool that backed to the wall. "Is this okay?" he asked. It was loud and he had to yell a little, but to my surprise, it *was* okay. Because of the way he positioned me, I could see everything that was going on without worrying about someone jostling me or invading my space. I had a wall to my left and Jonathan stood next to the table on my right, making me feel like I was in my own little protected corner. He ordered himself a beer and asked me what I wanted.

"Do they have wine coolers?" I asked.

"I'm sure they do. What flavor?"

"Cherry." Those were the kind Janice always brought home from the store.

It was nice sitting there eating nachos and drinking my wine cooler, but a short while later the band that had been setting up in the corner started playing. The whine of the guitar and the crash of the drums felt like knives slicing into my eardrums. I put my hands over my ears and squeezed my eyes shut, trying to will away the awful sounds.

Jonathan pulled my hands from my ears, shouting, "Annika, what's wrong?"

"Too loud." I put my hands back, because it felt like my brain might explode and leak out my ears. Jonathan put his arm around me and led me from the bar. In the lobby, he set me down on a bench and crouched in front of me.

"Are you okay?"

"It was just so loud!"

"Yes, it was loud." He grabbed my hands and held them. "Do you want to go back to our room?"

"Can we?"

"Of course. Stay here. I'm going to pay our share of the bill and then I'll come right back."

When we reached the blissful quiet of our room, the stillness soothed me and eased the ringing in my ears. Jonathan put his arms around me. "Better?"

I didn't answer his question. Instead I whispered, "I love you, Jonathan."

"I love you, too. I've been thinking about how I was going to tell you."

"If you've been thinking about it, why didn't you just say it?"

"Because the first time you say it to someone, you hope they'll say it back. And if you're not sure they will . . ."

"Why wouldn't I say it back? I *did* say it. Just now." I thought I was the one confused by relationships and everything that went along with them.

"Maybe there was a small part of me that worried you wouldn't. I don't always know what's going on up there," he said, tapping my temple gently.

"I never know what people are thinking. It's like visiting a country where you don't speak the language and you're trying so hard to understand but no matter how many times you ask for juice, they keep bringing you milk. And I hate it."

He smiled. "I love you, Annika. So much."

"I love you, too."

When I looked back on the time we spent at the Palmer House Hotel, I realized they were some of the best days of my life.

25

Annika

THE UNIVERSITY OF ILLINOIS
AT URBANA-CHAMPAIGN
1992

"Are you nervous?" Janice asked as we sat down in the small waiting area of the student health center.

"Why would I be nervous? You didn't tell me there was anything to be nervous about."

"No, it's just that I didn't think you'd ever had a pelvic exam before."

"I haven't." My mother had taken me to have a physical before I left for college. The doctor had asked if I was sexually active and I said no and that had been the end of it. "Why, does it hurt?"

"No. It can be a little uncomfortable, but just for a second. You'll be fine."

I filled out the form the receptionist had given me and returned it. "Is this where you went?" I asked Janice when I sat back down.

"Yes. It's where everybody goes. Or Planned Parenthood."

The nurse called my name. "I'll wait here," Janice said, thumbing through a magazine. "Come back and get me when you're done."

The nurse weighed me and took my blood pressure. She gave me a paper gown and told me to take off all of my clothing, so I hopped off the table and began shucking my clothes.

"Oh, I'll just . . . let me give you some privacy."

All I was wearing by then was my underwear, and I pulled it down and let it drop onto the growing pile on the floor. The paper gown was a little tricky, so she showed me how to slip it on so that it opened in front. Then she gave me a paper sheet to lay across my lap.

"Well, I guess I'll let the doctor know you're ready."

"Okay."

The doctor looked a little like my dad, and when I told Janice this later she said that would have freaked her out, but I didn't think much of it at the time. Mostly the doctor seemed kind and unthreatening.

I'd had a basic introduction to reproductive health in fifth grade, but it wasn't something my mother had spent much time on outside of helping me when I got my first period. Everything I'd learned about the actual mechanics of sex had come from Jonathan, and that had mostly worked itself out in a variety of experimental, hands-on ways.

I had so many questions for the doctor as he examined me, starting with a breast exam. What was he doing? What were things supposed to look like? What was the purpose of it all?

"Not many women take as strong an interest as you have today. I find it admirable that you're so eager to understand the process."

"It's my body. It's nice to know how it works." I didn't understand why everyone wouldn't want to know.

When the exam was over, the doctor told me I could scoot back up on the table. "Your paperwork indicates you're interested in obtaining birth control and that you're currently sexually active."

"Yes. With my boyfriend Jonathan. We love each other."

The doctor smiled. "It's always nice to hear that a couple is in love."

I had been so excited to return to school after winter break so I could tell Janice that Jonathan and I had said "I love you." But when I told her how it happened, the first thing she said was "Oh."

When someone said that word to me, I knew what it meant.

"Did I do it wrong?" I asked, my voice rising in panic. Of course I had. Why would this be any different from all the other things I'd screwed up?

"No, not at all. It's just that usually the guy says it first."

"Once I realized I loved him I wanted to tell him right away. I didn't know there were rules about this!"

Janice had grabbed my hands. "You know what? It's a stupid rule. It's not even a rule. It doesn't matter who said it first. All that matters is that you love him and he loves you."

I wanted to believe her. Since we got back to school, Jonathan had told me he loved me seven more times and he always said it first.

"What method of birth control are you currently using?" the doctor asked.

"Condoms. But my roommate Janice thinks I'm ready for the pill."

"Do you?"

"I think so."

The doctor explained the importance of taking the pills regularly, preferably at the same time of day. "You'll have to take these for thirty days before you're fully protected. If you miss a pill, be sure to use a backup method of contraception until you've finished the pack." Janice kept her pill pack on her nightstand and took one first thing every morning, but I decided I would keep mine in my purse. I spent many nights at Jonathan's, but sometimes he spent the night at my place. If I kept the pills in my purse, I would always have them with me no matter where we decided to sleep.

We talked about safe sex and that I could protect myself by making sure anyone I was intimate with had been tested for sexually transmitted diseases. The doctor asked if I had any questions, but I didn't. I felt so grown-up and responsible. Janice had been on the pill since her senior year of high school, but all of this was uncharted territory for me. I'd been granted entry into a special girls' club, and I was proud of my membership because I was tired of being behind on everything all the time.

So far, my senior year of college had been the best year of my life. I had a steady boyfriend, I'd attended a chess tournament, and while I hadn't contributed directly to the team's victory, my skill level had earned me the right to be a part of it. I was exhibiting a level of responsibility for my sexual health that gave me immense personal satisfaction, and every day I was one step closer to the career I'd coveted for so long.

Life was on an upswing, and I was starting to believe that my future was every bit as bright as Janice always promised it would be.

Later that day, Jonathan picked me up to walk to class. "I went to the student health center this morning," I said as I grabbed my jacket and backpack and locked the door behind us.

"Are you sick?"

"I went there so I could get on the pill."

He stopped walking. "The birth control pill?"

"Is there another kind of pill they call the pill?"

"No. I mean, not that I know of. Really? You went on the pill?"

"It's what women who are in monogamous relationships do. Janice said it would make things easier and that you would probably like it."

"Well, yeah. I like it a lot."

"It won't be safe until I've taken them for thirty days. And the doctor said you have to get tested. I got tested. I can't have sex without a condom unless I know you're free of sexually transmitted diseases."

"I assure you that I don't have any STDs."

"The doctor said you might say that."

"Annika, I will get tested. I promise." He squeezed my hand and kissed me. "This is going to be really great."

26

Annika

THE UNIVERSITY OF ILLINOIS
AT URBANA-CHAMPAIGN

A friend of Jonathan's was having a party, and he wanted us to go. He'd mentioned it that morning while we were eating breakfast, but I hadn't committed the details to memory, because I really wasn't interested. I felt tired and crampy and my back ached, and the gloomy weather wasn't helping things. It was much colder than usual for early April and had been raining all day, the cold drizzly kind of rain that falls during that in-between time when winter is over but spring hasn't fully arrived. I'd spent the day curled up in Jonathan's bed with him and a book, and spending the evening that way sounded much more appealing than anything we would encounter beyond the four walls of his bedroom.

"I'm going stir-crazy," he said after we ate dinner. "We don't have to stay for a long time, but I really want to introduce you to some more of my friends."

Janice said that Jonathan always seemed proud to be with me. That made me feel good, because until I met him, I never thought I would be the type of girl anyone would be proud to be seen with. And

Janice was always reminding me that relationships were all about compromise.

"Like when you said Joe wasn't a great kisser but had a bigger than average penis?"

"I said that?"

"You did. After seven wine coolers." Joe had been replaced a few weeks ago by a graduate student who rode a bicycle everywhere and whose penis according to Janice was merely average. "But his hands are magical," she said.

Jonathan made lots of concessions for me, and I didn't need Janice to tell me that. He kept me away from loud noises before they could overwhelm me. He was always kind—to people, to animals, to strangers. He made me feel special and smart.

Jonathan wanted to go to the party, and I wanted to be the kind of girlfriend who compromised, who made concessions. So at nine thirty we put on our jackets and we headed out into the rain and we went to the party.

I enjoyed it more than I thought I would. The host's name was Lincoln and I only spoke to him briefly, when Jonathan introduced us. For some reason, Lincoln's girlfriend took a shine to me when she found me sitting at the end of the hallway playing with the fattest cat I had ever seen. Her name was Lily and the cat—whose name was Tiger despite it not having one single stripe—belonged to her. It turned out she liked cats almost as much as I did. I told her about Mr. Bojangles and suggested she get Tiger one of those balls with the bell inside. "But take out the bell because you will hate the noise it makes and it will drive you crazy," I said.

"Tiger hates balls, but he loves string." She left abruptly, and when she returned a moment later, she had a stick with a piece of string tied to the end. Tiger went nuts, and we took turns holding the stick and dragging it along for him to chase.

I didn't know if her kindness was genuine. I still struggled with that, because I'd learned that sometimes people were kind only because they wanted something. "Don't you like parties?" I finally asked. If her boyfriend was the host, it surprised me that she'd want to spend time sitting in the hallway with a stranger.

"I like them, but I don't drink and Linc and his friends have a tendency to get loud after a few beers."

"I don't drink much either. I mean I will drink, but it's an acquired taste and I haven't finished acquiring it yet."

Jonathan poked his head into the hall. "Hey, there you are," he said. He crouched down beside Lily and me. "Looks like you've made a friend."

"Do you mean Lily or the cat?" I asked.

"Both," Lily said. Jonathan smiled really big when she said that.

"You doing okay?" he asked.

"Sure," I said, because I wanted to show him he could take me to parties, and that I could fit in. It didn't matter to me that so far, my only interaction had been with a girl and her cat.

Lily was right, though, because later it did get loud. Tiger disappeared around eleven thirty when the hallway became crowded with people going in and out of the bedrooms and bathroom. I found a small spot near the laundry room off the kitchen, and I hung out there for a while by myself. The living room was packed, and I didn't really want to fight my way through the crowd to look for Jonathan. Instead he found me fifteen minutes later.

"Where'd you go? I've been looking all over for you. I was worried."

"There are so many people in the living room. I thought I would hide out here until it was time to go."

"Let's go now. I'm ready to climb back in bed. I just want to say good-bye to Lincoln real quick."

Jonathan clasped my hand firmly in his and led me through the crowd. Lincoln was sitting on the couch with Lily on his lap. There were several guys seated next to him and a few standing in front of it talking to them.

"This is my girlfriend, Annika," Jonathan said.

"Hey, Annika," they said. Everyone smiled at me, and I was so glad we came.

"So, we're taking off," Jonathan said. "Thanks for the party. It was great."

"It was nice talking to you, Annika," Lily said. I felt so tongue-tied that all I could do was nod and smile.

A super tall guy with blond hair and a patchy beard winked at me. "When you get tired of Jonathan, give me a call. I may not be as smart, or as handsome, or a chess wunderkind, but I'll treat you right."

Everyone looked at me, but no one said anything. I didn't say anything either, because I loved Jonathan and wasn't ever going to get tired of him, and I certainly wasn't going to call up this guy who I'd just met for the first time and barely knew. Lily, though, seemed like someone I might actually want to get together with sometime. Unfortunately, I wasn't very good at making those kinds of things happen.

"I wouldn't wait by the phone if I were you," Jonathan said, slinging his arm over my shoulder. Everyone laughed and then Jonathan pulled me closer and asked if I was ready to go.

I said yes because Lily was right. It was really loud. Besides, I hadn't seen Tiger for a while and my back was hurting again.

On the way home, I watched the windshield wipers sweep the rain away, enjoying their rhythmic motion and the silence inside the truck. I found it very soothing. I tried to tell Jonathan about Lily and her cat, but he kept his eyes straight forward and only answered when I asked a direct question. I knew I'd done something wrong but didn't know what it was.

I got ready for bed and slipped beneath the covers, but Jonathan didn't join me. I read for a while and then went into the living room to see what he was doing. He was flipping through the TV channels, a beer on the coffee table in front of him.

"Aren't you coming to bed?"

He clicked through the channels on the TV. "Eventually."

"I don't understand why you're mad at me." I wanted to know what I'd done so I wouldn't do it again.

"I'm not mad," he said. But he was, and I wasn't so dense that I couldn't hear it in his voice.

"Yes, you are. I don't understand why you're upset. I don't know what I did!"

He set down the remote. "You've got to give me something to hold on to, Annika. You've turned me into this . . . this lovesick *fool,* and all I get in return for my romantic gestures is a blank look. When someone hits on you, especially when they come right out and reference your current boyfriend, it would be nice to hear you say that you'd never be interested in that person because you already have someone. Someone you claim to love. So, help me out here. Throw me some kind of *bone* once in a while."

I didn't get the bone thing at all, but I finally figured out that everyone had been waiting for me to make some kind of proclamation about how I felt about Jonathan. I squeezed my eyes shut, angry, so angry at myself. My eyes filled with frustrated tears.

"I did think that! I thought it in my head, but I was afraid if I said it out loud, I'd mess it up somehow and then everyone would think I was stupid. I've never been in love before, so I'm not sure what I'm supposed to do. What I'm supposed to say. But when you walk into the room my whole body relaxes because I think 'Jonathan is here.' And I never want you to leave, even when it's just to go to class or work or the pool. I want you to be with me. So when we go places or you introduce me to people, I'm so happy to have someone like you holding my hand or standing by my side that I don't think of those things. I just see you, and I think 'Jonathan wants to be with me.' I love you more than I've loved anything in my whole life except maybe Mr. Bojangles but that's because not a lot of people love him. Probably just me and my mom and maybe the vet, which isn't very many and that makes me so sad."

I was really bawling by then and Jonathan pulled me onto his lap and put his arms around me. "I'm sorry, Annika. I'm so sorry. I didn't mean to make you cry. I know you love me. You show me all the time in your own special way. I'm being an asshole." He pressed his forehead to mine and we stayed like that, our eyes closed, until I stopped crying.

"Are you okay?" he asked.

I was curled up in a little ball on his lap, and I never wanted to leave. "Yes."

"I love you, Annika Rose." He wiped away my tears and kissed my forehead, my cheek, my lips.

"I love you, Jonathan Hoffman."

He started laughing. "You put me in the same category of love as your *cat.*"

"But I love Mr. Bojangles!"

"I know you do. You love him as much as you love me. And that's funny because you make no attempt to hide it."

"But *why* is it funny?"

"Because most people like their boyfriends a little bit more than they like their pets. And if they don't, they probably don't say it out loud."

"You can love both."

"Yes, you can." Jonathan kissed me again and soon we weren't doing much talking at all. Janice had mentioned having more make-up sex with Joe than any other guy she'd dated. She told me it made the arguments worth it, and the way I felt that night, as we made up right on Jonathan's couch, I would have to agree even though the couch wasn't nearly as comfortable as his bed.

"I want to stay together after we graduate," Jonathan said afterward. "There are plenty of libraries in New York. We'll both get jobs and we can go to grad school at night. We'll probably have to live in a crappy apartment even smaller than this one, but someday I'll make enough for us to live anywhere we want. Say you'll come with me, Annika."

I told him I loved him again, and then I told him I would.

27

Jonathan

CHICAGO

AUGUST 2001

Nate and his new girlfriend are waiting at the bar when Annika and I arrive at the restaurant. The woman is completely Nate's type, or at least the type he's been dating since the divorce: late twenties, club attire, pretty. I won't know until we're seated and having a conversation if she's an improvement over the last one, who talked incessantly about the TV show *Survivor* and drank several frozen strawberry daiquiris that gave her "the most awful brain freeze."

Nate and I shake hands. "This is Sherry," he says.

"Jonathan," I say. "Nice to meet you. This is Annika."

Annika smiles, shakes hands, and maintains brief eye contact with both of them. She's wearing a long, full skirt, which is in direct contrast to Sherry's super short dress and skyscraper high heels, but Annika's top clings slightly in all the right places, and I've been glancing appreciatively down its deep-vee neckline since I arrived at her apartment. Nate appraises her and shoots me a quick, approving look, which I ignore because we're not twenty-two anymore. Also, he can't read my mind, so he doesn't know my thoughts about the cleavage.

Our table is ready and once we're seated, I take a look at the drink menu. Nate asks Sherry what she'd like to drink and she says "Chardonnay" as if she'd had the kind of day only wine could fix.

"Would you like a glass of wine or would you prefer this?" I ask Annika, pointing to the one nonalcoholic option the restaurant offers, a mix of mango, cranberry, and orange juice with a splash of ginger ale.

"I'll have the Chardonnay," Annika says.

"Jonathan tells me you're a librarian," Nate says.

"Yes."

Nate waits for Annika to provide details, but he's greeted with silence. "Where?" he finally asks.

"The Harold Washington Library."

"How long have you been there?"

"Six years, three months, and thirteen days. How long have you been at your job?"

Nate laughs. "I'm not sure I can answer that as thoroughly as you have. You've put me on the spot."

Annika shoots me a quick look as she tries to decipher whether he's kidding, so I smile at her. "Don't listen to him. I bet he can tell you the exact date of his retirement, right down to the minute."

"You got me," Nate says.

"What do you do, Sherry?" I ask.

"I'm a scientist."

Okay. Did not see that coming.

Nate doesn't even bother to hide his smirk and was probably near bursting from holding that little detail inside. The daiquiri girl was between jobs and seemed vastly uninterested in remedying the situation anytime soon. Nate broke up with her a short time later.

The waitress brings our drinks and Annika takes a tentative sip of her wine. "Do you like it?" I ask her.

"It's very good." She puckers her lips a little, because it's probably a bit drier than she expected.

"I need to use the restroom," Sherry says. She looks at Annika. "Would you like to come with me?"

"No," Annika says, grimacing and using the same tone you'd use to turn down an elective root canal.

Sherry looks at her in confusion. "No?"

Annika pauses. Removes the napkin from her lap and smiles. "Actually, yes. I should probably go now, too."

I keep my expression blank, but inside I'm laughing. Annika's honest response to what is essentially one of the most common female conventions is priceless, but she says it so sweetly—without a trace of sarcasm—that I may be the only one who realizes she didn't arbitrarily change her mind. It just took her a few extra seconds to shuffle through her brain for the appropriate social response. No wonder she was so tired after I took her to my company dinner. It must be exhausting, and it makes me feel extra protective of her.

"Does she always say what she means?" Nate asks after they've left the table.

I take a sip of my drink. "Always. What you see is what you get with her. If Annika likes you, she'll let you know." I laugh. "And she'll also let you know if she doesn't."

"No games, no bullshit. I bet it's nice. And you were right. She's beautiful."

"On the inside, too." Even with her bluntness, I can't imagine Annika ever saying an unkind word about anyone. She's been on the receiving end of too much bullying and abuse to ever make someone feel bad on purpose.

"So, I guess she did want to rekindle."

"We both did." I'll never tell Nate or Annika how close I came to shutting the door on giving us a second chance. It doesn't matter now.

Sherry and Annika come back from the bathroom. Sherry takes a big drink of her wine and Annika mimics her, choking slightly.

"This wine is amazing and just what I needed after the day I had," Sherry says.

"Me too," Annika says with a sigh.

"This is my favorite Chardonnay, but sometimes I prefer a nice crisp sauvignon blanc. Then there are those times when nothing but a giant glass of Cabernet will do," Sherry says. "What about you? Do you have any favorites?"

"It really doesn't matter to me. I drank wine coolers in college, but no one orders those anymore."

I pause with my own drink halfway to my lips as I wait for Sherry's response.

"Yes! Oh, that brings back memories. I *loved* the watermelon ones."

"I liked cherry. They turned my lips red," Annika says.

"But they're so sweet. I could never drink one now."

"Oh, me neither," Annika says a beat or two later, shuddering like she can't imagine such a thing.

She is so adorable right now. Also, I'm pretty sure she would drink a cherry wine cooler right this minute if I set one down in front of her.

She and Sherry finish their wine and when the waitress asks if they'd like another, they both say yes.

"So, you must like books if you work at a library," Sherry says.

"I like books more than I like most people," Annika says.

Nate and Sherry stifle a polite laugh, but there's nothing patronizing about their reaction. It really is nice to be with a woman who genuinely owns her choices. There were times when Liz's behavior was as chameleon in nature as Annika's, but in my ex-wife's case, it was less about fitting in and more about manipulating her business opponent. It's not fair of me to excuse one while vilifying the other, but I do it anyway.

Our dinner proceeds uneventfully. When we're done eating, no one takes the waitress up on her offer of dessert, so Nate orders a third round of drinks for the table instead. Annika isn't even done with her second. Her cheeks are flushed and she's leaning back in her chair instead of the usual stiff posture she displays in social situations. Nate, Sherry, and I probably have what could be described as a solid buzz, but Annika's size and low tolerance for alcohol has put her much closer to the intoxicated end of the spectrum. It's the most I've seen her drink, ever, and when she finishes off the second glass she looks warily at the third.

"It's okay if you don't want to drink that," I say to Annika, pointing at her glass.

"I don't." The blunt way she says it reminds me that I shouldn't automatically assume she needs me to come to her rescue.

She may not have wanted any more wine, but what she's already consumed is still working its way through her bloodstream. I ask Sherry some questions about her work, and she mentions a grant she's hoping to gain approval for. "But I'm having trouble convincing my boss."

"Never allow a person to tell you no who doesn't have the power to say yes," Annika says. In theory, yes, but in this case I'm pretty sure Sherry's boss has the power to say both.

"What's that?" Sherry says. She sounds hesitant, as if she's not sure where this is going.

"It's a quote from Eleanor Roosevelt," Annika says. "Are you familiar with them?"

"I know a few," Sherry says.

"My best friend bought me a book of them. 'Do one thing every day that scares you' is what got me through my twenties. 'Do what you feel in your heart to be right—for you'll be criticized anyway.'"

She had been doing so well, and it might have gone unnoticed if she'd only shared one or two of the quotes. But once Annika gets started on a topic that interests her, it's hard for her to stop. She shares quote after quote, her cheeks pink from the wine and her enthusiasm about the subject matter. Annika talks with her hands, and her movements are becoming more pronounced by the second. Sherry and Nate are every bit as polite as they have been throughout dinner, but then Annika stops talking abruptly and the color on her cheeks deepens from excited to self-conscious as she realizes she's let down her guard and gone totally off script.

No one knows what to say, including me.

While I'm still trying to decide the best way to handle this, Sherry leans toward Annika and squeezes her hand. "It's okay, I've got a nephew who's a lot like you."

For possibly the first time in our lives, Annika and I share the exact same shocked expression. Hers soon gives way to mortifying embarrassment, and she gets up from the table and rushes from the dining room.

"I'm so sorry," Sherry says. "Maybe I shouldn't have had that last glass either. I wasn't thinking."

"It's okay. It's just not something she talks much about."

Not even to me.

"Let me know what I owe for the bill," I say to Nate. "I'll settle up with you tomorrow. It was nice meeting you, Sherry."

I push my chair back, grab Annika's purse, and take off after her.

She's standing outside on the sidewalk, pacing and bouncing. I don't try to still her. I want to comfort her and wipe away the tears that are rolling down her face, but instead I hail a cab and when it pulls up to the curb, I hustle us inside it and give the driver her address.

28

Jonathan

CHICAGO

AUGUST 2001

By the time the cab pulls up in front of her building, her tears have subsided and she's taking lots of slow, deep breaths. Once we're inside her apartment, she sits down on the couch and curls herself into a little ball. She won't look at me. I sit down beside her and wait. It's a full five minutes before she speaks.

"All I wanted was to show you that I've changed. That I'm not the same person I was in college." She sounds defeated.

"Well, guess what? You haven't changed all that much. You're still the same girl I fell in love with at twenty-two. And here's a newsflash: I like that girl and always have, and I never once said I *wanted* her to change."

Annika turns her head toward me slightly, curious.

"Sherry should not have made that comment," I say. "It was incredibly assumptive and it wasn't the time or the place. But did you really think I didn't know?"

Her face crumples. Oh shit. She did.

"I try so hard to fit in. I spend hours studying appropriate behaviors." She makes little air quotes around the last two words. "I will never get it right! Do you know what that's like? It's the most frustrating thing in the world."

"I can't even imagine what that must be like," I admit.

"It's like everyone around you has a copy of the script of life, but no one gave it to you so you have to go in blind and hope you can muddle your way through. And you'll be wrong most of the time."

"My ex-wife could have written the script. She was an expert in navigating business *and* social situations. And if it was a mix of the two, that was even better because she was a goddamn superstar at playing the game and wasn't about to be outshone by anyone, not even her husband."

Especially not her husband.

"But you know what else? Liz would drive right by a wounded animal on the side of the road if stopping even remotely interfered with whatever she was doing at the time. No. You know what? She would never have stopped, not even if she had all the time in the world."

"What!" Annika cries. Because of my insensitive analogy, all she's thinking about now are hypothetically injured animals.

"I'm trying to explain that the way you navigate the world will never be more important than the type of person you are."

"How can you want to be with someone like me? How were you able to fall in love with someone who acts the way I do?"

"It was easier than you think."

She scoffs like she doesn't believe me.

Annika has shared so many painful truths with me. Maybe it's time I admit to some of my own. "There's something about being with you that has always made me feel better about myself."

"Because at least you're not like me?"

"No, but when we met I wasn't at my most confident. I figured I at least had a shot with you." She looks shocked, and I rake my hands through my hair as I exhale. "But it didn't take me long to realize I had greatly overestimated my chances and that I'd have to work hard if I wanted to make you mine because there was *nothing* easy about you. But that made it so much more special when you started to let me in. I watched you come out of your shell and I discovered so many great things about you, including how you loved me so fiercely. I never questioned your loyalty, even when I wished you'd show people how you really felt about me. I knew I would never hurt you."

She's back to not looking at me. "What if there's a woman out there who's somewhere between Liz and me?" Her question hits me hard, because it's something I've thought about. I hate that I have, but she's right.

"Maybe there is? But there's no guarantee I'm going to find her and certainly no guarantee that she'll fall for me, too."

"You can have anyone you want."

"That doesn't mean I can make them stay. Liz cheated on me. It was when we were still trying to work things out, before we gave up on the marriage counseling that wasn't helping and brought in the lawyers. It wasn't like I found an email I wasn't supposed to read or anything like that. She flat-out told me about it. It was some guy she worked with and the only reason she admitted it was because she knew it would hurt me. And it did exactly what she intended. That is one thing I've always known you would never do. I knew that if we reconciled there was a chance I might lose you again someday, but if I did it wouldn't be because I'd lose you to another man. It would be because I'd lose you to yourself. To the things going on in your head. Can you let me in all the way? Can you tell me straight up what you're dealing with, what you're feeling? I've figured out most of it, and I want you to know that I don't care if you need help sometimes."

"Tina said I'm probably on the autism spectrum. High functioning, but still. I can get tested to find out for sure, but why? It's not going to change anything."

"I really don't know what it would accomplish. Did she say what you might gain?"

"She said it might help me find peace."

"Then I think you should do it."

She hesitates. "What if it turns out that after going through the evaluation, I find out I'm not on the spectrum. That I really am just weird. I don't know if I can handle that."

"You're not weird."

"C'mon, Jonathan. All my life, I've been the *poster* girl for weird. It's not that people like me don't know how other people see us. But to us, *you're* the ones who are weird, and we're the ones who have to change if we want to fit in."

"You've overcome a lot of hardships to get where you are today. The bullying. The people who tried to take advantage of you. It's heartbreaking knowing that people treat others so horribly."

"I don't want you to be with me because you feel sorry for me."

"I don't feel sorry for you. I admire you. It takes incredible strength to do what you've done, and you deserve every bit of happiness that comes your way."

"It's hereditary." She says it quietly.

"I've known that since the day you introduced me to your dad."

"You'll regret it. A lifetime with me. A family with me. You'll get more than you bargained for the same way my mom did."

It's possibly the most intuitive thing she's ever said to me. Annika may struggle to *identify* what I'm feeling, to empathize, but she is quite capable of understanding what it means.

"The only thing I'll regret is passing up another opportunity to find out if we have what it takes to go the distance. I thought we were going to build a life together after college, but you changed your mind. Don't you think it's time we talked about it? Because if you're going to avoid the hard stuff, no matter how unpleasant the memories, I'm not sure how we're going to do this. And I want to do this. Very much. Do you?"

She nods. "I know I didn't handle it the right way, but I was just so devastated."

"I know. I was, too." I pull her closer and press my forehead against hers the way I used to all those years ago. Our eyes are closed and we stay that way until her breathing slows and I feel her exhale in a sigh of relief. "But come on. It's me, Annika."

"It's always been you," she says as she presses her lips to mine.

We can talk later. We *will* talk later. But right now there's only one thing I want to do. I've been waiting for ten years and I can't wait any longer.

We open our mouths and kiss for real. The kisses are the kind of kisses you don't exchange in public, and there's a rawness to them that wasn't there in college. Back then, everything I did in regard to Annika was conducted with care and caution, as if she were made of glass and might shatter. She's stronger now. She might not think so, but she is. I can see her strength in so many ways. I can *feel* it as her hands grip my arms.

We shift so that we're lying down. The small couch isn't ideal for any kind of sexual gymnastics, but that doesn't slow us down in the least. I inhale and take hit after hit of her scent, burying my face in her neck while I kiss it. The kissing turns to sucking and Annika arches her back when I remove her shirt and bra. I skim my thumbs across her nipples with a firm touch and she groans. Her full skirt has an elastic waist, so it's easy to strip her of it in one quick motion. Ditto her underwear. I'll have to make this couch work, because now that she's naked, I don't want to stop even for a minute. There is a total absence of shyness as Annika spreads her legs, and I smile, not just because of the view but because this is the girl I remember. I love the way she opens herself up to me so completely. When we were younger it took a while for us to reach the place where she felt comfortable enough to let go, but once she did, it made me feel like she trusted me more than anyone in the world. Rightly so, because I would never give her a reason to think otherwise.

Annika attempts to undress me without breaking contact with my mouth and within the confines of a surface that is shorter than our outstretched bodies. It's comical. She soldiers on because she's as determined to make this couch work as I am. She wraps her hand around me and I smile again because she hasn't forgotten the way I like to be touched, either.

Feeling around on the floor, I fish my wallet out of the pocket of my jeans. I could ask Annika if she's on birth control, but I'd use the condom anyway, and not just in the name of safe sex. If anyone would understand my reasoning, it's Annika.

There's really only one position that's going to work, and when I sit up and reach for her, she climbs on top as if she's read my mind, one thigh pressed up on either side of me as she lowers herself so quickly I groan, but not because it hurts.

I let out a breathless laugh. "And you claim you never know what I'm thinking." She laughs, too, but our laughter fades away, replaced with whispered words from me about how good she feels and how long it's been and how much I've missed her.

29

Annika

THE UNIVERSITY OF ILLINOIS
AT URBANA-CHAMPAIGN
1992

I awakened fully from a fitful sleep around 6:00 A.M. Jonathan slept soundly beside me, one foot touching mine. I'd been waking up off and on since shortly after midnight, because a persistent dull ache in my lower abdomen made it impossible to stay asleep. I'd shifted position, closed my eyes, and done everything I could to relieve the discomfort, but nothing had helped. My period had arrived the week before, lighter than normal and a slightly darker color, but the pain in my back had finally gone away. The discomfort I'd felt from the backache paled in comparison to what was happening in my stomach now, and the pain seemed to have intensified significantly in the last fifteen minutes.

Around seven, I walked to the bathroom, hoping that might solve the problem, although I really didn't feel like I had to go. My shoulder hurt and I felt strange as I walked, light-headed, almost like I might faint. I held on to the wall and gripped the doorjamb hard as I flicked on the bathroom light. I was wearing a pair of cotton bikini underwear and a T-shirt of Jonathan's that I'd appropriated for my own. Now that I was upright, gravity had taken over and the blood soaked my underwear and trickled down the inside of my legs. Maybe I was having another period, and the pain was due to cramping. Dark spots appeared before my eyes, and I managed to scream Jonathan's name as the floor rose up to meet me.

I didn't think I'd been out for more than a few seconds, and when I came to Jonathan was on the floor next to me. "What is it? What happened?" he yelled. He tried to help me sit upright and I felt him shift my legs a little as he gathered me into his arms, my back against his chest.

"Oh Jesus. Annika, tell me what's wrong!"

I couldn't answer him with words because the pain ripping through my abdomen made it impossible to speak. Instead, I screamed.

Jonathan laid me back down on the floor and ran.

I regained consciousness as the paramedics were putting the oxygen mask on me. "Annika, I'm right here. Everything's gonna be okay," Jonathan said somewhere off in the distance. I turned my head in the direction of his voice and spotted him next to the door, his hands covered in blood. He was wearing a pair of shorts and his legs were bloody, too. I thought for sure they would drop me as they carried the stretcher down the stairs on the outside of Jonathan's house, but I felt the thump as the wheels hit the pavement and they rolled me toward an ambulance waiting with its back doors open. A wave of pain hit me then, so severe that I began sobbing hysterically. As they loaded me inside, I tried to tell someone I thought I was dying. I tried to tell them how cold I was because it felt like my blood had been replaced with ice water, and that it was running through my veins in a miserably cold loop, but I must have only thought I'd spoken, because no one answered me. Once the stretcher was all the way in, they slammed the doors and we left, sirens wailing.

At the hospital, a nurse kept asking if I knew how far along I was. I was having a hard time focusing and there were so many people surrounding me, cutting off my T-shirt and underwear, taking my blood pressure. I tried to say no, that I wasn't pregnant because I was on the pill and had recently had a period, but I drifted in and out as they brought in a machine and ran a wand over my abdomen. Later, I would find out that the ultrasound was inconclusive because there was so much blood in my abdominal cavity they couldn't see anything.

Everyone seemed to be shouting. The nurses were giving instructions and Jonathan was trying to give them the information they wanted. I faded in and out as my pulse and blood pressure dropped dangerously low. Then they made Jonathan leave and I tried to yell, to tell them I wanted him to stay, but I was so cold and so tired.

They wheeled me into the operating room, where they performed emergency surgery to stop me from bleeding to death. I had most definitely been pregnant, and the period I thought I'd had wasn't a period at all, but rather the first sign that things had started to go wrong. The embryo had implanted in my fallopian tube and when it grew too large, the tube burst, more than likely right before they loaded me in the ambulance.

The doctors were unable to save it.

30

Annika

THE UNIVERSITY OF ILLINOIS
AT URBANA-CHAMPAIGN
1992

My parents and Jonathan were at my bedside when I woke up. I had been gravely ill and required a blood transfusion, but by the time my parents arrived at the hospital, my condition had stabilized. Because my tube had ruptured, I had a more invasive procedure than I would have had the ectopic pregnancy been caught sooner. The doctors had to cut me open instead of going in laparoscopically, and because of this, they said, I would need to stay in the hospital for several days and it could take up to six weeks before I recovered fully.

Janice was there, too. She wrapped her arms around me and cried so hard, I asked her if she was okay.

"I was just so worried when I got the call from Jonathan. I'm so sorry." She said it over and over.

I didn't know what she had to be sorry about, because I was the one who'd caused this. Jonathan had had the forethought to grab my purse before following the paramedics down the stairs. He'd assumed my wallet would contain my insurance card, and it had. But my birth control pills were also in there, and it didn't take the hospital staff long to piece together that I'd missed taking quite a few of them. I had been almost certain that I took one every day, because my intentions were to take them exactly the way I was supposed to. I hadn't forgotten on purpose, and I did not want a baby, because I could barely take care of myself. I'd simply forgotten in the way I sometimes forgot to brush my hair, or eat breakfast, or take out the trash when it was my turn.

And in the case of the pills, I had forgotten enough times that we made a baby.

My parents stayed at the hospital from sunrise to sundown and then retired to a nearby hotel rather than make the daily four-hour round trip home and back. Jonathan stayed by my side and only left briefly when he would run home to shower and change. He spent the nights sleeping in a recliner by my bedside as I drifted in and out of a painkiller-induced haze. The first night, after my parents had finally left after receiving enough assurances from the doctor that I was no longer in danger, he clutched my hand tightly in his and there were tears in his eyes. "I was so scared, Annika."

"Me too," I whispered. But what I didn't tell him was that my grief over what had happened outweighed the fear of what had not. During my more lucid moments, I'd thought about the baby growing in my fallopian tube. The doctor had told me that with an ectopic pregnancy there was no way to save the baby, and it was true that I was in no way equipped to have one.

But that didn't stop my heart from breaking for the tiny living thing that never had a chance.

Janice brought a pair of my pajamas and helped me change into them in the bathroom, leaving my parents and Jonathan to make small talk in my room. "I know you must hate wearing these," Janice said as she slipped the hospital gown from my shoulders and replaced it with the long-sleeved top to my pajamas. She held open the waistband of the bottoms, and I stepped into them—gingerly, because even the slightest movement caused a painful, pulling sensation in my incision.

I didn't mind the gowns, actually. They were loose and somewhat soft, probably from the repeated washings. What I hated the most about being in the hospital was the noises and smells. The sharp smell of the antiseptic and the repeated announcements over the intercom interfered with whatever semblance of calm I had been able to achieve. All I wanted was to stay asleep, to escape from this nightmare in the only way I knew how. But that didn't keep the nurses from coming in hourly to poke and prod me, to take my temperature and blood pressure. My wound needed its own care to make sure there was no infection. I had caught a glimpse of the angry line of stitches when the nurse helped me go to the bathroom for the first time after they removed the catheter, and I made sure never to look down again.

Janice opened the door and put her arm around my shoulders to help me walk out of the bathroom. I was still light-headed and the nurses warned that I should not get out of bed unless someone was at my side to make sure I didn't fall.

"I told your mom I'd go around and talk to all your professors and see what they wanted to do about keeping you in the loop for these last few weeks of school," she said. "I'm sure they'll allow you to turn in the work late and make some other concession for the final exams."

I didn't say anything, because I could only focus on one thing at a time, and at the moment all I really wanted was for Janice to put me back in bed.

"I'll leave as soon as classes are over on Friday," Jonathan said on the day they allowed me to go home.

"Leave to go where?"

"Your house. I want to be with you."

"Okay," I said. I was still tired and weak, and all I wanted to do when I got home was go back to sleep, but it would feel good to have Jonathan with me.

My parents arrived and while we waited for the discharge paperwork, Jonathan said, "Is it all right if I visit Annika this weekend?"

"Of course," my mother said.

When the nurse said it was okay for me to leave, my dad left to bring the car around.

"I'll just be out in the hallway," my mom said.

Jonathan pulled me close, crushing me in his hug. I didn't mind, though. When he let go, he kissed my forehead. "I love you. Everything's going to be okay."

"I love you too," I said. I didn't address the second part of his statement, because I didn't believe that anything would ever be okay again.

I climbed into the backseat of my parents' car, lay down across the seat, and went to sleep.

"What can I get you?" my mom asked after she tucked me into my bed like a child. The perfume Jonathan had given me for Christmas and I'd callously left behind was directly in my line of vision, and I asked her to give it to me.

I clutched the perfume bottle in my hand, and I cried myself to sleep over the sadness of what I'd done, and for the baby Jonathan and I had made and lost.

He came on Friday just like he promised, and he was there when I woke up from one of my many naps. He brushed the hair back from my face. "How's my Sleeping Beauty?"

I smiled, because his face was one of the few things that still brought me joy. He pulled back the covers and climbed into my bed, and I settled my head in the small crook between his neck and shoulder. "I'm fine," I said, though I had never lied to him before.

The first lie made the ones that followed so much easier to tell.

The door opened late on Saturday night. "Annika?" Jonathan said, his voice only slightly louder than a whisper.

"I'm awake," I said. My mom had put Jonathan's things in Will's room when he arrived, but my parents weren't overly strict about that sort of thing, and I knew my mom wouldn't care if she found us together in my bed or Will's. The reason I was awake when Jonathan came in was because I'd slept so much of the day away that for once, I couldn't sleep. Instead I'd been lying in bed ruminating over the state of my life. Other people's mistakes seemed small in comparison to the ones I'd made. Mine seemed to be getting bigger, and now they were hurting other people.

He slipped under the covers. "I know it won't be easy to get caught up, but you can do it. You can graduate and you can still come to New York on time."

Jonathan had big plans, and goals he'd been working toward since high school. I wasn't so clueless and out of touch that I couldn't see how my involvement in his life might negatively affect those things. Even if I managed to catch up with my schoolwork and graduate on time, I would only be a hindrance to him and would never be able to pull my weight in New York. And if I was being honest with myself, it seemed overwhelmingly exhausting to even consider it. I would need way more time to recover from not only the physical effects of what had happened, but also the emotional.

I simply did not have anything left to give, even to Jonathan, whom I'd finally realized I loved much more than I would ever love Mr. Bojangles.

The veil of depression that descended upon me was heavy, dark black, and suffocating. I did not leave my bedroom other than to attend my follow-up medical appointments, and only then because my mother threatened to have my dad physically place me in the car. The hospital had sent us home with a bottle of pain pills and I'd watched my mother put them in the cupboard when I said I could manage my pain without them. I could go into the bathroom and open that cupboard and swallow all of them. A sleep that would top all the others. Permanent. I spent two whole days thinking about it. Turning it over in my mind. It would be so easy! It probably wouldn't even hurt.

I had gone so far as to get out from under the covers to walk to the bathroom when my dad came into my room to check on me. He was never one to talk, and that day he didn't say anything at all. But he pulled my desk chair over to the side of the bed and reached for my hand, holding it loosely in his smooth, dry palm as the tears slid down my cheeks.

He stayed all day.

I never told anyone that my dad was the one who kept me tethered to this life, but I did tell my mom she should dispose of the pills because I didn't need them anymore.

Jonathan finally confronted me when it was clear I'd done none of the things I said I would do. "I know you're still recovering, but there's no way you can catch up when you haven't even started." I didn't respond. "Annika, I need you to talk to me."

"I want you to go to New York and start your job. I'll go back to school next fall and when I graduate in December, I promise I'll join you then."

He looked as defeated as I'd ever seen him look. "I want to believe you," he said.

So on a beautiful Saturday in May, Jonathan received his degree.

The next day, he boarded a plane to New York to crash on a friend's couch while he started his new job and looked for a place for us to live. No one read my name aloud on graduation day. I would have to repeat the semester in order to complete my undergraduate education. Janice told me later that she spoke with Jonathan after the ceremony. "I invited him and his mom to come to dinner with my family, but he politely declined."

"How did he look?" I asked.

"Not as happy as he should have."

May turned to June, and then July. I might have decided to live, but my mom grew frustrated with me because I was still sleeping way too much. "You cannot lie in this bed and let life pass you by," she shouted.

"What, this life?" I shouted back, gesturing toward the four walls. "A life inside this room is the only life I'm equipped for." I pointed toward the door, the windows. "I hate everything out there. Everything out there sucks! You know why? Because you never told me what to expect. You never helped me develop any coping skills. You just . . . you let me stay in this house playing school, isolated from everything, and then you sent me off to college, completely unprepared. Janice is the only one who ever taught me anything about real life."

And Jonathan, a small voice said inside my head.

"I had no choice. I couldn't let you stay at that school, let those bitches torment you or hurt you again. Seventh grade!" she cried. "How can children be that cruel at such a young age? I had to take you out, keep you here with me where I knew you'd be safe." My mom had never spoken to me using such language before, and she was wrong because the girls were worse than bitches. They were evil.

She sat down on the edge of my bed. "Your dad told me of the bullying and abuse he'd suffered as a child, and how no one did anything about it because boys were strong and they were expected to tough it out. I swore I would never let that happen to you. Someday when you have children of your own, you will understand."

"If I can even have them," I said.

"You've still got one tube. You will have them if you want them." She wiped the corner of her eye. "I started preparing you for life outside these four walls from the day you were born. I did what I thought was right, and I did it until I couldn't do it anymore because there *was* no more. You were ready and the only way to help you was to send you out into the world. Do you think I wasn't scared? Do you think I wanted to put your welfare in the hands of an eighteen-year-old girl? Someone who was essentially a stranger to us both?"

I had no idea what my mom was talking about. "What do you mean?"

"I called Janice's mother the day after we received your roommate assignment from the university. My hand was shaking as I held the phone because I didn't know how she'd respond to what I was about to ask her for. I just wanted another set of eyes on you. It was a lot to ask of Janice and I wanted to make sure her mother didn't mind. She agreed and so did Janice. I called your dorm room after you asked us to come get you that day three weeks into your freshman year, when you wanted to give up. Thankfully Janice answered the phone."

I remembered that day. The phone ringing and Janice taking it out into the hall. Asking me to walk to the union for lemonade. Finding the chess club.

"And before you start thinking she was only your friend because I asked her to be, I want you to know that Janice loves you like the sister she never had. I remember the end of your freshman year when I called to see if she might consider rooming with you again. She said, 'Linda, I can't imagine living with anyone else. Annika is a true friend.' She has told me multiple times how much she cares about you and how much your friendship means to her."

Now my mother and I were both wiping our eyes. The amount of gratitude I felt toward Janice and what she'd done to get me through college was immeasurable.

"You have wonderful gifts to offer people, Annika. You are honest and loyal. Not everyone will appreciate that, and there are people who will dislike you anyway. Life isn't easy for anyone. We all have challenges. We all face adversity. It's how we overcome it that makes us who we are."

I was still too young back then, too self-centered, too overwhelmed by the trauma of losing the baby and the daily battle to fight my way back toward the light, to understand that my mother had given me the greatest gift a parent could give a child. But years later I would recognize and appreciate that everything my mother had hoped for me had come to fruition only *because* she'd kicked me out of the nest, and it had mostly worked, despite a few bumps along the way.

"You will always have to do things you don't want to do, and they'll be harder for you than they are for your brother, or Janice, or Jonathan, or me. But I truly believe there will always be people in your life who will help you. Who will love you just the way you are."

It was only after she left the room that I realized she hadn't included my father in that list.

31

Annika

THE UNIVERSITY OF ILLINOIS
AT URBANA-CHAMPAIGN
1992

I returned to the University of Illinois campus for the fall semester, in August of 1992. I rented a one-bedroom apartment in the same complex Janice and I had lived in. Jonathan was the first person to leave a message on my new answering machine.

"Hey, it's me. I hope you're all settled in. I have some good news. I finally found an apartment for us. It's a dump, Annika. I'm not gonna lie. But I told you it probably would be. Hey, at least we won't have to share my buddy's couch, so there's that. When you get out here we can fix it up together. I don't have a lot of time to do it now anyway. It's like a competition to see who can be the first one here in the morning and the last one out the door at night. Weekends, too. I'm sure it won't always be like this. Call me when you can. I miss you so much. I love you."

I glanced at the clock and called him back even though I knew he probably wouldn't be home. "Hi, it's Annika. I'm all moved in. The apartment's nice. It looks a lot like my old one. I'm glad you found a place and don't have to sleep on the couch anymore. I miss you, too. I love you, Jonathan."

He was still planning for the day when I would join him, but I couldn't think about the future. Getting back on my feet in the present took everything I had, and moving to New York would mean starting over yet again. Even though Jonathan would be by my side to help, the very thought of it exhausted me. I could only address the here and now and would have to worry about the rest later.

I was walking out of a lecture hall a few weeks later when I spotted Tim, a member of the chess club. It was too late to turn around or pretend I hadn't seen him, which was my go-to maneuver for avoiding people I didn't want to talk to.

"Hey, Annika," he said. "I thought you graduated."

"I have a few classes I still need to finish."

"It's like you dropped off the face of the earth last spring."

"I had some health issues," I said, hoping he wouldn't ask for details. "I'm fine now."

"Good. I'm happy to hear that." He hoisted his backpack higher on his shoulder. "Well, hey, I'm late for class but hopefully I'll see you at the union on Sunday for chess club. You missed the first couple of meetings. We need you."

"Okay," I said. "See you then."

But I did not rejoin the chess club, and this time there was no one around to talk me into it.

One day in October, I came back from the library and discovered there was something wrong with the lock on my apartment door. When I inserted my key, the lock didn't make the same sound it had made previously. Or did it? I stood in the hallway turning the question over and over in my mind as I locked and then unlocked the door, listening for the click that never came. No matter which way I turned the key, the door always opened with ease.

When the sun went down that night, the darkness that filled my apartment settled on me like an inky black film of anxiety. I shoved a chair under the doorknob of the front door and also the one leading into my bedroom. I dozed fitfully with the lights on, burrowed under the covers like an animal in its nest. Every noise sounded like an intruder slowly letting themselves in to my apartment.

Every day that week when I left the apartment, I fiddled with the lock, hoping to hear the sound of it thumping into place. And every day that I didn't, my fear increased. I stopped opening the curtains in the morning because the setting sun and the fretfulness that accompanied it unnerved me to the point that it was better to keep them closed all the time.

It's not that I didn't know what to do, it was that I didn't know *how* to make it happen, and I was too paralyzed to ask someone. Janice had always taken care of these things. Once, when she'd gone home for the weekend, she discovered upon her return that the heat had stopped working. She found me under the blankets in my bed wearing three sweaters, my wool stocking cap, and a pair of fingerless gloves. My fingertips were icy, but I'd found it difficult to turn the pages of my book with mittens on, so I'd had no choice.

"It is fifty-two degrees in our apartment!"

"Why are you shouting at me?"

"Because it's fifty-two degrees in our apartment."

"You already said that."

"I'll be right back," she said. When she returned, she told me that the maintenance man had put in a call to the furnace repair company, and by the time we woke up the next morning the apartment was a toasty seventy-two. I had never asked her what she'd done to make that happen, because as soon as it was taken care of, I forgot all about it.

I took several deep breaths and walked down the stairs to the manager's office near the entrance of the building. What if I couldn't explain the problem properly? What if they told me there was nothing wrong with the lock, and I was just too dense to know how to turn a key?

There was a tenant ahead of me in line, a young woman I'd seen in the hallway a few times. "I need to put in a work order," she said. "The faucet in the kitchen is leaking."

"Sure," the man said. "Just fill this out." He handed her a form and she scribbled something on it and gave it back. He glanced at it and said someone would be there later that day to take a look.

"I need to put in a work order too," I said, the words tumbling out in a barely coherent rush when I stepped up to the desk.

He handed me the same form he'd handed the young woman, and I wrote down my name and apartment number. "There's something wrong with the lock on my door."

"Just note it on the work order and we'll get it taken care of immediately. Security issues always take priority."

I wrote down "broken front door lock" and handed him the form. A few hours later, I had a fully functioning lock and a whole lot of peace. *That wasn't hard at all,* I thought, chastising myself for acting so helpless instead of tackling the problem head-on.

The next morning, I opened all the curtains and let the sun fill the apartment with light.

The epiphany that the world was full of people I could emulate the way I had with Janice and Jonathan gave me renewed hope. Once I opened my eyes, I realized it was all laid out right in front of me: Watch the person in line ahead of me buying their coffee. Pay attention to the way people were dressed, so that I'd never be caught off guard by changes in the weather. Listen to how other people responded before mimicking their answers and speech patterns, body language and behavior. The constant vigilance and my heightened anxiety that I'd screw it up anyway exhausted me, but I persevered.

Because I was always looking, always observing, I saw things I didn't want to see. The female students laughing and chatting on their way to class or sharing a meal in a restaurant the way Janice and I used to. The couples walking hand in hand, stopping to share a kiss before going their separate ways. The young man carrying a girl piggyback through the grass as she laughed and nuzzled her face in his neck. The guy in one of my classes who always dropped a tender kiss on his girlfriend's forehead before they parted. *I used to have that*, I'd think. The hollow ache I felt due to Jonathan's absence made my lip quiver and I'd blink back tears.

I made endless lists to remind me what I needed to do every day. They were the things Janice used to do, in the order she'd always done them, and when we lived together, I followed her example. But Janice wasn't there anymore, so I checked off each item on my list: Drop rent check into the slot on the metal box mounted outside the rental office. Pay utilities. Buy groceries. Take out the trash. On Sunday nights, I lined up a week's worth of mugs containing a single tea bag. I put spoons in cereal bowls and stacked them seven high, taking one off the top every morning before pouring in the cereal and adding milk. Monday was for laundry. Wednesday was for cleaning. Eventually, I learned to love living alone. It was always quiet. My routines were solidly in place, and nothing ever interrupted them.

Though I had things mostly under control, the lack of companionship wore on me. Janice, I could speak to by phone, but Jonathan's calls were a different story. I always called him back, but now I found myself returning his calls when I knew he wouldn't be there and eventually, we communicated more with our answering machines than we did with each other. At the time, I told myself I didn't want to interfere with his life and was doing it for him, but that was another lie. It wasn't that I was still afraid of holding Jonathan back; it was what I needed in order to soar.

The milk I'd taken from the refrigerator to pour on the cereal I'd decided to have for dinner one evening smelled sour, because even though "buy milk" was clearly listed on the grocery list I'd brought to the store with me the day before, sometimes I still forgot to buy it. The sun had set and I didn't want to go out, but the cereal was already in the bowl, so I shrugged into my coat and left.

On the way home from the corner store, I passed a man who was sipping something from a flask he pulled from the pocket of his dirty jean jacket. He looked older than me, maybe a worker from one of the nearby bars. He raised the flask in my direction and started toward me. "Come drink with me, beauty," he said.

I quickened my pace, desperate to put more distance between us, but it only seemed to egg him on. "Come on, I won't bite," he yelled. "Unless you're into that kind of thing." His voice sounded closer now.

I wore a whistle on a chain around my neck, and as the footsteps grew louder, I pulled it out from under my shirt and put it in my mouth. It was silver, pretty, shiny. Almost like a necklace, although I never wore it on the outside of my clothes.

I felt a tug on my sleeve, and though it was gentle, I spun around, the shrill blast of the whistle piercing the otherwise quiet sidewalk. I blew as hard as I could, and I took a step toward him, stopping only to take a deep breath so I could blow it again. Bystanders and passersby stopped what they were doing and a few of them began to approach. But it wasn't the man with the flask. The man who had tugged on my sleeve looked no older than me, and he held up his hands and yelled, "Hey, sorry! I thought you were someone else."

"You shouldn't sneak up behind people like that! It's very rude."

"Jesus Christ, chill out." He turned on his heel and stomped away like he was mad. At me! I looked around and calmly dropped the whistle back down into my shirt. Then I went home and ate my cereal.

You might think the whistle was Janice's idea, but it had actually been my mother's. It was the last thing she gave to me before she and my dad got back in the car to go home after moving me into my apartment. "You must speak up if something should happen that frightens or endangers you," she said. "If you can't, let this be your voice."

"I don't want it," I said, shoving it back into her palm. Why did my mother insist on scaring me like that? Giving me a whistle only filled my head with swirling thoughts of danger lurking on every corner, confirmed that the world was an unsafe place for people like me to navigate on their own. *There's no Janice to babysit you this time, Annika. So, here, have a whistle.*

"Take it anyway," she said, slipping the chain over my head. "Someday you might need it and you'll be thankful you have it."

My mother, as always, had been right.

Jonathan left a final message on my machine shortly before Christmas. I'd postponed my move to New York indefinitely by enrolling in graduate school. I finally felt like I was in control of my life, and I'd proven I could live independently. Leaving now would disrupt the routines that brought me such calm, rock the boat I'd worked so hard to keep steady. "I just need some more time," I'd said into his machine. "I think I should complete my education before I move anywhere."

Now, I listened to the message he'd left for me, tears running in a torrent down my cheeks. It should not have been a surprise; even I knew he would not wait forever.

Though my heart felt like it was splitting in two, I did not regret my decision. But I paid a steep price for my independence, and losing Jonathan was harder than all the things that had come before it, combined.

32

Annika

THE UNIVERSITY OF ILLINOIS
AT URBANA-CHAMPAIGN
1992

Will showed up at my apartment to drive me home for Christmas. I'd been expecting my parents, but when I opened the door I found my brother instead.

"What are you doing here?"

"Happy holidays to you too, sister."

"Mom said she and Dad were coming."

"Yeah, well. Mom's busy cooking and Dad's busy . . . being Dad. The roads are shit and I was bored, so I volunteered."

"You never come home this early."

"Clearly, I did this year."

Will picked up my suitcase and I locked the apartment and followed him out to his car.

"Is Jonathan going to join us over break?" Will asked as he merged onto the snowy highway.

"No. That's over." I had never said it out loud. Now that I had, it meant that it was real and it hurt. I played Jonathan's last message again in my head. *Definitely over.*

"By the way, in case you were wondering. It wasn't that I couldn't hold on to Jonathan. It was that I decided to let him go."

Will had never been home in time to go get the tree. My dad and I were usually the ones who cut it down and dragged it back to the car, but it was bitterly cold and Will told our parents to stay home. "Annika and I can handle it."

We drove to the same tree farm we'd been buying our trees from my whole life, and we walked down the rows until I found the perfect tree, a seven-foot Canaan fir. I waited patiently while Will sawed it down.

"I got fired," he said as we watched the tree fall.

"Oh."

"Don't you want to know why?"

That felt like a trick question. "Do you *want* me to know why?" We each picked up one end of the tree and headed toward the parking lot.

"I made a mistake. A big one. It cost the company a lot of money. I didn't tell Mom and Dad. I just said I quit because I didn't like the job."

I didn't say anything. It was cold enough for us to see our breath as we panted and dragged the unwieldy tree through the snow.

"Do you have any thoughts on this?"

"I make mistakes all the time, Will. Been making them pretty steadily my whole life."

"Yeah, well, when you make them in investment banking, it's a big deal." He set down his end of the tree. I couldn't carry it without him, so I did, too.

"I didn't take my birth control pills the way I was supposed to, and I got pregnant."

"I know that. Did you think Mom and Dad wouldn't tell me? They said you could have died. I was worried about you."

"You never told me you were worried. You didn't call me. Or come home to visit me."

"No. I didn't and I should have. I'm sorry."

"So, what are you going to do now? Just give up?" I asked.

"What? No. What's that supposed to mean?"

I picked up my end of the tree again. "It just means that life goes on."

After we got home, we decorated the tree. Will didn't like the way Dad and I did it last year and convinced me to do it the old boring way. "That's just not very creative at all, but whatever." It was a nice way to spend the afternoon, though. I liked hanging the shiny ornaments, felt the thrill of plugging in a strand of lights and watching the resultant burst of color. My mother kept offering to throw another log on the fire crackling in the hearth; to bring cocoa; to ask if we'd like her to put on some Christmas music. I said yes to the cocoa but no to the music.

"Mom's so happy," Will said.

"How can you tell?"

"Are you kidding me?"

"No." I pulled a chair over next to the tree so I could place the angel on the top. "Isn't Mom always happy?"

"No one is always happy."

When we finished decorating the tree, Will sat down next to me on the couch. I covered my lap with the old wool blanket that my mother always kept folded over the back of the couch in the winter. Will balanced a paper plate of Christmas cookies on his knee and cracked open a beer. He took a bite of the cookie and a drink of the beer, and my stomach turned over.

"That looks revolting."

"Don't knock it 'til you try it. There's more beer in the fridge." He offered me the plate of cookies and I took one.

"I only like wine coolers," I said around a mouthful of frosting. "Preferably cherry."

"I saw a bottle of peach wine in the fridge. That sounds . . . horrible. But maybe you'd like it?" Will got up and went into the kitchen. When he returned, he held a wineglass full of light-amber liquid.

I sniffed it, and it smelled okay. Definitely peach. The first sip went down a little rough, but the more I drank the more the flavor grew on me.

"Give me some of that blanket," Will said. I shoved it over and he shook it out a little so that it covered both of us.

"What did you get Mom and Dad for Christmas?" he asked.

"I got Dad a book and Mom some dish towels."

"Isn't that what you got both of them last year?"

How did Will remember something like that? I'd had to rack my brain to remember what I'd bought them last year when I was trying to come up with something to get them this year.

"Yes, but it's a safe choice. They both seemed to like their gifts last year." Truthfully, I was a little worried about it and would have to come up with something different next year. The same gifts three years in a row would probably be pushing it.

"I should tell Janice about this wine."

Will drained the last of his beer and I handed him my empty glass. "Looks like someone needs a refill," he said.

We did all of the Christmassy things in the days leading up to the actual holiday. Will was right, because my mom did seem happy. She was always smiling or humming and she kept coming into the living room whenever Will and I were in there. She'd stand at the door and just *look* at us and then Will would laugh and say, "Enough, Mom."

The four of us watched *It's a Wonderful Life,* and I had a hard time watching George Bailey on that bridge. But I was surrounded by my family and for the first time ever, I felt like we were all in this life together.

When break was over Will volunteered to drive me back to school. "The roads still aren't great. I'll take Annika." He was in a good mood, because he had an interview with a big firm in New York the next week and would be flying home the next day to prepare. He'd told me to keep my fingers crossed for him and I said I would even though that wouldn't have anything to do with him actually getting the job.

My mother squished me with her hug. "This has been a truly wonderful Christmas. I got everything I ever wished for this year, Annika. Everything."

I don't know why I worried so much, because those dish towels were obviously the perfect gift after all.

"Why have you been so nice to me?" I asked Will on the way back to campus. It was calming not to have such an antagonistic relationship with my brother, but I didn't understand how it had happened and I wanted him to explain it to me.

"Maybe I understand you better now. I'm not sure I really did before."

"I don't really understand anyone."

"I want you to know that I'm here for you if you ever need me, Annika. Someday, when Mom and Dad are gone, it'll just be the two of us."

"Okay, Will. Thanks."

I had no memory of ever hugging my brother, but before he left he reached out his arms and I stepped into them, and his hug was every bit as crushing as my mother's.

Two years later, when I completed my education at the University of Illinois, I had earned my bachelor's and master's degrees. I started looking for an apartment in the city and began interviewing for the librarian career I'd coveted for so long.

And when I walked across campus for the last time, I held my head high.

33

Jonathan

CHICAGO
AUGUST 2001

I wake up wrapped around Annika the morning after our dinner with Nate and Sherry. We finally abandoned the couch and moved to the comfort of Annika's bed for rounds two and three, and we collapsed in a heap of exhaustion a few hours later. She'll be tired for days. When she finally stirs around noon we take a shower together and after making coffee and tea, we go straight back to bed.

Annika tells me she's sorry for forgetting to take her birth control pills. Before they rushed her into surgery, she hadn't been in any condition to read the expressions of the medical staff, and it's doubtful she would have understood what they meant. But I saw something on the doctor's face when he laid it all out and explained how the pregnancy had happened, and everyone else in the room would have recognized it easily: it was thinking you had your life all planned out and then standing by helplessly while the universe laughed in your face.

"There's no need to apologize," I say. "We're not the first couple to have a lapse in birth control."

"I have the implant now." She holds up her arm and points to the spot where the doctor inserted the small rods under her skin. "Out of sight, out of mind."

I take a drink of my coffee. "We were so young. I had this idea that we'd conquer the city together. That we'd wake up beside each other every day in another crappy apartment. But I wasn't thinking about what would be best for you. All I could focus on was why you stopped loving me." Here's her chance to remove that pebble once and for all.

"I was just in a really bad place that summer after I lost the baby. Worse than what you saw. A dark place that scared me so much. I thought maybe I'd go to sleep and if I never woke up, I wouldn't have to hurt anymore, and I wouldn't hurt anyone else."

I understand what she's saying and it guts me. For a split second I can't breathe as the weight of her words settles on me. I feel like I might throw up. "I'm so sorry for what you went through," I say.

"I never stopped loving you, but I couldn't go to New York. I had to prove to myself that I could finish something on my own without you and Janice."

I set my coffee cup on her nightstand and reach for her. I don't trust myself to talk, so I hold her tight and rub her back, thinking how selfish my thoughts were because all I wanted when I landed in New York was for her to be there with me.

"You never gave up on me," Annika says.

"Yes, I did."

When I met Liz at a mixer for new employees, she was everything I thought I wanted. The high school valedictorian from a small town in Nebraska shared more with me than her Midwestern roots. She had student loans to pay and ambition to burn, and she was also working on her master's at night. We spent hours together studying, promising ourselves that when we'd earned those degrees, there was nothing that would hold us back. In the meantime, we clawed our way higher and higher in the company, working more hours than any of our peers. Liz was every bit as smart as I was, and it didn't hurt that her intelligence was wrapped in a pretty package. She knew what she wanted, and she had the answer for everything. Eventually I would find her direct approach abrasive, her confidence bordering on arrogance. But that came later. In the early days of our relationship, she thought I was something special, and to me, it felt like a life preserver thrown from the sinking ship of my failed relationship with Annika. I grabbed for it with both hands.

Annika wasn't ever going to join me in New York. I'd known it for a long time, but until I met Liz I still held out hope that she might. In early December, I called Annika and got her answering machine again. "It's me. I wanted to let you know I met someone. I just thought I should tell you in case you thought you might still come. I'd love to hear from you, but I'll understand if I don't. Bye, Annika."

I would never have left such an important message on a recording, but she rarely picked up the phone, and the last time I'd called, she hadn't called me back. I told myself that being honest with her had to count for something.

It was the last time I ever dialed her number.

"That message devastated me. I wanted to call you back and tell you I still loved you," Annika says. "But I just couldn't. I knew what I had to do for myself, but I didn't think about how my decision would make you *feel*. I didn't understand that you could be hurt by my actions until Tina explained it to me."

"It's okay. I got through it." It seems almost silly now, the extent of my heartbreak. The hours I spent listening to songs that reminded me of Annika. Her pillow that traveled to New York with me and that I laid my head on every night, missing her. The blond girls on the subway that all looked like her.

"I did call you back, but it was years later and whoever answered said you were no longer at that number. I probably could have tracked you down by calling information, but even Tina couldn't help me figure out what I wanted to say, so I didn't. I focused on what I'd accomplished by then, living independently and my job at the library, but I missed you terribly. When I ran into you that day at the grocery store, I was so happy to see you again."

"Seeing you was like seeing a ghost. I wasn't sure it was you at first."

"I knew right away it was you," she says. "And I've been grateful ever since."

34

Annika

CHICAGO
SEPTEMBER 2001

I'm meeting with Tina today to tell her about the results of my evaluation. I took Jonathan's advice about getting tested and when I told Tina I'd finally decided to do it, she referred me to a neuropsychologist named Dr. Sorenson. Tina said autism is a developmental disorder and not a mental illness, and diagnosing autism-spectrum disorders is something neuropsychologists specialize in. When I called to make my appointment, I learned that testing would take four or five hours but that they would split it up over two sessions. They would also mail me a multipage questionnaire that I would fill out in advance and bring to my appointment.

Dr. Sorenson's office was nothing like Tina's. The furniture was stiff, the lights were bright, and there was a lot of chrome and glass. I kept catching my reflection on the shiny surfaces, and every single time I'd startle, wondering who the other woman was. Finally, I just looked down at my hands, which were folded in my lap, and tried not to flick my fingertips.

The tests were grueling and they exhausted me, but I felt good afterward. Like I'd finally confronted an issue that had plagued me my whole life. When I speculated about the results of my evaluation, my nervousness returned. What if the fears I shared with Jonathan were about to come true? What if there was nothing wrong with me and I really was just a weird girl whose childhood tormentors had been right on the money?

When I returned for my follow-up appointment to hear my diagnosis, Dr. Sorenson sat down behind his desk and opened a folder. "The testing shows that you fit the criteria for someone who has an autism-spectrum disorder. You're very high functioning and likely employ a number of coping strategies and workarounds, but there are things we can do to make it easier to manage your everyday life. I believe you're also suffering from a generalized anxiety disorder and that it's causing more difficulty for you than being on the spectrum."

"I have an anxiety disorder too?"

"They often go hand in hand. My point is that you don't have to go through life feeling this way."

What I learned that day in Dr. Sorenson's office made me feel peaceful. Hopeful. I had known for a long time that my brain worked differently, but to hear it confirmed provided immense relief.

I wished I'd sought an official diagnosis years ago. If I'd known then what I know now, I might not have spent so many years convinced there was something horribly wrong with me. I could have developed better coping skills at a much younger age. With the knowledge I gained in Dr. Sorenson's office, I might have excelled instead of merely gotten by.

I certainly would not have been so ashamed.

"Dr. Sorenson also prescribed an antianxiety medication," I tell Tina after I fill her in on everything I learned. "He said it might help calm the chatter in my brain. Make my thoughts clearer."

"And has it?" Tina asks.

"I haven't been taking it for very long and he said it could take up to a month before I see the full effects, but I already feel different. Calmer." I was starting to not second-guess everything I said and did. I felt more confident in my interactions with other people. Or maybe I just wasn't as worried about saying the wrong thing.

"Have you shared the results of your evaluation with Jonathan?"

"Yes. I told him everything, and I told him how happy I was that he encouraged me to go through with it. I wish my mother had had me evaluated when I was younger."

"Knowing what I know about your mother, she more than likely tried. There were fewer resources and there was even less awareness of spectrum disorders back then. I think your mom did the best she could to prepare you for the world."

"I should have pursued an evaluation when I first started seeing you. Why can I only see that now?"

"Because hindsight is a wonderfully illuminating thing."

"There's a woman I work with at the library. Her name is Stacy. People smile at her in our staff meetings and everyone's always wandering into her office to chat or offer her cookies they've brought from home. I've been trying to make friends with her since she started working at the library a few years ago. I always tried to copy everybody else's behavior, but it never seemed to work when I did it. The other day, when we were in the break room, I felt so much calmer that I just said hi while I waited for the microwave to heat water for my tea."

"And then what happened?"

"She said hi. And then she asked me how my day was going and I said fine. Then the microwave dinged and I took my mug and told her to have a great rest of the day before I walked out."

Tina seems delighted by this revelation. "How did that make you feel?"

"I can't describe how it felt other than to say it felt natural. In the past, I would have misread her signals and started rambling. Then I would worry about what I'd said, which would make me ramble even more, making it worse. This time I didn't. A couple days later, Stacy and I were walking out at the same time and she held the door for me and asked me if I had plans for the weekend. I told her I'd probably do something with my boyfriend and she asked me his name and how we met. I told her a little about Jonathan and how we'd dated in college. She thought that was so romantic. Then, before she got into her car, she said, 'Have fun with your boyfriend,' and I said, 'Have fun with your boyfriend too!,' because of course I did."

"What's wrong with that?" Tina asks.

"Stacy is *married*," I say.

"So close," Tina says, and then we both crack up and we are still laughing when my time is up.

35

Annika

CHICAGO
SEPTEMBER 2001

"You are . . . not great at this," Jonathan says when I try to pull his car up alongside the curb and bounce off it instead.

"Sorry!" I say.

"It's okay. You can't really hurt it unless you hit something big."

Jonathan's car is nicer than the old truck he used to drive. It's a shiny silver color and when I asked what kind it was, he said it was a sedan.

He doesn't drive it that often because he usually takes the train. I like the way it smells inside: new, although Jonathan said he bought it when he moved back from New York.

"I told you I was a bad driver. If I remember correctly, those were my exact words."

"You're not that bad. You just don't do it enough."

We're visiting my parents this weekend, and Jonathan decided the town of Downers Grove would be the perfect place for some basic driving lessons before we tackle something harder. I don't tell him I'm hoping he'll give up on me before we reach that point. Chicago traffic has a paralyzing effect on me; I literally cannot drive the city streets.

Between cabs, the L, and my own two feet, I shouldn't have to, but Jonathan thinks I need to broaden my horizons a little.

"Annika, stop!" Jonathan slams his foot down on the floor in front of him, hard. It startles me.

"Why did you do that?" I ask, stopping so suddenly my seat belt locks up. Oh. Maybe because that wasn't my light that turned green.

"You don't know how much I wish there was a brake pedal on my side."

Another fifteen minutes of jerky starts and sudden stops is all either of us can take, and Jonathan switches places with me. I'm limp with relief and slump against the seat as he drives us back to eat lunch with my parents.

My mom and dad were thrilled to hear that Jonathan and I had reconnected, and even more thrilled when I told them we were driving over to see them. That's how this whole driving-lesson thing got started. I told Jonathan that my mom and dad usually drove over to Chicago to pick me up whenever I wanted to come home.

"It's only half an hour," he said. "Why don't you get a Zipcar and drive over yourself? It would be good practice."

"Because I hate driving. I found a job and an apartment downtown so that I wouldn't have to do it."

"It's not about the driving."

"It's not? What is it about?" I seriously didn't know.

"It's about doing one thing every day that scares you. Wasn't there a famous woman who said that? I feel like there was."

"It was Eleanor Roosevelt and you know it. And I'm not scared."

"Mmmmmm."

"I know what that sound means."

"Then you know there are going to be more driving lessons in your future."

Jonathan wants us to head home by four so he'll have time to go into the office for a few hours. He said something this morning about Brad wanting him to get a jump on Monday, which sounded like a good way to ruin a perfectly lovely Sunday. We say good-bye to my parents and get back in the car. I'm thrilled that Jonathan doesn't suggest that I get behind the wheel.

"Why can't you tell Brad you don't want to work on Sundays?" It would be nice if he and I could watch a movie or do some other relaxing activity together when we get home.

"Nobody would admit that to their boss. It would mean we weren't team players and that our personal lives are more important."

I wrinkle my forehead in confusion. "Aren't they?"

"Of course they are, but we can't admit it."

"I don't understand this at all, and I don't think it has anything to do with the way my brain works."

Jonathan laughs. "It's corporate culture. No one has to understand it as long as we play by the rules."

"It sounds horrible."

"It's just the way it is."

"What if you decided you didn't want to do it anymore? What else could you be?"

"I don't know. I've never thought about it. What would you do if you decided you didn't want to work in a library anymore?"

"I would write plays. All day long, just"—I mimic pounding on the keys. "But I can't imagine ever leaving the library. I love it too much."

"You're lucky," he says.

I shrug. "I just know I couldn't spend my life doing something that doesn't make me happy."

36

Jonathan

CHICAGO
SEPTEMBER 10, 2001

"That's not going to help us at all," Brad says after a junior member of the team makes a suggestion that contradicts what Brad has proposed but will, in fact, help us quite a bit. Our petulant boss punctuates his statement by throwing a stack of reports across the conference room table like a child throwing a tantrum. Brad suffers from a raging case of impostor syndrome, and he's terrified someone will discover that, most of the time, he's talking out of his ass. But he's what they call "good in a room," energetic and animated, and it's masked his overall incompetence and made him look smarter than he is. It doesn't hurt that the solutions I generate for this team, through my own hard work, are often delivered via his big mouth, making him look like the superstar he only wishes he could be.

The whole team is catching the last flight to New York tonight so we can be sitting in our seats in a conference room by eight thirty tomorrow morning to give our presentation and, even more important, dazzle our clients. Unfortunately, we're not adequately prepared, which is why our fearless leader is in such a rotten mood. During our last five-minute break, I ducked into my office, shut the door, and called Annika.

"Don't expect me tonight. Things are *not* going well and there's no way I can break away to meet you for dinner. I'm sorry."

"But then how will you eat?" It kills me that Annika's focus is on whether or not I'll be able to feed myself.

"I don't know. Brad usually has dinner brought in, but he decided not to order anything because he didn't want us to be distracted by the food. The way things are going I can tell you right now that none of us will be leaving until we have no choice because we have to head for the airport. I'll eat something there."

"That's ridiculous," Annika says.

"It's okay." Really, dinner is the last of my worries at this point. Brad has hinted repeatedly that my contributions and performance in New York will be directly tied to the likelihood of me being named director of the division, which is only one step below his position. There are three of us gunning for the job, and Brad has been wielding his decision-making power like the most giant of tyrants. Lots of musing out loud about our strengths and weaknesses, but with a hint of uncertainty sprinkled in to keep us guessing. I hate pandering to him, but I want this job and he knows it. Brad might be more surprised if he knew what I *really* wanted, which is his job. This department would flourish under the leadership of someone who cared more about making smart decisions for the company than making sure everyone knew how much power he had.

Brad's extra cranked up tonight because while we're in New York, he'll be attending meetings with his boss and he's panicking. He'll have to navigate those on his own, and I'm sure he's worried about being able to think on his feet without the rest of us there to feed him the information.

"I've gotta go," I tell Annika after glancing at my watch. I've been gone for five minutes and if I'm the last one back in my seat, I'd better have a good reason why, and talking to my girlfriend on the phone will not be an acceptable option. "I'll call you from the airport."

"Okay, bye."

Somehow, I get lucky, because when I return to the conference room, everyone is in their seats, but Brad is nowhere to be found. Brian, who is also up for the promotion, leans over and whispers, "Heard he's on the phone with his wife. Kid's got pinkeye or something."

Brad comes back into the room five minutes later, red-faced and a little flustered. We're really cutting it close with this presentation, and the result is starting to show on his face. Over the next hour, we provide enough viable options and solid research for Brad to cobble together a halfway-decent pitch. We lean back in our chairs. Push our legal pads toward the center of the table.

We're all a little punch-drunk and exhausted from the late nights and seven-day work weeks, and when I catch of glimpse of Annika outside the conference room's glass walls, I do a double take to make sure I'm not hallucinating. She's smiling and holding a take-out bag from Dominick's. She spots me and waves enthusiastically. I wave back, but before I can excuse myself and intercept her out in the hall, she pushes open the door. Every man at that table turns to look at her, and boy is she a sight for sore eyes with her big smile and her swinging ponytail as she bounces into the room. I have no idea how she managed to get past the security guard and into the building, and I don't care. The almost childlike glee on her face is the only thing that's put a smile on mine all day.

Wives and girlfriends have occasionally swung by the office to say hello, to deliver an item forgotten at home, or show off a new baby. But rarely has one ever walked right into a conference room during a meeting. They would know it was something that simply isn't done. But not my Annika. And there's something about the fact that she doesn't that makes me admire her even more. Because really, when did we start taking things so seriously? It's not like it's ten in the morning. It's six o'clock at night and we've been working for ten hours straight. Longer than that, actually, because every single person in this room probably started working before they left their homes this morning. Can we not drop the façade for a moment and admit that we're human? That not everything we do has to be done to show how hard we're working?

A few starving members of the team have resorted to raiding the vending machines, and the conference room table is littered with empty Coke cans and candy wrappers, but whatever's in the bag Annika's holding smells incredible. I know these people well and have worked with several of them for years. Their amused expressions are also kind, because they know what I went through with Liz, and also because how can anyone not see how sweet—if ill-timed—Annika's gesture is?

Well, for starters, Brad can't.

"Hi," he says, and the tone of his voice sets me on edge immediately. I sit up straighter in my chair. "Monica, is it?"

He gives her one of those fake and condescending smiles, and it's at that moment that my blood begins to heat up. Annika smiles back at him, although her smile is sincere. "Annika. No 'M.' Everyone thinks it's Monica, but it's not."

"Okay. Well, Annika, we're in the middle of a meeting here."

"I can tell," she says. "But I'm sure Jonathan is hungry since there's no food, so I brought him some dinner."

"Let's take a break, guys," Brad says. The team pushes back their chairs, stretches. Most of them start to leave, but the nosier ones hang around. Annika walks over to me and sets the bag down on the table. "It's ham and cheese."

I push my chair back and stand so I can kiss her on the cheek. Before I can grab her hand and coax her gently out of the room, Brad comes over and stands next to us.

Annika is wearing a dress and while the neckline isn't low, there's a gap in the front because it's a little loose on her. If she moves at all, the material moves with her and I catch a glimpse of her bra and the tops of her breasts. Brad's height makes it possible for him to look straight down into the gap, and he's taking full advantage of it, as if Annika's interruption somehow gives him the right—as if it would give *anyone* the right—to do that. I want to smack the entitled look off his face.

"Jonathan, I'd like to see you in my office," Brad says. He's doing his best "you're about to get in trouble" routine, like he's the principal and I've been caught skipping class.

I lead Annika to my office.

"I got you in trouble, didn't I? I just wanted to do something nice."

"Annika, it's okay. Really. It was a sweet thing that you did, and I'm going to eat the hell out of that sandwich."

Probably not in front of Brad, but still.

"Are you mad? I can't tell if you're mad." She sounds so worried.

I reach for her hands and squeeze them. "I'm not mad." And I'm not, at least not at her. Mostly I'm mad at myself for being willing to walk on the eggshells Brad has thrown down and worrying more about my professional life than the things that really matter.

"Wait here." She sits down in my chair and looks at me so fearfully that I tell her everything's fine and I'll be back in a minute.

I enter Brad's office. He's sitting at his desk looking down at some papers he's shuffling. I stand there like a naughty child waiting for him to acknowledge me. "Why don't you close the door," he says without looking up.

Jesus. He's going full-on manipulative asshole.

When he finally looks up, he leans back in his chair and twirls a pen idly. "I'm just wondering if your . . . What is that woman to you?"

"My girlfriend," I say, because I can't deny any longer that it's what I want her to be. I say it slowly and pointedly, the way you would if someone is dense and you want to make sure they understand. Two can play at this game, Brad. I see by his expression that he doesn't care for my tone.

"I'm just wondering if your *girlfriend* will be making a habit of dropping in on you while you're at work."

"I don't know. I can't say for sure that she'll never try to bring me dinner again."

"I'm not mad about the interruption. We've all been working long hours, and I like to think of us as a family. But there's a certain kind of image we need to uphold at this firm. Someone who's in a director position like you might be will be attending a lot of social events, often accompanied by their significant other."

"What are you trying to say?" I ask even though I know what he's getting at. Is it even okay for him to say that? I'm pretty sure HR would be interested in this conversation. Wouldn't they?

"I'm just saying there are certain behaviors we need to adhere to in a business setting."

I let out a short laugh, although I doubt Brad finds this situation funny. "Yeah, well, you might want to rethink looking down her dress because it's certainly not appropriate behavior for any setting."

Brad doesn't know what to say. I'm well within my rights to call him out on this, and he knows it. But as my boss, to concede to me in any way would diminish some of his power, and he can't have that.

"I wasn't looking down her dress, Jon."

"I guess we'll have to agree to disagree, *Brad.* I'm sure it won't happen again."

I almost want to laugh again, because now I'm just poking the bear, and we're both aware of it. The thing is, Brad knows I'm the best person for the job. And putting someone like me under him will allow his own workload to decrease, although I can only imagine the amount of work he'll pile on me. He'll make me miserable while I wait to find out if I got the job, but I'm almost certain he'll choose me in the end. He'll let me stew about it, and he'll definitely make me wait until we get back from New York before he makes the announcement, because that will be my punishment for this altercation. Brad swivels around in his chair so that his back is to me, busying himself with a stack of files on his credenza. I take that as my cue to go.

When I return to my office, Annika isn't there.

37

Jonathan

CHICAGO

SEPTEMBER 10, 2001

Brad finally dismissed everyone ten minutes ago. It's almost seven, and I'm cutting it close, because I should be on my way to the airport for my 8:52 flight to New York, but instead I'm in a cab racing toward Annika's apartment.

She buzzes me in and when she opens the door, eyes shiny with tears that look like they're about to spill over, fresh anger toward Brad wells up inside me for what this has done to her.

"Why did you leave?" I shout.

She flinches, because yelling is not something I usually do, especially not at her.

"You said you weren't mad, but you are!"

"I can deal with Brad, but I'm upset because you left. Do you know how that makes me feel?" She doesn't answer me, because of course she doesn't know how I feel, and she won't unless I tell her. "It makes me feel like you think I'm not worth fighting for. You can tell me a hundred different ways that I matter to you. But I need you to show me. I need to know you're willing to face whatever shit comes our way.

You can't run, you can't bury your head in the sand every time something happens that overwhelms you. You don't get to go to sleep and hope it's all been taken care of when you wake up. We didn't have to rekindle this relationship, but I wanted to because I happen to think *you're* worth fighting for and I love you just the way you are."

"You love me?" she says, as if she can't believe it.

"I never really stopped loving you. Sometimes I don't know why, but I do. You're going to have to accept that I'm a grown man and can handle whatever you throw at me. You need things from me, and I get that. But so do I. I need you to show me that you're not going to crumble every time you're faced with a little adversity. I need you to show me that we're in this together."

She looks me straight in the eye and says, "I love you too, Jonathan. I'm sorry. I promise I won't run and hide when things get bad."

I pull her into my arms and squeeze her tight. "I have to go. I'll be back in two days, and we can talk more then." I have a feeling that no matter what happens on this trip, I'll be in dire need of her affection when I return. I kiss her like I mean it and then take off down the hall.

I luck out, because my cabdriver is insane and when I tell him he needs to get me to the airport in record time, he floors it and doesn't let up until we're screeching into O'Hare.

I've cut it about as close as anyone can and actually still hope to get on the plane. I make it through security and reach the gate with mere seconds to spare, which is good, because if I'd missed this flight, Brad would probably fire me.

38

Annika

CHICAGO
SEPTEMBER 11, 2001

I call in sick the next morning, which is something I almost never do, but the situation I created with Jonathan had me in such a state I couldn't fall asleep. I'm ashamed of myself, because he's right. I do run from things. I hide. I always have. I do believe that he loves me and doesn't want me to change, but that didn't stop me from lying there wide awake ruminating on what I'd done and the trouble I'd caused for him. The forecast for Chicago on this September day is sunny and mild, and my boss probably thinks I'm playing hooky to take advantage of the gorgeous weather, but that's not it at all. I'm just so mad at myself, and I can't let it go. Last night's humiliating incident will play for days on an endless loop in my brain.

I make tea and crawl back in bed with it to call Janice the way I always do when I've messed up. She's making breakfast with a clinging Natalia, who she says is riding her hip like a monkey.

"If you ask me, these businessmen take everything way too seriously," she says after I spill the whole embarrassing story. "I wouldn't worry about it. You did a nice thing for Jonathan. Jesus, they're putting together deals, not curing cancer or solving world peace."

"Your husband works in the financial district."

"I know. That's why I'm allowed to make that statement. Clay and I laugh about some of the things he hears in those conference rooms. It's eye-rolling for sure. But they have to play the game."

"Then you of all people can understand why it would be so terribly confusing to me."

"Jonathan is treating you like an equal partner because that's how he sees you. Not when he first met you, maybe, which he's admitted. But now he feels differently. So start acting like his equal."

"Wow, tough love."

"You know I'm right."

"I shouldn't have left, but I got scared. I don't want to mess things up for him."

"He's a big boy. He can take care of himself."

And me, I think. Because there will always have to be someone in my life who's tasked with taking care of me.

But I don't have the courage to say it out loud, not even to Janice, who would certainly understand.

After we hang up, I go into the kitchen to make another cup of tea. When it's ready, I pick up the cat I recently adopted and also named Mr. Bojangles in honor of the original MBJ, who died a couple of years ago, and settle him on my lap. I click on the TV. Matt Lauer and Katie Couric are making small talk on the *Today* show. Feeling guilty about playing hooky, I tell myself that taking a mental health day is almost the same thing as taking a day for a sinus infection or the stomach flu, and those are two things my coworkers are always citing for their absences. Matt cuts Katie off midsentence—something is happening in lower Manhattan. I lean forward a little, watching the broadcast with curiosity and a strange sense of foreboding. The cat leaps off my lap because I'm squishing him.

Someone has called in to the show to report a big boom near the World Trade Center, which is where Jonathan mentioned his team would be having their meetings. He has some kind of fancy phone called a BlackBerry, and I think maybe I should call him to see if he heard it. But if I interrupt another meeting, his boss will really hate me and maybe Jonathan won't get the promotion he's hoping for.

Matt and Katie are perplexed. No one seems to know what's going on down there, but another caller thinks a small commuter plane might have hit the building. I pick up the handset of my cordless phone and place it in my lap. So what if I call Jonathan. Janice was right. They need to stop making such a big deal out of everything.

Then Matt and Katie cut to a picture of the World Trade Center, and there's a hole in the building and flames are coming out of it! It scares me so badly that when I try to lift the phone to my ear, I drop it and it bounces onto the floor. Will works on Wall Street and so does Clay. Though I don't exactly know how close that is to the World Trade Center, I'm scared for them, too.

This is bad. I know this is bad because there's a fire and when there's a fire, the first thing you have to do is get out. One of the things my parents made me do when I first started living alone was come up with a plan for the order in which I'd need to do things in the event of an emergency. If there is a tornado warning, I need to go to the most interior room in my apartment, which is the bathroom. If the smoke alarm ever goes off, I need to grab any pets I might have and leave immediately. I am not supposed to stop and call the fire department or put on a bra or any of the other dumb things I'd probably think I should do. Once I'm outside, only then should I call the fire department, from a neighbor's house.

I scramble to pick up the handset, and I hit the preprogrammed numbers I've stored in my phone for Jonathan: office, home, and cell. I punch the button for his BlackBerry, but it rings and rings and finally goes to his voice mail. I hang up and try again. Matt and Katie have a woman on the line and she's saying the aircraft was bigger than a commuter plane but that doesn't seem possible because how would a pilot not see buildings as tall as the World Trade Center. Also, I don't know which tower Jonathan is in. Whatever is happening seems to be happening in the North Tower.

He finally—finally!—picks up. "Annika." He sounds weird and out of breath. It's very noisy in the background, and I can barely hear him.

"What tower are you in?" I scream it into the phone.

"The south. We heard a giant boom ten minutes ago. Brad went to see if he could find out what's going on."

"Jonathan, I'm watching it right now on TV. It was a plane."

"Are you sure?"

"Yes! Matt and Katie are saying a plane has hit the North Tower. There are flames pouring out the side of the building."

"That's what Tom's wife said. She said a small plane coming out of JFK might have gone off course. Some problem with air traffic control or something. We're looking out the windows, but we can't see anything from where we are. There's no TV in this conference room."

"The buildings are way too close. You've got to get out. Right now. Tell the others. Make them go with you."

Jonathan shouts to his coworkers. "Hey! It *was* a plane. There's a ton of fire. Go, get out. Take the stairs."

"Go with them," I say.

"What?" I hear him say to someone in the background. "Brad just came back. We're supposed to stay put because there might be falling debris outside. They're working on getting the fire contained. He said they told him we aren't in imminent danger of the fire spreading to this building."

My logical mind cannot wrap itself around the directive they've been given to stay put, because it makes no sense at all. Brad doesn't know what I know, what all of us watching TV know because it's unfolding live before our eyes. This is not a fire that will be contained.

"Jonathan, listen to me. For the first time since the day you met me, I know I am finally right about something. Just do what I say. You can see what things are like on the ground once you get down." I'm sure he thinks I'm overreacting. That I've misread this.

But I know I haven't.

Fire means go. Fire means get out, get lower.

"All right, we'll go." In the background, the shouting grows even louder. Jonathan is telling everyone to leave the room, take the stairs, head for the lobby, where they'll reunite to assess the situation. I hear Brad telling them to stay, and Jonathan telling him to fuck off. That makes me happy because *Jonathan believes me.*

"We're heading toward the stairwell. I couldn't get everyone to go with me. Some of them stayed behind. Brad wouldn't leave."

"Okay," I say. I'm breathing so fast and trying to listen to what Matt and Katie are saying now. Jonathan's phone is breaking up and I can't hear everything he's saying. I dig the cell phone Jonathan bought for me out of my purse, but I don't have the mental capacity to simultaneously handle another call. As soon as I know Jonathan has reached the bottom floor, I'll call Janice, Will, my mom.

I wish I had more phones.

"Jonathan, where are you now?" I scream, but maybe he can't hear me, because he doesn't answer. "Jonathan, tell me what floor!"

It takes me a few seconds to realize that Jonathan isn't answering because something has severed our connection.

And I know exactly what it is because Matt and Katie have cut to a brand-new clip, and the thing that has severed our connection is another plane, except that this one has just hit the South Tower, which is the building Jonathan is in.

I'm flicking my hands so frantically, I can hardly dial the phone. I'm trying to reach my mother but receive only a busy signal. Pacing from one side of the room to another, I redial for what seems like forever but is in reality less than five minutes.

"I was on the phone with your brother," she says in lieu of a normal greeting. "He's okay." Though I'm desperately worried about Jonathan, and Clay, too, I'm relieved to know my brother is safe.

"Okay, good," I say. I'm panting and shaking, because there is so much adrenaline flowing through me and my body doesn't know what to do with it. "Mom. Jonathan is in New York right now, and he is in the South Tower."

Deadly silence greets my announcement. Then my mother says, "Annika," and I can hear that she's crying. "Don't go anywhere. We're coming."

I remain glued to the TV while I wait for my parents to arrive. Though I know the phone lines are jammed, I call Jonathan's number every thirty seconds with my cordless phone, and Janice's with my cell. Busy signals from both.

When my parents arrive, my dad is moving slowly and with apparent difficulty. I've completely forgotten about the hip-replacement surgery he had a couple of weeks ago, because even though I don't mean to be, sometimes I am a horrible daughter.

The surgery went off without a hitch.

My mother is waiting on him hand and foot.

I moved on.

It is my mom's idea to try to reach someone in Jonathan's Chicago office after she gets my dad settled on the couch. "Surely they have information for family members," she reasons. She calls, but it's to no avail. They are every bit as confused as we are, and the information trickling out of New York is hampered by the fire, the crush of emergency vehicles, the people streaming from the buildings. It's all happening so fast, yet there is an agonizing slowness as well.

My mom makes tea, but I can't drink it. I want to pace and flick. Rock and bounce. I do all of those things, some of them at the same time, but none of it helps.

I decide to call Will. Maybe he can go down to the World Trade Center and tell me if Jonathan has made it out of the building.

The call won't go through, and I slam my hand down on the arm of the couch. On the TV, they are showing things falling out of the towers. Paper rains down like some kind of nightmarish ticker-tape parade.

The heat has become too intense, and people are jumping out of the windows and the gaping hole in the side of the building. Some of them are holding hands. A woman's skirt billows up as her body plummets toward the ground. How can they show this on TV?

I cannot watch any footage of the jumpers. The thought of Jonathan being one of them, the thought of *anyone* choosing that option because it was preferable to the others, reduces me to a rocking, sobbing, hysterical puddle on my kitchen floor. No amount of comforting from my mother will calm me, and the intensity of my emotions puts me in an almost catatonic state.

I am not equipped for this.

No one is equipped for this.

I think that it cannot possibly get worse than people jumping out of buildings, but I am so wrong, because at 9:59 A.M., on live TV, the South Tower, which Jonathan was in, collapses and falls. Twenty-nine minutes later, the North Tower follows suit.

39

Annika

CHICAGO
SEPTEMBER 12, 2001

We have been up all night, and around six thirty in the morning, my call to Will finally goes through.

"I'm okay. I've already talked to Mom and Dad. I wasn't anywhere near the towers. I tried to call you yesterday, but I couldn't get through."

"Mom told me. She and Dad are here with me now." My voice cracks and I begin to whimper.

"Annika, everything's okay. I promise."

"Jonathan flew to New York Monday night. He was in the South Tower for a meeting. I spoke to him yesterday and told him to get out of the building. We were on the phone when the second plane hit. I haven't heard from him since."

"What? Oh God. Oh shit."

"Can you go down there? Can you look for him?"

"Annika, the towers *fell.* Even if I could get near them, which I can't, I have no idea what I'd do. It's absolute pandemonium down there. There's smoke and fire and . . . The National Guard is here." He stops talking when I start sobbing. "I'm so sorry," he yells in an attempt to be heard over the noise I'm making.

I hand the phone to my mom and I sit in the corner of my living room, MBJ 2.0 in my lap, and I rock. The reality of what I'm facing is too much for me to handle, and even though I promised Jonathan that I would be brave, that I would not run and hide from the things that scare me, I escape in the same way I always have when things go wrong.

I shut my eyes and I let sleep's darkness swallow me.

When I wake up several hours later, still on the floor but with a pillow under my head and a blanket covering me, my body feels like a lead weight. I struggle to sit up. My dad is stretched out asleep on the couch, but my mom is on the phone. She looks at me and the first thing I notice is that her expression seems different. I don't know what it means, but then she smiles, and when she hangs up, she gives me the first bit of hopeful news we've received since the planes hit the towers. While I slept, she decided to try Jonathan's Chicago office again, and she tells me that he's been accounted for by someone named Bradford Klein.

"That's his boss," I say.

"They told me everyone with direct reports is supposed to use their BlackBerrys to communicate with the Chicago office by email."

My phone will do no such thing, but Jonathan's BlackBerry can do things the phone he gave me cannot. I don't care how they're doing it as long as they provide an open channel of communication. A feeling of absolutely unmitigated joy rises in me with such force that I clap my hands while running around the room. My dad jolts awake. "What? What is it? What's happened?"

"It's good news," my mom says. "They think Jonathan made it out okay."

"He *did* make it out okay. Brad said so." I start pacing again, impatient for details. "Where is he now? Is he hurt?"

"They couldn't tell me much. They just said his name is on a list of employees who made it out of the building."

"How can they not know where he is?"

"There's still a lot of uncertainty," my mom says. "Many of the survivors left on foot and are no longer in the area, especially once the towers fell. Does Jonathan know anyone in the city?"

"He knows Will, but I'm not sure if he'd know how to contact him. He knows that Janice lives in Hoboken. I don't know if there's any transportation available to take him there. I can ask Janice once I get through to her. I'm sure Jonathan has other friends or business acquaintances because he used to live there, but I don't know their names or phone numbers." Maybe his ex-wife will be nice enough to let him stay with her. I wonder if Liz was at the World Trade Center. I hope she got out of the building, too.

"Your brother will let us know if he turns up, and so will Janice. In the meantime, we'll have to be patient. Jonathan will go *somewhere*, and I'm sure he'll call as soon as he gets there."

I am never able to get through to Janice, but an hour later, she calls me. "Clay is here. He was able to catch the ferry after spending the night on a friend's couch a few miles from Ground Zero. That's what they're calling it. What about Jonathan? Have you heard from him?"

"He got out! My mom spoke to someone from his company's Chicago office. We're just waiting for him to call and let us know where he is."

"Oh, thank God." She's crying now in relief. So am I. "I can't get any incoming calls, but the outgoing calls seem to be going through now. You'll hear from him soon. I'll try you every hour. It'll be okay."

"It'll be okay," I parrot.

"It *will.*"

"I know," I say, because I believe her and because it simply has to.

So, we wait. My mom makes lunch and forces me to eat it. The food feels like a lump going down my throat, because Jonathan really should have called by now.

There's a *reason* he hasn't.

I know that's what we're all thinking, but no one can say it, because that would mean admitting that maybe Jonathan *didn't* make it out of the building.

We wait some more.

Janice calls again. "Have you heard from him?"

"No. Not yet."

"Clay says lots of people had to find shelter with friends, even strangers. The phone lines are just . . . they're still a mess."

"That's what Will said. He checked in half an hour ago. Took him a while to get through. I'm sure Jonathan will call." My voice sounds oddly flat and unconvincing, even to my own ears.

"I'm sorry, Annika." She is silent for a few moments. "I wish we could wait this out together and I could comfort you."

She may get her wish, because if I don't hear from Jonathan soon, the next time she calls, I'm going to tell her what I've decided to do.

Jonathan does not call. It's nearly eight o'clock at night by then. When I break the news to my parents that I'm going to drive to Hoboken, New Jersey, and then go to Ground Zero to find Jonathan myself, they protest. Loudly and rather emphatically. I don't blame them. It's an outlandish, foolhardy plan. Surely they don't believe I'm even capable of it, and why would they? There are lots of things no one thinks I'm capable of, and for the most part, they would be right. But in the words of Eleanor Roosevelt, "A woman is like a tea bag; you never know how strong it is until it's in hot water." This is the hottest water I've ever been in. I'm scared, and driving to Hoboken seems impossible.

But I'm going to do it anyway.

"Then what will you do?" my mom asks.

"Janice will help me. We'll look for Jonathan. We'll check all the hospitals. We'll put up signs." I have gleaned from the news broadcasts and newspaper articles that this is what people are doing. They're holding candlelight vigils and they're trading information and they're helping one another.

"I can't go with you. I can't leave your dad, and he can't be in a car that long right now."

"Yes, I can," my dad says, but it would be too painful for him. He doesn't even look comfortable sitting on the couch. And she will not leave him by himself.

"I'm not asking you to go with me. I don't *want* you to go with me." That's a straight-up lie, because I have no idea if I have the ability to do this. Even more important than ability is whether or not I have the *courage.* This revelation makes me feel ashamed. I'm a grown woman, and it's time to prove—if not to everyone else then at least to myself—that I can do things on my own. Janice said that Jonathan needs me to step up, to be the kind of person he can depend on not to retreat when things get rough. This time, I won't hide in my childhood bed hoping the world will right itself. Jonathan would do anything to help me, but now he's the one who needs help, and I'm going to dig deep and be the one to give it to him.

Janice reacts even more strongly than my parents when I tell her. "I don't think you have any idea what it's like here. Clay said the footage on TV can't remotely compare to what he saw with his own eyes. We won't be able to get anywhere near Ground Zero unless we can prove we live in the neighborhood. And I'm not even sure that's enough."

"What if Jonathan is hurt? What if he's at the hospital but for some reason he can't speak." I don't like to think about what those reasons might be. I tell myself that his voice might be too hoarse from the smoke and dust and it's given him laryngitis and that's why he hasn't called. "He has no one. No siblings, no parents. No one is looking for him but me."

"Annika." She sounds tired.

"His name is on the list. He got out."

"What if his name is there by mistake?"

"Why would it be there by mistake? His boss was supposed to put down the names of everyone who got out and email it to the Chicago office, and that's what he did. He wouldn't lie about something like that." Janice doesn't say anything. "If I can get there, will you help me?"

"Of course I will."

Before we hang up, I tell her when to expect me and that I'll have my cell phone so I can call her from the road. "Be careful," she says.

My mom's subsequent calls to the Chicago office go unanswered. The phone just rings and rings now. "I can't blame them," she says. "They must be terribly busy."

Jonathan's company has set up a hotline and also a command center of sorts at a hotel. Family members of missing employees have been instructed to go there.

I want to go there.

40

Annika

SEPTEMBER 13, 2001

Because there is a ban on airline travel, I'm not the only one who's decided they will rent a car to get where they need to go. The line at Hertz is thirty-seven people deep. Some of them curse and drop out, walking away rolling their carry-on luggage behind them, wheels thumping out the door and down the curb. I want to run after them and ask where they're going, because maybe they know of some shorter line or magic supply of cars I haven't thought of. But I don't and now there are only twenty-nine customers in front of me, and that makes me feel a little better. I will wait as long as I have to and then I will drive straight to Hoboken using the directions my mom printed out for me using something called MapQuest. Clay and Natalia will stay home while Janice and I go into the city to find Jonathan.

I just don't think it's going to be as hard as people are saying.

I arrived at Hertz at seven thirty this morning, and it is almost one before it's my turn. I'm the last customer, because everyone who was behind me bailed a long time ago. I think that's a bad sign, but I've waited this long and it seems dumb to give up now that I've finally reached the counter. The man standing behind it says they have only one car left.

"That's okay," I say, because there's only one of me.

"It's a standard transmission."

"What does that mean?"

"A stick shift."

"I can't drive a stick-shift car. I can barely drive a regular car. My boyfriend was in the South Tower and I'm driving there to look for him." This means I will have to find another car-rental place and start over. I sit down right there on the floor, because my legs feel wobbly, and the Hertz man leans over the counter and looks down at me. "Miss?"

"I'll switch with you," the man who had been in front of me in line says. After he received his car keys he stayed to make a call on his cell and I guess he's overheard our conversation. "I can drive a stick. You can have mine."

Impulsively, I throw my arms around him. He does not recoil or go rigid the way I would if a stranger ever did that to me. He briefly returns my embrace, pats my back a couple of times, and says, "Be careful out there. I hope you find him. Godspeed."

I leave Chicago a little after one o'clock and head east on I-90 to begin the twelve-hour drive to Hoboken. For the most part, I'll stay on I-90 or I-80. I don't mind driving on the interstate. I'm getting passed a lot, but I stay in the right lane and keep going. I don't even mind when I come to the first toll, because I know how they work and made sure I had plenty of dollars and coins on hand before I left. The only time I get nervous is when another car is trying to merge onto the road. Two people have honked at me because there was a car to my left and I couldn't get over in time, but nobody crashed or anything.

Depending on how many stops I make, I will be in Hoboken sometime tomorrow afternoon. My mom made me a hotel reservation in Pennsylvania, where I'll spend the night. If I weren't leaving so late in the day, I would try to drive straight through, because I am *doing* something and I feel energized by that, but my parents had a fit when I mentioned it, and they made me promise to stop at the hotel and call them when I get there.

I'm not as confident driving in the dark. It's also raining a little, and that puts a weird glare on things. I'm only going forty-five now. I've needed to pee for about ten miles, and as much as I'd like to avoid the whole pulling-off-the-interstate thing, I have no choice. There's an exit up ahead, so I put on my blinker.

At the end of the ramp, a man is sitting by the side of the road. He's wearing a jacket with the hood up, but he's not holding a sign asking for food or money. When the car in front of me stops, the man shuffles to the driver's-side door so he can accept whatever the driver is offering. It's then that I realize that there are legs wrapped around the man's waist, and that he's shielding a child with his coat.

The light turns green and I follow the car ahead of me through the intersection and down the street to the gas station. I still have half a tank, but since I'm here I decide to fill up. As I wait for the pump to shut off, I think about the man and child. Why are they out in the rain? What happened to their car? Where will they spend the night? They must be cold. I fidget like crazy, because I should have peed before worrying about the gas.

I finally put the cap back on the gas tank and run inside to the bathroom. I'm not paying as much attention as I should, because I can't stop thinking of the man and child, and when I stand up to zip my pants, my phone flips out of my pocket and falls into the toilet. I'm not sure if it's ruined, but I imagine how it will feel to reach in and pluck it out of the dirty gas station toilet bowl.

I can't do it, so I leave it there.

I'm still thinking about the man and the child two miles down the road. There have been horrible stories in the news about all the bad things the terrorists caused, but there have also been stories about people coming together to help other people. People inviting strangers into their homes in New York to shelter them, feed them. Give them clothes and shoes. I want to be a part of this. I want to show I can help people, too.

If I give this man and child a ride, it will probably be one of the few good things that's happened to them today, so at the next exit, I pull off and turn around to go get them.

The man doesn't really want to get into my car. He tells me that the last person who gave them a ride made them get out when the little boy threw up. "I don't think he's got anything left in him, but I can't be sure," he says.

I say I don't mind even though I will certainly have trouble with the smell if it happens again. They're on their way to stay with the man's aunt in Allentown so he can look for work and she can watch the child. Their car broke down a few miles back and he has no money to fix it.

"I'm on my way to Hoboken. My best friend and I are going to look for my boyfriend who was in the South Tower on Tuesday. He's missing. I have a hotel reservation just across the Ohio-Pennsylvania border. That's as far as I'm going tonight."

"Your boyfriend was in one of the towers?"

"Yes, but he got out okay because his name is on a list. I just have to find him because he hasn't called."

"I . . . I'm sure you'll find him. I can call my aunt and have her pick us up at the hotel. We just need to get out of the rain tonight."

His name is Ray and the little boy is Henry. He looks feverish and pale as we strap him into the backseat.

"I had to leave his booster seat on the side of the road. Henry couldn't walk anymore and I couldn't carry everything. I sure hated to leave it behind."

"I'm sure it will be fine," I say, although I have no idea what the rules are about this kind of thing and had no idea Henry even needed a special seat.

Ray doesn't look like a serial killer or anything. I caught a glimpse of his face when the door was open and the interior light came on. He looks close to my age or maybe a few years younger. I'm not good at guessing that kind of thing. He has a scar on his chin. It's so hard to know what a person is like by looking at them. People are either kind or they're not. Some people look shiny on the outside but are rotten to the core. Some people pretend to be kind, but they're only faking it. Janice and Jonathan taught me a lot of things, but I don't think there's any way to truly know whether someone is kind until you put your trust in them and show them kindness of your own.

"You're gonna be okay, buddy," Ray says to Henry. "You'll be warm now."

"I'm thirsty, Daddy." He closes his eyes. Maybe he'll sleep. I wish I had something for him to drink, but I don't.

Ray doesn't comment on my jerky acceleration or the fact that I consistently drive five miles under the speed limit. We travel in companionable silence. Even if I enjoyed small talk, I'd have trouble keeping up a conversation. I have to concentrate on the road and the fact that I'm now responsible for the safety of two more people.

From the backseat, Henry begins to whimper. Maybe there's something left in his stomach after all. Ray turns around. "Do you think you're going to throw up?"

"I'm thirsty, Daddy," Henry says again. "I want some juice."

"Shh," Ray says.

"I can stop."

"I don't have any way to pay for it. I gave the last of my cash to the other driver that stopped for us. I wouldn't have if I'd known they were going to make us get out."

"Don't worry. I have plenty of money."

I get off at the next exit and pull into a gas station. It occurs to me as I walk down the aisles placing crackers and apple juice and water in my basket that it was wise of me not to give Ray my cash or credit card and let him be the one to go inside. What if he didn't want to give it back when he came out? What if he told me he would and when we got to the hotel he pretended he'd forgotten? But maybe I shouldn't have left them in the car, because what if he takes off with it? I push those thoughts away and pay for the groceries and when I come back out, there they are, right where I left them.

Ray gives Henry a few sips of water and when it doesn't come back up immediately, he gives him a little more. Henry wants to drink it all down because he says it tastes so good. Ray doesn't want to try the juice yet, but he gives Henry one of the saltines to nibble on.

"Would you like me to drive?" Ray asks.

"Do you want to drive?"

"Yes, but only if it's okay with you."

"Sure." I climb into the backseat and as Ray drives us down the dark interstate, I recite for Henry the play I'm currently writing, the one about the blue duck who knows he could be a good friend to the yellow ducks if they'd only give him a chance. Henry takes sips of the water I offer and eats another cracker. I sneak him some of the juice, because I can't say no to him when he asks. He does not throw up, which is good, because if he does, there's a one hundred percent chance I will, too. I'll feel bad about it, but I won't be able to help it.

We cross the state line into Pennsylvania at midnight. I read off the directions for Ray so he can find the hotel, and we pull into the parking lot. Ray lifts a sleeping Henry from the backseat. "His forehead's cool," Ray says.

They have another available room, so I slide my credit card across the counter and tell the man we'll take it. Ray doesn't protest. Instead he says, "Thank you," in a voice so soft I can barely hear him. He probably doesn't want to wake Henry.

"I'll call my aunt and let her know where she can pick us up," Ray says when we get off the elevator on our floor.

"Okay." I'm beyond exhausted and I've reached my limit for interacting with people today. It has been a good distraction from worrying about Jonathan, but I'm fading fast. I slide my key card into the door of my room and go inside, leaving Ray and Henry in the hallway.

My parents say they have never been so happy to hear from me. They've been calling my cell phone for hours, and I tell them it's at the bottom of a gas station toilet. Then I tell my mom about Ray and Henry, and all she says after that is "Oh my God," over and over.

"It's okay. Henry is fine now. He didn't throw up again and Ray said his fever was gone."

"You can't take risks like that."

"Everything turned out fine." My mom probably thinks she was right and I'm not capable of making a trip like this on my own without someone to guide me and keep me safe. But someday they'll be gone, and I'll have to live my life without their guidance. Maybe without Jonathan's, although that thought fills me with immeasurable pain and sadness. This road trip isn't my first or only attempt at independence, but it's an important step toward laying down a foundation for the years to come. And I'm not so dense that I don't know that most people are younger than thirty-two when they achieve it.

I've lagged behind everyone my whole life, so why would my adulthood be any different?

"I spoke to Janice. She's been frantic with worry because she couldn't reach you on your cell phone. I'll call her and let her know you're okay. Do you know what time you'll reach Hoboken?"

"I'm going to leave here by nine. Tell her I'll call her right before I get back on the road."

"Okay." My mom sounds really tired.

"I need to go to bed," I say.

"I'm so happy you're safe. Don't pick up anyone else. Please be careful and call me the minute you arrive at Janice's."

"I will. Bye."

There's a knock at the door, and when I open it, Ray is standing there, alone. "Henry's asleep. I locked the door in case he wakes up and tries to leave."

I'm not sure what this means. Am I supposed to invite him in? I don't want to. I'm too tired.

"I just wanted to thank you."

"Oh. You're welcome."

"Annika. Listen to me. Don't pick up anyone else, okay? You have a wonderful heart and your kindness astounds me. But what you did was very dangerous and there are people in this world who would not have cared about your safety."

"I know that." I mean, I know that *now*.

"Could I have your address? I'll pay you back when I get on my feet."

I tear a page from the notepad on the dresser and write it down for him.

He takes the piece of paper, folds it, and puts it in his pocket. "I better get back to Henry. I hope you find your boyfriend. No one deserves a miracle more than you."

41

Annika

SEPTEMBER 14, 2001

I leave the hotel an hour later than I planned, because I was so exhausted I somehow shut off the alarm and fell back asleep, although I have no memory of it.

It's hard to follow the MapQuest directions, because I don't want to take my eyes off the road and Janice's urban neighborhood has a lot of streets. She's waiting for me in the driveway when I pull in, Natalia on her hip.

"Thank God," she says when I get out of the car.

"I did it," I say. "No one thought I could, but here I am."

Janice squeezes me tight and says, "Yes. Here you are."

Clay and Natalia accompany us as far as they can, and then Janice and I head toward lower Manhattan on foot. Clay made us take surgical masks, and as we draw as close to Ground Zero as they'll let us, which isn't really close at all, I finally understand why. The smell of acrid smoke is overpowering, and ash fills the air like we're walking around near some kind of smoldering urban volcano. It coats our skin and hair, and I cough uncontrollably. Soldiers stand on corners with assault rifles slung over their shoulders. There are shrines and missing-person posters. We make the rounds of the hospitals closest to the World Trade Center, but we don't find Jonathan and I blink back tears because I've made it too far to just give up now.

We go uptown, to the hotel where Jonathan's company has set up an emergency center in the grand ballroom on the second floor. No one is wearing a tuxedo or fancy gown, but there are bottles of water and soft drinks in buckets on buffet tables; waiters circulate with trays of sandwiches no one wants. The round tables for eight are all numbered, and it takes me a moment to realize these are the floor numbers where the missing had been seen last.

"Do you know what floor he was on?" Janice asks.

"No." We pick a table at random and introduce ourselves to the people standing next to it. We share what we know, which isn't much, and in return we receive snippets of information, most of it things we already know: They tried to leave the building. They went down, were forced back up. A man from New Hampshire draws a diagram for us on a paper napkin showing the possible routes they could have taken. "If someone is strong, they could have survived if they made it low enough. We can't give up hope."

The people in this room are wearing the same clothes they've worn for days and many of them have shadows under their eyes. Jonathan's company has lost approximately seven hundred of its employees. We are just two out of hundreds, all despondent and desperate for information.

A long table near the front of the room holds information packets. There are phone numbers for surrounding hospitals, and we check them against the list Janice typed up, making sure that we've been to them all. We stand in line to fill out a missing-person report; it's eight pages thick. Unfortunately, Jonathan has very few unique identification markers. No tattoos, piercings, or facial hair that will separate him from all the other dark-haired, blue-eyed clean-shaven men who shared his fate. He does have a scar on his knee from a torn ACL he suffered during his sophomore year of college when he went skiing, but it's a common injury and is hardly worth mentioning. I list it anyway.

On the walls, people are putting up pieces of paper with pictures of their loved ones and their names and details. Janice made one for Jonathan with her computer using a photo I brought, and we tack it up with pushpins we take from a box on the floor. There are so many pictures, and I feel compelled to look at each one and read the information.

Someone lays a hand on my arm, and I flinch. "I'm sorry," she says. The middle-aged woman wears a name tag that says Eileen. "I'm a grief counselor if you'd like to talk."

"I don't need a grief counselor," I say, because I don't. "That's for people whose loved ones have died."

She pats my arm again and drifts toward a sobbing couple standing a few feet to my right.

A man steps up to the podium near the front of the room. "Please, if you haven't filled out a missing-person report, you need to do that now."

The crowd murmurs their assent, but then angry voices overpower them. "Why isn't the company trying harder to rescue the survivors?" a woman yells from somewhere in the middle. "Bring in experts. People trained to comb through the rubble."

"We are a financial services company. We are not in the business of search and rescue," the man says.

"But the company has considerable financial assets at their disposal. Why aren't they using them to help the people who made all this money for the company?"

The crowd erupts into shouting and the man leaves the podium.

No one knows what to do after that, including Janice and me, so we do the only thing we can.

We pray, we talk, and we listen, and for as beneficial as that is, I can't help but feel that we're wasting precious time.

42

Annika

SEPTEMBER 15, 2001

We return to the ballroom at the hotel early the next morning, because we don't know where else to go. Shortly after ten, as Janice and I sip Styrofoam cups of lukewarm tea, a man steps up to the podium and introduces himself as the head of the company. Then he announces that they're no longer looking for survivors. Four days after the attack, hopes are waning that anyone else will be pulled from the rubble alive, but hearing someone say it out loud causes a swift and heartbreaking reaction from the crowd. The keening sobs and cries of despair drown out whatever the man is still trying to say. Janice puts her arm around me and holds me upright, as if she's afraid my knees will buckle, but they don't, because I don't believe what this man is saying. It may be true for some employees, but not Jonathan.

"Annika," she says.

"He was in the stairwell," I argue. "Jonathan said he would go down and he was in the process of doing that when we got cut off. Based on the time the towers fell, he would have had time to reach the lobby, go outside, and get clear of them. Brad got out, and he didn't even head down with Jonathan. He stayed behind and he still got out!" I'm shouting and crying.

A man lays his hand on my arm, and I whirl around with so much force that he takes a quick step back. "I'm sorry, but who did you say you were looking for?"

"My boyfriend Jonathan."

"My son and a man named Jonathan helped my son's coworker, who was having a panic attack in the stairwell."

"Do you know what floor that was on?" Janice asks.

"Fifty-two."

"I don't know what floor my boyfriend was on, but I'm sure it was lower than that."

"My son was too, but according to some of the people they were with, he and this Jonathan went back up."

"Have you been able to find your son?" I ask, my voice trembling with fear.

The man's eyes fill with tears. "No."

And there it is. The reason Jonathan never called and we can't find him is because he's buried in the smoldering rubble of the South Tower.

"I'm sorry," he says. Janice squeezes the man's hand and puts her arm around my shoulders.

We leave the ballroom and sit on a bench outside the door where it's quieter. Janice has given up. I know this because she does not tell me what our next step should be. She has suggested everything she thinks we can do, and now with this devastating news, there is nothing left. She can't return to this hotel with me forever. She has a child to take care of. Mourning of her own to do for the friends she lost in the attacks. I have never felt so hopeless in my life.

Janice's phone rings. She answers and says, "No. We're still at the hotel." She listens to the caller for another minute. "I think that would be really great." Then she hands the phone to me.

"Hello?" I say.

"Stay where you are," my brother says. "I'm on my way to meet you."

43

Annika

Janice goes home and Will finds me in the hallway near the ballroom and leads me outside. I blink against the sunlight and inhale, but the air is a bit cleaner and we don't need our masks yet. The posters of missing people are everywhere. They're stapled to lampposts, taped to railings and windows. The ones that have come unmoored from their surfaces litter the street and blow away in bursts of wind. I try to avoid stepping on the pictures of the faces as Will and I make our way downtown on foot. There are people carrying candles, unlit for now but destined for tonight's new wave of vigils.

My brother revisits the theory: that Jonathan is not in the rubble but has instead been transported to a hospital. "He may be injured and unable to communicate," Will says.

"We went to all the hospitals," I say.

"You went to them two days ago, when it was utter chaos. Some of those people have died. New patients have been brought in. There's been a lot of confusion. Let's check again."

I agree, because Will's idea has merit and there's nothing else for us to do. I'll be fine as long as we keep moving, keep trying to find Jonathan. "Where do we start?" I ask.

Will smiles. "I've always found the beginning to be a good place."

I smile, too, because the beginning is, indeed, a good place to start, and for the first time in our lives, it seems Will and I are on the exact same page.

The sheet of paper I pull from my pocket lists the hospitals Janice and I already visited, a check mark next to all fifteen of them. It's gray from our dirty hands and tattered from being folded repeatedly. I hand it to Will, and he studies it. He turns the paper over and scribbles the names of nearby landmarks and streets, and draws a circle around it and an X to indicate where we are. He adds the names of the hospitals whose locations he already knows and numbers them in the order of the likelihood we'll find Jonathan there. He points to number one.

"All right," he says. "Let's go."

My resolve is starting to falter. We're standing in the hallway of the ninth hospital. My feet ache and I want nothing more than to go back to Janice's and collapse into bed. But I can't sleep until we're done.

"Can we sit down for a minute?" I ask.

"Sure," Will says. There are no chairs in the hallway, so I slide my back down the wall until my butt hits the hard tile floor. Will does the same.

I don't even care that at the moment, we're accomplishing nothing. We've been turned down so many times today, and I need a break to recharge.

I want to be strong for Will because he's been so nice to help me, but I have reached my limit, and the tears slide down my cheeks. Soon, the floodgates open and I'm sobbing. Will puts his arm around me. We can check again at the remaining six hospitals on the list, but if Jonathan isn't in any of them, it's over. As soon as they lift the travel ban, I'll fly home.

A nurse pokes her head out of a room at the end of the hall and walks toward us. "What did you say he looked like?"

I scramble to my feet on shaky legs. Will stands up, too. "He has dark brown hair. Blue eyes. A couple inches over six feet. He has a scar on his knee from a torn ACL."

"How old is he?"

"Thirty-two."

"Wait here," she said.

I forget how to breathe. I tell myself not to get my hopes up, but they soar anyway. Will reaches for my hand and we stand there like that until the nurse returns and says, "Come with me."

We follow her down the hallway and onto an elevator. I'm afraid to open my mouth, because the words are right there, waiting to tumble out in a frenzy of "Where are we going, what are we doing, do you think it's him?"

The door opens two floors below, and we follow the nurse out of the elevator. "One of my friends works in intensive care on this floor. She mentioned a John Doe they're keeping under sedation for breathing difficulty and pain and that a few people have come to check his identity, but so far there hasn't been a match. She said he has dark hair. He matches the height and age. No clue about his eyes because they're closed. I can only let one of you in at a time."

"Go, Annika," Will says when we reach the doorway of the patient's room. "I'll be waiting right here."

Once we're inside the room, I hesitate because whoever this is, he's in rough shape. Medical equipment surrounds the bed; a cacophony of whooshes and beeps. The antiseptic smell seeps into my nose, reminding me of my own hospital stay years ago, and I gasp for fresh air. That only makes it worse, because there is none.

In the dim light of the room, I can make out the shape of a man. I don't think it's Jonathan, because the hair looks wrong—dull and gray instead of dark brown—but the nurse motions for me to approach the bed. She's been so nice, and I don't want to seem ungrateful or cowardly, so I do it.

This man has been gravely injured. The hair looks wrong because it's coated in ash and concrete dust, but underneath it I can see that the color is, in fact, a deep dark brown. It's also dotted with dried blood. He's on a ventilator, the tube down his throat held in place by some sort of white adhesive tape.

I look closely, feeling a glimmer of hope as I mentally catalogue the planes and angles of Jonathan's face, and I try to identify them under the bruises and the blood and the dirt. I don't want to touch him because it would surely bring him pain, but I trace those planes and angles, my finger hovering inches above his skin. Jonathan's face is like a Polaroid picture that slowly develops into something recognizable right before my eyes.

It's him. I know it's him.

Lastly, I lift the sheet and cry harder when I see the scar on his left knee. It's also apparent that his legs and maybe his pelvis are badly broken.

"Is this the man you're looking for?" the nurse asks.

Tears roll down my face and splash onto the sheet covering Jonathan's chest. "Yes. Can my brother please come in? Just for a second?"

"Just for a second," she echoes.

I throw myself into Will's arms. It's a strange sensation, this hug. I can't remember ever feeling so loving toward my brother or wanting to express it in such a physical way. It's comforting beyond words.

"I can't believe it," Will says.

"I can."

The nurse comes back in the room. "A doctor and a hospital administrator would like to speak with you. It won't take long. You can come back when you're done."

Dr. Arnett introduces himself and tells us that Jonathan's respiratory injuries are severe, and he is in critical but stable condition. He warns that there are complications that could arise at any time, and that Jonathan is not out of the woods yet. He is already showing signs of pneumonia, and the risk of an additional infection is high.

From the administrator, we learn that Jonathan was carried out alive late on the day the towers fell. He was found in a small pocket of space surrounded by shattered concrete and crumpled steel. His clothes were cut off as paramedics tended to him before bundling him into an ambulance and sending him on his way. With no wallet or employee badge, he has been treated here at this hospital while the staff waited for someone to claim him.

"I claim him," I say, and from that moment on, I don't ever leave his side.

44

Annika

Will invites me to stay at his apartment so I can be closer to the hospital, but for the most part, I sleep at Jonathan's bedside the way he did for me all those years ago. I can't make actual medical decisions for him, but I will be Jonathan's medical advocate, and I tell him I'll take care of everything I can. I'm not sure if he can hear me, but I talk to him anyway and repeat everything the doctors tell me. I tell him we're going to be here awhile.

I couldn't wait to share the news with my parents and Janice and Clay. I don't think anyone but me thought that I'd ever find Jonathan, and my mom and Janice mostly cried into the phone.

"I'm going to call the Chicago office right now," my mom says. I'm glad she's on top of things, because that hadn't even occurred to me. When she calls me back later, she tells me that no one there believed Jonathan was alive either. I hope they celebrated.

Bradford flew back to Chicago as soon as they lifted the travel ban. He calls me the next day on the new cell phone Will picked up for me. My mom has given him the number.

"We're all overjoyed that he's alive. We would have lost even more employees if not for his directive to leave the building," Brad says. Maybe he's no longer mad at me for interrupting that meeting. I guess a national tragedy will do that to a person.

"You said he got out of the building. That his name was on the list."

"There was so much confusion. He went down before I did. I . . . I really thought he got out." His voice sounds pretty wobbly.

"Well, he did not."

"Please let me know if there's anything we can do for Jonathan, or for you."

"Thank you. That's very nice of you. I'm sure Jonathan isn't thinking about work or that promotion right now."

"No," Brad says. "I'm sure he isn't."

Before we hang up, Brad tells me that Liz, Jonathan's ex-wife, did not make it out of the building and that she is presumed dead. "I thought Jonathan might want to know."

I promise Brad I will tell Jonathan when he wakes up.

I didn't know Liz, but Jonathan once loved her, so when we hang up, I cry for her anyway.

Jonathan's medical team has been slowly lifting the sedation, and two days later Jonathan opens his eyes a little. He looks at me so oddly, I worry that maybe it isn't him and I've been wrong this whole time. But the nurse warned me he would be confused, so I reach gently for his hand and say, "It's me, Annika. I'm here. I love you, and you're going to be okay." He closes his eyes and doesn't open them again that day.

The next day it's a little better and he keeps them open for almost an hour. He understands, I think, because he's looking into my eyes like he knows it's me. I don't dare look away. I stare straight back into them, and I hold his gaze and say, "It's Annika. It's me. I'm here and I won't leave."

He gets better every day and I tell him to squeeze my hand if he understands what I'm saying, what the doctors are saying. His grip is as weak as a baby's, but he does what I ask. The doctors have gradually been turning down the ventilator and now they want to extubate Jonathan to see if he can breathe on his own. The sounds he makes when they remove the tube and he tries to breathe are terrible, and I can hear them clear out in the hallway, where they asked me to wait. If the staff notices my physical reaction—the flicking and bouncing I'm doing—they don't mention it. When they let me come back into the room, Jonathan gasps and tries to speak, but no sound comes out, and he closes his eyes and goes back to sleep. It scares me, but they said he did okay and is just tired because breathing is really hard work.

The next time he wakes up, he seems a little more coherent. Not much, but enough that he utters, "Annika?" His voice is so hoarse from the tube that I can barely hear him.

"Yes, yes it's me. It's Annika. You're okay. I mean, you have a lot of broken bones and some respiratory issues, but you're going to be fine."

Jonathan's pelvis is not so much broken as it is shattered, and the legs are a mess, too. Pretty much every bone from the waist down has some kind of damage, but the doctors say he will heal in time. His respiratory health is still the biggest hurdle he'll have to overcome.

"How did you get here so fast?" he asks, because it must be confusing to lose so many days the way Jonathan has. Maybe he thinks it's still September eleventh.

"I didn't arrive until three days after the planes hit. No one could fly after that. I had to drive."

He blinks like he's confused. "For a minute, I thought you said you drove."

"I did. You needed me, Jonathan, and here I am."

45

Annika

Jonathan is discharged from the hospital three months later and we fly home on a gray drizzly day in December. It doesn't feel dreary to us, though. It feels like heaven to finally leave the confines of his hospital room and walk outside, to breathe fresh winter air that is only vaguely tinged with the smell of smoke. Or maybe I'm just imagining it.

There have been endless, grueling weeks of physical therapy and breathing treatments. There have been some setbacks, including another very scary bout of pneumonia. The antibiotics weren't working, and Dr. Arnett, whom I had come to know very well, pulled me aside and warned me that Jonathan might not survive.

"I know this is difficult to hear," he said. "But I want you to be prepared. His condition is very grave."

That seemed so unfair to me. To make it out of the tower only for your lungs to succumb to an infection one month later. Janice and Clay came to the hospital; Will was already at my side. Everyone seemed resigned to the fact that Jonathan would not be granted another reprieve. His fever rose and nothing the doctors tried was working, and I spent the better part of a day sobbing on someone's shoulder.

But Jonathan is the strongest person I know, and he did survive. And now we are leaving the hospital hand in hand, the way I always told him we would even on those days I wasn't so sure I believed it myself.

Will arranged for a car to take us to the airport. He came by earlier to say good-bye. I cried in my brother's arms, overcome by all he had done for me, and when he pulled away there were tears in his eyes, too. I feel like Jonathan and Will are almost brothers now, considering how much time they spent together. Will was great about watching over Jonathan while I ran to his apartment to grab clean clothes or take a shower.

I used every bit of vacation I had, and when it ran out, I put in my resignation at the library. They said they'll hire me back when I'm ready to return to work, and Jonathan said it shows how much they value me as an employee. It makes me feel really good to hear things like that, because I never really know what people think of me, at least the ones who don't say rude things to my face. I will go back, because I love my job at the library, but I'll wait until Jonathan is fully recovered, because right now he still needs me a lot.

His bones are healing and he's walking okay. A little slow, but who cares. Well, he does. But I know he'll get faster.

He doesn't know what he wants to do, but he's not going to work for Brad anymore.

Life's too short, he said.

My parents are there to pick us up at the airport. It makes me sad that Jonathan's mom isn't here, too, and that he doesn't really have any family left. We're going to live at my apartment. Jonathan knows how attached I am to it, and since he still has a lot of recovering to do, he said he doesn't care at all where we live as long as we're together. By the time we arrive home from the airport and I walk Jonathan into the bedroom, he's leaning heavily on me. He doesn't admit that he's hurting, but sadly, I know all too well what Jonathan's pain face looks like. I get him settled in bed and crawl under the covers with him. He wraps his arms around me and kisses the top of my head.

"You amaze me," he says. He's probably said it twenty times by now, but it always makes me smile. "It feels so good to hold you again."

It feels good to me, too. It's been so long since we've been able to stretch out alongside each other. "It's the best feeling in the world," I say. We kiss for a while, which is something else we haven't done in a long time. They're the kind of slow, deep kisses that say more than words ever will, and they make me feel loved and cherished. He's half-asleep when we finally stop. We have the rest of our lives to kiss, so I whisper that it's time for him to take a nap. He murmurs his assent without opening his eyes, and I slip from the bed and leave the room.

He coughs for a while and then I don't hear any sound coming from the bedroom. I sneak back in and check on him, watching his chest until I see it rise and fall. Then I softly close the door.

While Jonathan sleeps, I go through the mail my mom has been collecting for me and find an envelope with no return address. I pry open the flap, and inside are two crisp one-hundred-dollar bills and the words "thank you" written on a piece of paper. There is also a child's drawing. It's of a woman with blond hair and she is driving a car. There's a princess crown on her head and a man in the passenger seat.

And a duck in the backseat that's blue.

Acknowledgments

I have taken creative liberties with this story. The Illini chess club does not meet in the food court of the University of Illinois Student Union but rather in a specific room. Vivek Rao, who is a real person, appears in the book as a member of the chess team who represented the University of Illinois in the 1991 Pan American Championship. From what I learned via research, he is a truly phenomenal chess player. The other members of the team who appear in the book are all fictional. I owe a huge debt of gratitude to Eric Rosen, who was a member of the University of Illinois chess club and team and whose knowledge and input was so beneficial in the writing of this book.

Thank you to my editor, Leslie Gelbman. I am deeply grateful that you connected so strongly with this story. It has been a real pleasure to work with you.

To the wonderful and talented folks at St. Martin's Press and Macmillan, thank you for welcoming me with open arms. Special thanks to Lisa Senz, Brant Janeway, Marissa Sangiacomo, and Tiffany Shelton.

To Brooke Achenbach, thank you for advising me on all things related to the University of Illinois at Urbana-Champaign campus. I hope you enjoyed the trip down memory lane as you provided the names of lecture halls, dining establishments, and bars.

To Jana Waterreus, thank you for providing information about the role of a librarian and the academic path one would follow in order to make this their career. I appreciate it so much.

To Tammara Webber, thank you for not only reading the manuscript, but for encouraging me regarding my vision for this book. Your input was invaluable.

To Hillary Faber, thank you for lending your expertise and experience in working with students who are on the autism spectrum. You helped ensure that Annika's character portrayal was authentic, and I appreciate it so much.

To Elisa Abner-Taschwer, your cheer game is stronger than ever. Thanks for believing in me from the beginning and continuing to provide feedback seven books later. Your support and enthusiasm is immeasurable.

To Stacy Elliott Alvarez, thank you for always assuring me that writing is what I should be doing.

I am also deeply grateful for the contributions, assistance, and support of the following individuals:

David Graves, because his ongoing encouragement means more to me than he'll ever know. Also, you're a pretty good typo-catcher.

My children, Matthew and Lauren. Thank you for always understanding when I'm on a deadline or caught up in the imaginary worlds in my mind. None of those things will ever be more important than the two of you. I love you both.

Jane Dystel, Miriam Goderich, and Lauren Abramo. You are truly the trifecta of literary-agent awesomeness. Thank you for your continued guidance and support.

I am eternally grateful to the book bloggers who have been so instrumental in my ability to reach readers. You work tirelessly every day to spread the word about books, and the writing community is a better place because of you. I also want to give a special shout-out to the readers' groups who are so passionate about championing the books they love: Andrea Peskind Katz of Great Thoughts' Great Readers, Susan Walters Peterson of Sue's Booking Agency, and Jenn Gaffney of REden' with the Garden Girls.

I want to express my sincere thanks and appreciation to the booksellers who hand-sell my books and the librarians who put them on their shelves.

My heartfelt gratitude goes out to all of you for helping to make *The Girl He Used to Know* the book I hoped it would be. Words cannot express how truly blessed I am to have such wonderful and enthusiastic people in my life.

And last, but certainly not least, my readers. Without you, none of this would be possible.

Credits

Trapeze would like to thank everyone at Orion who worked on the publication of *The Girl He Used to Know*.

Editorial
Katie Brown
Charlie Panayiotou
Jane Hughes
Alice Davis

Audio
Paul Stark
Amber Bates

Contracts
Anne Goddard
Paul Bulos
Ellen Harber

Design
Charlotte Abrams-Simpson
Lucie Stericker
Joanna Ridley
Nick May
Clare Sivell
Helen Ewing

Finance
Naomi Mercer
Jasdip Nandra
Afeera Ahmed
Elizabeth Beaumont
Sue Baker
Victor Falola

Marketing
Amy Davies

Production
Claire Keep
Fiona Macintosh

Publicity
Alainna Hadjigeorgiou

Sales
Jen Wilson
Esther Waters
Rachael Hum
Ellie Kyrke-Smith
Frances Doyle
Viki Cheung
Ben Goddard
Georgina Cutler
Jo Carpenter
Tal Hart
Barbara Ronan
Andrew Hally
Dominic Smith
Maggy Park

Operations
Jo Jacobs
Sharon Willis
Lucy Tucker
Lisa Pryde